To my A.......

wo

MW00878462

PHOTO: KIM TRUJILLO

" *I couldn't put this book down. It's such an accurate depiction of an amazing period of American history. It's funny, full of love and compassion. It's terrifying, and it's an incredible read for anyone, whether you were living at that time or not.* **"**

–Terese Kristensen

The
Foot Soldier

BY
TOM TRUJILLO

email: tomkim2@comcast.net
www.tomtrujillo.com

BOOK & COVER DESIGN:
TOM TRUJILLO

A SPECIAL THANKS TO SUSAN DORAN, AND BRUCE PIDGEON
FOR EDITING AND PROOFING.

FICTION
ISBN-13: 978-1548026714
ISBN-10: 1548026719

The Man in the Tree
1967

T he man in the tree is wondering how the insignificant act of responding to a classified ad seeking a bilingual lawyer in the United States had resulted in where he now finds himself. If only he hadn't picked up the paper, and instead ripped it into a thousand pieces. He is surprised he remembers that moment at all. He does recall the day he read the letter to his daughter, telling her that he had been accepted and the look of excitement on her face. She suggested they celebrate the good news by having lunch on the *muelle*, where he could watch the surfers ride the waves breaking along the rocks. Even though he felt the need to get their affairs in order to prepare for the move, his daughter pleaded, "Please Popi, the sun is shining and the weather is perfect for a picnic."

He remembers it was a warm afternoon without a cloud in the sky. They enjoyed fried shrimp *tortas* and lemonade and laughed while shooing away the pesky gulls.

But now he's looking at himself hanging on a branch with a wire wrapped around his neck. It sickens him that yellow jackets and flies are feeding on his once handsome face.

"I don't suppose you remember what happened to you, eh amigo?" says a gravely voice. "You got a name?"

"Yes, of course I do," he replies.

Surprised he's not alone, the man looks up and discovers an old Mexican cowboy squatting on a large branch, camouflaged in the leaves.

The old cowboy patiently nods his head waiting for him to spit out his name.

"I ... I don't remember," sighs the man in the tree.

"It will come to you. You must have really riled up those *pendejos* who hung you here to rot, because no one who has spent their last moments on Earth were men of meek spirit. "

"I was a lawyer, that I know. How did you get here?"

The old cowboy smiles proudly.

"I am here because a door opened. My name is Juan Nepomuceno Cortina, a cavalry rider for General Mariano Aritisto. I fought bravely against the invasion in the battles of Resca de Palma and Palo Alto."

"Am I dead?"

"Oh, very much so," replies Juan Cortina. "You must have guessed it by now, don't you think? What I do know is that you are the most recent of many hombres the Texans have strung up in this remarkable tree. The last bastard was pissed off that after fighting for independence from Spain, he was still considered an enemy by the Texans. In the throws of a mescal nightmare he went *loco* and broke into a white man's cabin. That fool murdered the lot of 'em. When they strung him up, he cried out, 'remember the Alamo!' He wasn't a hero, he was simply a drunken, murdering bastard who spent many years up here before turning to dust."

"I can't be dead. This is just a bad dream is all. There is still so much left for me to do."

"*Bueno*, but trust me, you no longer walk the earth with a beating heart."

"My God, I've left everything in such a mess," moans the man, "My beautiful Ramona. What will happen to her? Who will tell her of my demise?"

"I am sorry for you," Juan Cortina replies sympathetically. "It looks like you put everything on the line and lost. At least, that seems to be the case."

"I cannot even remember my last words to her. Did I tell her that I loved her more than life itself?"

"Probably not. Who knows when one's final moment of life is at hand? I believe you to be the victim of depraved, desperate men.

I pray it will not be long before you recall the events leading up to your death and those responsible for it."

Juan Cortina begins to fade away into the leaves. Just before he completely disappears the man in the tree hears him say, "It is important you remember who you are. Only then can I be of any assistance."

The sun rises and the sun sets many times after Juan Cortina departs—time is meaningless to the dead. Day after day, night after night sail by as easily as water flows to the ocean.

Then, this afternoon in fact, he heard glorious music in the distance and prayed that his time in limbo or purgatory was coming to an end, and that angels would soon be taking him to heaven.

If his heart were beating it would be leaping with excitement to see the glowing silver chariot coming his way on a cloud to whisk him away. Unfortunately for the man in the tree, angels do not appear, and his time in this tree is not yet over.

His hopes are dashed when emerging from the cloud, which turns out to be dust, is a 1965 Ford Galaxy with a huge chrome bumper and grill that stops abruptly near the tree. The driver cuts the engine and brings to an end the sounds of a steel guitar that was sending sweet notes through the woods. A tall, muscular man emerges, and walks briskly around the front of the car. He holds out his hand to a young blond woman wearing a low-cut summer blouse and a skirt covered in red polka dots.

The tall man points up into the tree and tells the woman in a gravelly Texas drawl, "See that honey? That is what happens to you when you're an ungrateful Mexican who steps too far out of bounds."

The woman averts her eyes and covers her face with the back of her hand before peeking out between her fingers. "Oh Pete, what a horrible sight! My goodness, I had no idea you had to make such difficult life and death decisions to keep us safe. I'm proud to work by your side."

Feeling safe and secure in his arms, she hugs him tightly and buries her head against his chest. He returns her embrace, then turns her face to him and kisses her before moving his hands to her blouse-covered breasts.

The woman pushes him away and cries, "I'm sorry, I don't think I can do this. Not with that creature staring at us."

The tall man ignores her plea and mumbles, "That scarecrow ain't lookin' at nobody darlin'."

He kisses her on the neck and reaches down and pulls away the loose neckline of her blouse and touches the smooth skin of her breasts.

The man in the tree would prefer to turn away out of decency, but he is unable to do so because his head is held in the viselike grip of the wire noose. He closes his eyes, but that is when his hellish nightmare returns. In it he fights with all his strength against a dark, raging torrent—a river of humanity sweeping thousands to oblivion. Against his will he opens his eyes, forced to watch the disturbing scene taking place at his feet.

The couple breaks their embrace when the tall man goes to the trunk of the car and pulls out a blanket. He lays it on the ground at the base the tree and invites the woman to lie next to him. She giggles like a teenager and eagerly takes his hand as he guides her to him. Immediately they begin pawing at each other and articles of clothing are removed, tossed aside carelessly, until both are completely naked. The tall man awkwardly rolls on top and she wraps her legs around his waist as he begins thrusting himself into her, growling with each lunge.

Each brutish grunt jogs his memory and the man in the tree

begins to remember the sound his killer made as he straddled his chest in the back seat of a car, cursing him as he punched and beat him senseless until he lost consciousness.

The afternoon wind begins shaking the leaves, or maybe it's the man in the tree boiling with fury as he recalls the horrific events leading to his death.

The lovers' sexual embrace turns cruel when the tall man grabs the girl's ponytail and pulls her head back forcing a frightened, quiet yelp. "Stop! Please stop, Pete!"

She gasps when the hanging man begins swaying in the breeze. "God damn it, Pete, stop, you're scarin' me!"

Pete ignores her pleas, but he also hears the leaves rattling. He turns a fierce gaze to the man in the tree and sniggers, mocking his victim, the trouble-making Mexican who is now just a heap of nothing hanging from a limb.

This offensive cruelty nearly jolts the man in the tree off his perch, but the provocation has indeed ended any further confusion about who he is:

"My name is César Gaspard, and I vow to avenge my death and the sorrow you have heaped upon me and my daughter. I pray for God to set me free me from this nightmare, but not before you suffer a wretched and agonizing death!"

Three Months Later

Under a deep blue sky outside the city limits of Beeville, Texas, white clouds lazily float above a colorful meadow of waist-high grasses and wildflowers. Bees, crickets, and hundreds of other insect neighbors busy themselves, as is their nature with territorial battles, gathering nectar, and the more serious issue of looking to fertilize a willing mate. Their rhythmical buzzing and chirping fills the atmosphere with a din of non-stop chatter. Barely audible in this clamor is a faint scream, growing in intensity until it overwhelms the insects' small world and shocks them to silence.

A Navy fighter jet is falling from the sky, plummeting nose-first toward the earth. Two hundred feet above the ground the pilot ejects from the cockpit still attached to his seat. His unopened chute trails behind like the long white tail on a kite. Unfortunately, he's projected himself directly in front of the plane's trajectory, and both pilot and jet are on the same path: heading into the woods surrounding the meadow.

The impact of a high speed jet slamming into solid earth is a sound unlike anything ever heard before in the meadow. Even more horrifying is the explosion of jet fuel followed by a huge ball of flame rocketing skyward. Burning fragments of the plane shoot high above the trees and thick black smoke rises up to compete with the blue sky for attention. Within a few moments an immense herd of yellow jackets race out of the woods, scattering in all directions seeking a less hostile environment.

It's not long before the insects of the meadow resume their life until another irritating racket disrupts their peace. The pilot, with his face blackened and flight suit torn to shreds, races out of the woods screaming and running as far away and as possible from his terrifying experience.

Ten Clicks
from Song Cau Do
1966

F ace down in a muddy rice paddy ten clicks from Song Cau Do, a bullet in his leg, Paul thinks about the Marine recruiter who showed up at his high school to promote patriotism and bravery—qualities Uncle Sam needed in his fight against the rising tide of communism in Southeast Asia. The dominoes were tumbling as hordes of commies crossed into Vietnam preparing to overthrow the government of America's strongest ally in Southeast Asia. Paul and his classmates didn't know squat about the politics of US involvement in that part of the world, but when the country calls on you to protect your way of life, you're expected you to do your duty.

Paul thinks about a tune titled, "April Love," by Pat Boone. He changes the lyrics and title to, "Song Cau Do." It's the song he tells himself he will sing out while strangling that recruiter asshole who brainwashed him into this shit hole.

Song Cau Do,
is why I'm going to strangle you,
strangle you because of
Song Cau Do!

Paul lost his gung ho attitude early on in his rotation. He was instructed in how to dehumanize the enemy—don't call them Vietnamese. Call them Charlie or Mr. Charles—VC in Marine lingo stands for Victor Charlie. Most everyone however, simply called them gooks. Everyone got a nickname, not only Charlie. The artillery were "big boys." "Chuck," was the derogatory term black soldiers called the white soldiers. As a low-level infantrymen, Paul was a "grunt" as if using more than one syllable for cannon fodder would be a waste of energy.

Paul is lying face down in a muddy rice paddy because of Operation Golden Fleece, the bigwigs' bright idea of protecting the rice harvest for the locals and to deny Charlie a source of food and income. The Ninth Marine's intended mission was to protect the precious rice by conducting search and clearing operations in the vicinity of the harvest, and provide security for the villages.

Ten clicks south of Song Cau Do, supposedly safe within a secured perimeter, Paul and his squad ran into a low-level ambush— Charlie was hiding in the rice. The moment the shit hit the fan he felt his leg kick sideways out from under him. He was struck with an insanely painful burning in his thigh. He gasped at the intensity of it while yelling out, "Hit the deck!"

In spite of the volcanic piece of metal in his thigh shooting agonizing lightning bolts throughout his body, Paul responded to the attack with appropriate fire power. He aimed his weapon two feet off the ground in the VC's general direction and emptied his clip. Paul had no idea if he got the sniper or not, but the shooting stopped. It was then he began attending to his wounds. He pulled his pants down to his knees and studied the small hole in his leg which thankfully wasn't bleeding. He flushed the dirt away with water from his canteen and packed the wound with gauze before covering it with waterproof tape. He gave himself a good pop of morphine purchased on the black market and wrapped the rest of the gauze tightly around his thigh to just below the knee as a splint of sorts. After pulling his pants up, he covered himself in mud and rice stalks as camouflage and lay silent. Charlie might still be hanging around.

Paul listened for any sounds that might indicate VC presence. They move more quietly than Americans. He listened for the breaking of rice stalks, the sudden flight of a bird, or the quieting of insect chatter for ten or twenty minutes before deciding it might be safe enough to crawl out of the rice paddy. Paul heard someone moaning in pain and cautiously moved toward the source. Parting the stalks, he discovered an emaciated, barefoot, VC lying on his back clutching a serious stomach wound with bloody hands. Upon spotting Paul, the VC began screaming at him in Vietnamese.

Paul didn't know what the hell the guy was ranting about until Charlie screamed out, "Fuck you, American! Fuck you! Go home," before doubling up in pain and choking out his last breath. Paul rolled onto his back and stared at the sky, thinking how messed up his life was. *Jesus,* he thought, *only two years ago my biggest concern was getting someone over twenty-one to score me a case of beer.*

Morphine doesn't last forever, and Paul needed to get out of the rice paddy regardless of what was lurking in the grass. Like some ancient primordial ooze, he slowly rose up from the muck to peer over the bright green straw. While doing so he marveled at its strength—standing tall, though dozens of bullets had just zipped its life. He studied every dew drop on the blades, awestruck when he saw his image captured within, as if each drop of water carried a part of his soul. At that moment he appreciated those droplets more than anything else in life. Certain this might be his final moments on earth he wished he could have experienced being in love just once in his life.

"Hey, Gill! You still here?"

◆

Recovery from his non-crippling wound was serious enough to warrant a few months in a Da Nang hospital with hours of mental and physical therapy. It was a time of pastel green rooms filled with too many seriously injured young soldiers, and days of lying on the beach and getting high.

In the winter of 1966, Paul took his medical discharge, his limp, and a large stash of hazardous duty pay and headed straight to

Roger's house in Marin County. Roger was a childhood friend who had written to him about his neighbor who had accidentally started the hippie revolution.

Two years earlier at Stanford University the CIA began mind-altering drug experiments using lysergic acid diethylamide looking for an effective truth serum. The scientists shortened it to LSD, and the dozens of student volunteers who signed up for the experiments simply called it, "acid."

Word quickly spread about incredible psychedelic trips and it wasn't long before one of the volunteers swiped a dose and took it to a chemistry student's house in Berkeley, who was now Roger's neighbor, a fellow named Stanley Owsley. Owsley began manufacturing the same CIA quality LSD for the San Francisco underground and beatnik community, and Roger was getting rich selling his "Purple Haze."

Roger drove Paul to a windswept, deserted beach in Marin County for his first acid trip. There, sitting on a rock overlooking the ocean, he heard the most beautiful voice imaginable—a lone barnacle was using the wind to sing sweetly to him from its rocky perch. When Paul expanded his view, he was brought to tears when thousands of barnacle neighbors joined in, forming one of the most incredible choirs to be heard on earth. As day turned to night, he heard music coming from Roger's car radio parked nearby playing Bob Dylan's, "Mr. Tambourine Man."

> Yes, to dance beneath the diamond sky
> with one hand waving free
> Silhouetted by the sea, circled by the circus sands
> With all memory and fate, driven deep beneath the waves
> Let me forget about today until tomorrow.

And that is what he decided to do for as long as possible.

San Francisco, California 1967

F ive thousand young men and women have gathered on in front of San Francisco City Hall to protest the war in Vietnam. They are the first generation to be raised on television, rock 'n roll, and annihilation by the A-bomb and have assembled to give a loud voice to the growing anti-war movement spreading across the country.

On the top steps of the City Hall, four large public address speakers surround a bearded, bushy-haired man that square culture would call a beatnik. Now a "radical protestor, is almost screaming into his microphone as he addresses the large crowd below. "LBJ, congress and the right-wing media are saying that they're ashamed of us and the image we portray to the world! I say it is LBJ and those senators and congressmen waging war and imposing misery and destruction upon millions of innocent Vietnamese who should be ashamed!"

He pauses and holds a fist skyward and chants, "End the war! Bring the troops home!"

The large crowd begins chanting in unison, "HELL NO, WE WON'T GO! HELL NO, WE WON'T GO!"

"Who starts the war?" yells the speaker.

"THE RICH!" replies the crowd.

"Who fights the war?"

"THE POOR!"

"Who dies?"

"THE YOUNG!"screams the crowd.

"We are FOOT SOLDIERS! We are the ones willing to fight and die for justice! The time has come to stand our ground. We are no longer dissenters, but resisters, battling the hideous war machine that is destroying our young men!"

On the perimeter of the plaza is a wall of heavily armed police. They have their shields and billy clubs ready for any trouble as they face a wall of angry protestors. One angry male protester carrying a sign in reading, "End The War" shoves it into a cop's plastic shield and knocks him backwards. The protester is rewarded with a firm shove that sends him tumbling to the ground. This small battle is all it takes for the police to lose their cool and start jabbing and swinging their night sticks at anyone within reach.

The speaker hears screaming and cursing coming from the back of the crowd, and from his vantage point on the top stairs also sees that the large gathering is falling apart at the edges. Angry voices from the hundreds of battling protestors and cops drown him out even though he's the one with four large speakers.

"Hey! Be cool!" he pleads. "Don't give the pigs a reason to hassle us!"

The crowd begins chanting repeatedly, "FUCK THE PIGS, FUCK THE PIGS!"

Sensing their lives to be in danger, the cops begin shoving the crowd out of the plaza, but not everyone cooperates. A few protestors, both men and women, stand their ground until they're overwhelmed and driven to the ground under an assault of punches then unceremoniously dragged to a nearby paddy wagon. Dozens of young people fall to the ground while being pushed hard by the police. In their enthusiasm, some of the cops trip over those on the ground and they go down. The police are now out of control, trampling over fallen protesters and giving chase to those suspected of being agitators.

The speaker screams, "Be cool! Be cool!" But no one is listening anymore as the majority of the gathering are fleeing out of the plaza.

But the cops and the protestors are far beyond being cool. The stampede turns into a rout and today's anti-war protest ends abruptly. Not simply content to just clear the plaza, the cops begin chasing protestors through the streets, hitting and trampling anyone who happens to be in their way.

David Macias is one of thousands of young men who have fled the draft by moving to an anti-war community like the Haight-Ashbury in San Francisco. Over the past year, he has changed his address three times, registering with a new draft board with every move. It takes months for the Selective Service officials to forward his name to the new draft board, then David would give them another address.

Like others of his generation, David has let his hair grow long, but has given up on any facial hair as his Hispanic blood refuses to grow anything resembling a beard.

David dropped a tab of acid an hour ago halfway through the anti-war rally. When the sun burned away the cool morning marine layer, he thought a cold drink would satisfy his gnawing thirst and walked a few blocks to a Foster Freeze stand.

"Can I help you?" asks a young hippie girl peeking through the small opening of the window counter with a smile.

"Lemonade please," says David.

"Would you like a straw with that?"

"No thanks."

"I didn't think so. You don't look like a straw man to me," she says softly.

Her words vibrate straight to his heart, past the sunrise aura glowing like a fire surrounding her cheerful blushing face.

"I get off work at five, if you're in the neighborhood," she smiles as she slides the lemonade to him

David likes that she thinks he's not a straw man, whatever

that means. "Okay," he says lamely, but it's all he can manage at the moment considering the effects of the acid.

Walking slowly through an alley with drink in hand, he's still thinking about the girl's comment when he's suddenly faced with a human wave of protesters racing toward him in panic. In another time, he might have taken some kind of action, such as moving up against the wall of a building to avoid being trampled. But the stars have aligned in Aquarius and this is a magical time, so he stands firmly in place and allows the mass of swift-moving bodies to part around him like salmon swimming around a boulder in a river. Puzzled, he watches them race out of the alley. When he turns around, he's met by a large number of police charging into the alley in pursuit of their prey. Once again, David makes no effort to avoid them, and they too part around him as if he were invisible.

Returning to the protest, David is shocked to find dozens of broken signs and piles of litter strewn about the nearly empty plaza. A young woman stumbles to the grass holding her bleeding head. As quickly as the acid took hold of him it magically dissipates. The rest of his trip will have to wait. He runs to the woman's side and discovers a shallow gash on her skull, bleeding profusely. Most head wounds stop bleeding as quickly as they begin, but why he knows this, he can't remember—health class? Boy Scouts? He removes his T-shirt and tears off a piece to dab at the cut—it's not as serious as it looks, and soon the bleeding slows. David wraps the rest of his shirt around her head, and it's just in time too, as the acid begins to rush through his blood once more.

He smiles into her expanding and contracting rainbow eyes and asks, "Can you stand up?"

"I think so," she answers while rising to her feet, a bit wobbly, even with David's assistance.

"Are you a healer?" she asks.

It's a question he's never been asked, but what he's just done, and on acid too. David puts his arm around her waist and together they leave the plaza. Arm in arm they slowly walk a couple of blocks and flag down a cab that takes them to a nearby hospital.

Everyone is tripping. Young men and women glide along the avenue in various states of being stoned—pot, acid, mescaline, or just blazing on good vibes. Hippies crowd the sidewalks, porch steps, and the many head shops filling the colorful neighborhood known as, "The Haight." Psychedelic rock music is pouring out of every open doorway and window, and it seems like every other person is buying or selling pot or acid. The groovy flow of the long-haired, colorfully dressed street people swirl around Paul and David as they make their way back to Vivian's after today's riot.

"Was your girl okay?" asks Paul, brushing his shoulder length hair back. The final, shitty US Marine Corp haircut they gave him is long in the past. It's been over the year since his discharge he still believes they cut it extra short on purpose because he was getting out of Vietnam early.

A noisy Volkswagen bug sails quickly down the street. In it are four young girls laugh and sing along to Bob Dylan's, "Like A Rolling Stone" playing on their radio. David wonders how this all happened in such a brief period of time. Two years ago, most of these kids were in high school listening to The Beatles or Herman's Hermits, making-out in cars at the drive-in, or cruising some hot spot in their home towns. The hippie movement has exploded almost overnight, in almost every major city on the planet. First, young people began smoking pot and then LSD cut them loose from a lame existence in the suburbs The parents too, are responsible for this migration

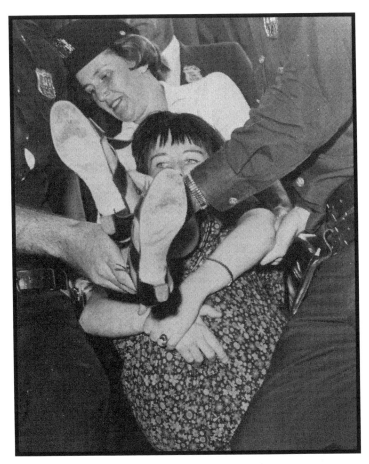

STOP THE WAR! BUSTED IN SAN FRANCISCO

to "Love City." The generation who survived the Great Depression and World War II, threw a dark cloud over everyone with the threat of atom bomb obliteration. The kids learned about the history of racism and segregation, and were horrified that the economy was being run by the defense industry promoting fear to justify the Vietnam War. The nail in the coffin was the draft.

"David. What about the girl?" asks Paul again.

"Oh, sorry. I got sidetracked. Yeah, she got bashed pretty good, but the emergency guys told me she was lucky I performed some pretty decent triage."

"Do you even know what triage is?" laughs Paul.

"Not until I'd performed it, smart ass. I don't think she was even a protester."

"The cops rioted like they always do," grumbles Paul.

"How come they always side with the assholes?"

David and Paul stop in front of a large Victorian house when a voice calls out to them. "Hey! Handsome guy!"

An olive-skin, enchantress with long black–hair, wearing a see-through Indian print Caftan with nothing underneath steps onto the sidewalk and takes David by the arm and pulls him close.

"Where have you been, lover?"

The aroma of her patchouli with other exotic oils captures David's attention. "Hi Sasha, I've been house painting."

"Oh, the queen of hippies—still working on her house?"

"I swear, I'm going to end up spending my life on that thing."

"It must be your karma or some dreadful sin you committed in a past life. How many colors is she up to anyway?"

"I don't know, I lost count months ago. It is pretty spectacular though. You should check it out with me."

"That sounds groovy. Are you asking me out on a date?"

David laughs and tugs on Paul's jacket.

"Sasha, this is my friend Paul. Paul, say hi to Sasha."

Paul smiles. "Hi Sasha."

Sasha gazes at Paul with an uncomfortable intensity.

"Is your army jacket authentic?" she asks.

"The real deal, but it's Marine Corps issue."

"Hmm, it has some bad voodoo attached to it, but more importantly it's masking your beautiful soul. When you're ready to shed that protective skin we should have a funeral for it—you know, burn it as a sacrifice to all the suffering we're causing in Vietnam."

Paul is immediately attracted to Sasha, liking her directness which is unique in the hippie world, where, "whatever" is a response to anything not mellow.

"This jacket means a lot to me. It reminds me that every day I'm alive is a miracle."

David whispers to Sasha, "Be nice to my friend, okay?"

"I could easily be very nice to him, handsome. He's lucky to have a friend like you. By the way, my girlfriend up there on the steps thinks you're hot and wants to ball you. I guess that's what I get for bragging about you. Her name is Amy."

David directs his gaze to a group of young hippie girls sitting on the steps. One girl is smiling flirtatiously at him.

"Is that Amy?" he asks. "The one with the cut-off shorts?"

"Pretty isn't she?"

"Beautiful is more like it." replies David.

"I want to talk to Paul. Go introduce yourself to Amy."

While David and Amy become acquainted, Sasha leads Paul up the stairs into the most colorful psychedelic house he's ever seen. The long hallway is painted in multi-colored geometric patterns with Art Nouveau swirls on the ceiling. Sasha wraps her arms around his waist and guides him into a room that is nothing like the hallway.

"My pad," she says as she closes the door. Her "pad" is

painted a dark eggplant with a half dozen, large abstract paintings on the walls, a black lacquered coffee table and a high-end stereo system sitting on the low shelf. There's no other furniture except for a dozen overstuffed pillows lying about on the floor. On the ceiling a copper tumbleweed sculpture hangs directly over the coffee table.

"Sit anywhere," she says while lighting a candle. Paul looks around at the pillow-covered floor and pulls one close to the table.

"I didn't mean to rush you away, but Amy is super uptight about the war because her friend was just killed over there. I felt your jacket was going to lead to trouble."

"I was in the war, too. You'll not find anyone more against Vietnam than me."

"David will be able to soothe her and she'll do the same to him—she's insane in the sack."

"Lucky David. Why aren't you uptight about my jacket?"

Sasha shrugs nonchalantly. "It's just a jacket to me. I know it has significance to you, but I don't know if it belongs in the Haight. We are peaceful flower children after all.

"So I've heard," replies Paul. "It's always struck me as kind of a lame term."

"Oh, it is! It was created by *Time* magazine after reporting on a Love-in. What I find charming is how right-on it actually is—we are in a garden, one of love and peace, and we are flowers: young, beautiful, all very different and probably too delicate to last. But when a garden grows, it spreads its magic like a miracle. Our little movement has affected music, art, and just about every facet of society. Isn't that adorable?" she laughs.

Sasha pulls out a small wooden box from under the coffee table and removes an intricately detailed ceramic pipe filled with hashish. She lights it with a long wooden match and presents it to Paul like an offering. Her graceful movements has Paul transfixed as she stares into his eyes, watching him inhale.

"I like your intensity," she says. "I wanted you because you're real—you've seen humanity, good and bad. I'm tired of rock stars screwing little girls just because they've sold a few records. They're so starved for fame—it's really sad and not at all revolutionary like they'd like to claim. But I don't think the Haight is the place for you. You know the horrors of war, and I also believe that your time as a soldier is not yet over."

Sasha takes the pipe from Paul's hands and places it on the table, then lies back and gently pulls Paul close to her in one smooth motion. They lie silently for a few moments enjoying the tumbleweed sculpture casting shadows of snakelike tentacles that dance about the ceiling.

"Find the source of your pain, your soul cries out for it. When you do, you'll discover absolute love, which is the only answer."

"I wish I could," says Paul.

"Give me your hand," she says and begins studying his palm. "Too bad, it looks like it's not in the stars for you and me, but you do have a very powerful love line. I believe there is a lover from a past life searching for you. I hope you can find her."

Paul watches her long fingers travel across lines in his palm.

"See this here? This is your life line." Sasha furrows her brow and says, "You should stop dropping acid. Do you see this split? It means that powerful forces are about to change your life. You need to take the right path because one is very short and filled with pain, while the other," Sasha says turning his hand over, "while the other travels all the way to here—a very long life indeed—filled with love and adventure."

Sasha places a tender kiss on Paul's hand, then on his lips, thrusting her tongue deep into his mouth before straddling him and moving her hips into his in a most enjoyable way. Paul gasps when her caftan floats off her body like magic and the expanding and contracting snake shadows travel from the ceiling, down the walls, and begin crawling about her naked torso. From somewhere African stringed instruments begin to play although Paul doesn't remember seeing her turn on the record player.

Sasha gives Paul a final kiss and slowly closes the door. He wonders if maybe, against her own advice, Sasha put a little taste of acid on her tongue before taking him on a heaving and surging, intricate journey to every aroused cell in her body before releasing him out into the hallway two hours later.

Out on the street David is waiting for him, leaning against a car smoking a cigarette. Paul stops on the stairs and turns back to stare at Sasha's house. "That is one intense witches coven. We're lucky we made it out alive, 'cause those chicks could have devoured us, one piece at a time."

David nods in agreement.

"Did you have fun with Sasha? Did she read your aura?"

"Oh, she is definitely a witch. She told me something about myself that was right on—said I'm still a soldier."

David tosses his cigarette to the sidewalk and crushes out the glowing ash. "You know, while we're here jerking around, dancing in the park and getting high, the war is only getting worse. You've mentioned more than once doing something to stop it, and I think I'm beginning to get it."

"What in the hell did Amy do to you in there? Was she not as good as Sasha said she was?"

"She was everything Sasha said she was. But after the insane sex she started crying uncontrollably about her childhood friend who was killed in Vietnam. All I could do was hold her and when her grief washed over me I felt like I'd been kicked in the chest. I swear it hit me right in the heart and made me see how little I'm doing to end this shitty war. Seriously, we need to do something meaningful and put an end to this nonsense."

Paul hugs David and exclaims, "God bless Amy, a very good witch indeed. Right on man, let's do it."

David met Vivian when he landed in San Francisco a year ago with very little money, no job skills, and no place to call home He ended up sleeping in a "crash pad" for a couple of weeks, a dump of a house filled with runaways and draft dodgers like himself, all hanging around getting high and engaging in casual sex. Then he saw a posting listed in a hippie paper called *The Oracle* for a house painter. As most of the kids really didn't want a job when they could be getting high and grooving on music, David easily landed the job, and met the only other interested job-seeker, Paul.

Vivian, the owner of the house, offered them a place to stay as partial trade for painting. David jumped at the offer. Paul, who had been living in his VW camper van for the past year, was more than happy with the arraignment.

"David, that act you pulled off at the rally was pure magic," says Vivian. "Everyone is talking about the way the pigs moved around you like you were parting the Red Sea."

Vivian's long dark hair flows over her shoulders and frames her ghostly white skin. She moves across the Victorian apartment with silver bracelets covering wrists and jingling like a tambourine. She takes a seat on an antique upholstered chair and hands David a glowing joint.

"That was pure magic, man. You tapped into another realm," says Vivian.

"I became invisible, I'm almost sure of it," says David. "Did you know that predators can't see slow moving prey because they're searching for the quick movements of panic or escape?"

"I should have tried that in Nam," laughs Paul. "But everyone saw it. That wave of cops parted around you like you *were* invisible, and they weren't tripping."

A dart bounces off a poster of Lyndon Johnson, President of the United States and the enemy of everyone against the war. Paul stoops to pick it up and stares at it, wondering if it's dull or not. Puzzled, he shakes his head and tosses the dart at the poster again, missing Johnson completely and landing two inches from his left ear.

"Can you imagine all the anti-war freaks disappearing right in front of the pigs?" asks Vivian.

"It makes as much sense as that guy preaching to the choir," complains Paul.

"That's a little harsh, man. Look at the crowd he got to come hear him," replies Vivian.

"Vivian, what good is an anti-war rally in a city full of draft dodgers and anti-war supporters? He needs to speak where the kids are still signing up to go to war. That's what David and I are planning to do; teach them how to avoid the draft."

"What are you talking about?" asks Vivian.

Paul throws another dart at the poster. This one sticks a few inches to the right of Johnson's ear. "I'm talking about splitting. The City is cool, but these rallies are nothing more than a social gathering. It's like another love-in; a groovy place to party, pick up chicks and get high."

"The pigs didn't think it was another love-in," says Vivian. "Those psychos could have killed someone."

Paul brushes back his shoulder-length hair and replies with a click of his tongue, "They're just pissed off 'cause everyone hates them, including the chicks."

David holds his hand out for the darts. He takes his time and nails Johnson in the eye.

Paul frowns. "You prick."

"Okay Paul, so how will splitting from the City accomplish anything?" asks Vivian.

"We'll go where the kids are still buying Johnson's bullshit. I'd love to find my recruiter and kick his ass for brainwashing me," he replies with a demonstration of stomping at the floor. Paul jabs his finger on the poster.

"This shit-for-brains is escalating the war because he's a dumb Texas redneck. I say we go tear up his backyard and see how he likes it."

"You guys can't be serious," complains Vivian. "Years from now people will still be talking about this time and place, and no one will give a shit about Texas. Why would you leave just as it's beginning to happen?"

"Oh, come on Vivian," replies Paul, "you don't like all the flower-power shit going on in your precious Haight-Ashbury. What part of the summer of love are you so much in love with anyway?"

"Okay, there are a lot of phonies taking advantage of our groovy scene, but that doesn't mean it's not a remarkable time and place to be alive. Most of the kids are at least searching for a better way to live without destroying the planet. What's your story, Paul? You joined the Marines—you didn't listen when people told you Vietnam was bullshit. How will you convince the cowboys to go all anti-war?"

"First of all, no one was telling me not to go. But I've been there and know it's a futile shit storm. If those kids will just listen, there will be fewer rednecks itching for a fight."

"You guys are nuts. David, tell me you're just talking, right?"

pleads Vivian. "I thought we had a pretty groovy thing going on."

David takes Vivian's hands. "I love you Vivian, but I need to do something to end this. Whatever we can do to make a difference is important to me."

Vivian paces the room for a few moments before huffing out an exasperated breath. "Okay, you guys go stumble off to Texas. But when those cowboys run your asses out of their miserable state, and I know they will, you better come straight back home to me. I promise I'll welcome you back into my loving arms, but I will also rub your noses in this dumb-ass decision."

David wraps his arms around Vivian's waist and gives her a gentle kiss.

"Thanks, Viv. You know we love you, right?"

"I love you, too. You guys are going to need some traveling money, so I suggest you get cracking and finish painting my house."

David let out a hoot. "Ha! We will if you stop adding colors. I don't even know how many are on it anymore!"

"Eighteen. That's how old I was when I bought this place."

Paul shakes his head in amusement and laughs, "How did you manage to buy a house in San Francisco at the age of eighteen?"

Vivian steps up close to Paul and pokes him in the chest. "I managed because I kick ass, and you had better do the same down in Texas, or whatever shit-kicking state you end up getting stuck in. And you better make sure you bring my magic painter man back to me. You are in charge of his safety."

Life
Unfolds

T he cowboy watches the smoke swirl and bounce off the windshield before scattering out the open window. The view is the same one he's been staring at for as long as he can remember—a faded white line on a two-lane road stretching off for miles before vanishing into the horizon. He pauses before the next inhale and fiddles with the radio. He hasn't picked up a signal in a very long time and seeing as he's sitting in the middle of nowhere, he isn't surprised either—that's how life works in Limbo or wherever he is. He gives up on the radio and puts an Old Gold to his mouth for another deep drag, exhaling with an audible, "Ahhh," one of life's great pleasures.

His momentary gratification is interrupted by a voice from the back seat. "This light burns my eyes."

"I am not interested in what rock you've crawled out from under," replies the cowboy.

"If you hear me though, that is enough."

"Spit it out then, I have places to go."

"Where would that be?" inquires the voice.

"Where those lie helpless. Maybe they thirst."

"And you have food and water to bring them?"

The cowboy pauses, wondering for a moment if he has any provisions. "There is always something one can do."

"How could you help? You yourself are famished."

"There is a thirst, even water cannot quench it," replies the cowboy.

"Why do you listen to that voice and not mine?"

"Truth is a sweeter tasting wine."

The cowboy jolts in surprise, when, for the first time in ages, the radio comes to life. A station with a clear signal begins playing an upbeat soul hit, "Just Give Me a Little Sign" by Brenton Wood.

Just give me a little sign..ah..a sign ah.

Show me that you love me, oh yeah.
Just give me a little sign...ah...a sign.

The cowboy hurries to start the car. The big engine sounds strong with a deep purr. He races the engine a couple of times to clear out the pipes and looks in the side mirror for any traffic. He laughs to himself as if there would be any. The good thing is that he seems to be free of that voice which has been pestering him. Not all from the other side are good spirits. Some spread mayhem and madness that are known as Tricksters. God only knows how long he has been sitting on the side of the road staring off into space.

A 1965 Volkswagen van sputters a few times and comes to a halt on a desolate stretch of highway in the Sonora Desert.

Paul angrily throws his cigarette on the ground as he jumps out of the van. "This sucks! Stupid-ass generator belt! I put a new one on in Barstow!"

A moment later, David slides out of the passenger door and accidentally slams it against the side of the van. Paul gives David a stern look and says quietly, "She's not liking your treatment. Be nice."

David steps out into the bright sun shielding his eyes with his hand. "Sorry, I lost my grip. I don't think we put the belt on right the last time."

Paul pats the side of the van. "Sorry I can't put a belt on you correctly, honey," he says affectionately. He looks up and down the highway and complains, "This is so messed up, man. We're in the middle of nowhere."

David takes a deep breath and studies the arid landscape, which due to the acid he dropped when they left Barstow, vibrates with radiating multi-color geometric patterns. But Paul is right, they are in the middle of nowhere. David looks down at the ground and gasps at the asphalt glistening in the sun like glowing stones.

"Look, a highway of diamonds!" he exclaims.

David returns to the van and pulls out a floppy canvas hat. He scrunches it down over his thick long hair. He takes a light jacket out of an old box being used as a suitcase and casually walks to the center of the road with a cigarette dangling from his mouth. He rolls the jacket into a pillow and lies down on the faded white lines. He closes his eyes and says, "Hmmm, God, this road feels good."

"You can't beat Mr. Owsley's acid," says Paul.

David takes a deep inhale off his cigarette and watches the smoke rise into the deep blue sky, dancing with the wind currents until disappearing. "I love watching smoke on acid."

"You're so weird. I can't stand to smoke on acid," adds Paul.

Not a single car or truck has materialized in the past hour. The sun has not let up its efforts to destroy the two stranded travelers and shade is nearly non-existent. Paul sits in the narrow shadow created by the van, picking up small rocks and tossing them into the arid landscape. He sighs out a frustrated breath and walks out to the middle of the highway and scans down the road for an oncoming car or truck, and shakes his head in wonder. He looks down at David, still lying on the road with a hat over his face.

"Maybe we should start walking. There's got to be a town somewhere out in this hellhole."

"Don't waste your energy," says David from under his hat.

"We can't stay here and fry," says Paul, throwing his cigarette on the ground and cursing their predicament.

"Paul, you're scaring off shit," says David.

"I should've dropped too, at least I'd die happy," complains Paul.

"Someone had to drive. I'll take the next shift. Lie here next to me, the road is warm and the portals are opening. We'll call in for some help."

"I need a joint."

Paul climbs onto the passenger seat and pulls a baggie of weed from the glove compartment. He lights up a fat one and takes in a few deep tokes, closes his eyes and holds the smoke in for as long as he can before exhaling.

"Ahhh, that hit the spot," he says.

Paul returns to David and sits down Buddha style. He closes his eyes and begins a quite chant based on an old rock song titled, "Come Softly," by the Fleetwoods. "Come softly, darling, Come softly, darling. I need, I need you so much, wanna feel, your warm touch."

"God, that's beautiful," says David.

Paul didn't think he was singing out loud and asks, "What is?"

"The insects. Listen, do you hear them? Their rhythm?"

"Oh, yeah."

"It's like everything in nature—the insects, our heartbeat, all with the same rhythm."

"Yeah."

Wondering if his call for assistance had been answered, David lifts his head and focuses on an object emerging from a shimmering mirage in the distance. A car does seem to be wobbling down the road, its image knocked side to side by the waves of heat.

"That looks like something," he says calmly.

"Are you still tripping?" asks Paul.

Paul squints and scans down the highway and shouts with joy, "Jesus, it's a car!"

A few moments later, a garish, two-tone, gold and maroon 1954 Oldsmobile pulls off the road and parks behind the van. The door opens and a tall, lanky cowboy wearing a gaudy, silver cowboy shirt slowly climbs out of the car.

The cowboy looks down at the ground and studies it for a moment, wondering if the Trickster is messing with him again. Satisfied when he feels solid matter, he breaks into a wide grin and asks, "Howdy, you boys in trouble?"

Paul points out his disabled van.

"Man, we've been stuck here all day. Could you give us a ride? We need a generator belt!"

The cowboy walks over and appraises the van quietly before closing his eyes and placing his hand on the chrome VW logo .

David and Paul are confused by this behavior, but the guy does have a car and it looks like they're not going to die out in the middle of the desert after all.

Finally the cowboy says, "I think I might have something that could work." He turns away and walks back to his Olds and opens the trunk. He begins moving things around until he locates the object of his desire. He slams down the trunk and steps out onto the highway with a brand new fan belt, smiling proudly as he holds the it up in the air like a prize he's just won at the county fair.

"This might do," he grins.

Paul and David follow the cowboy as he goes to the rear of their van. He squats down in front of the open engine hatch and compares his belt to the damaged one.

"Yep, this is perfect," he says. "Have ya got a wrench?"

Paul pulls opens his toolbox and hands the cowboy a large crescent wench.

"An amazing tool," says the cowboy. "Adjustable. Fixes most anything, and when confronted by desperados is a good weapon."

Paul wonders if giving this stranger a weapon was the right thing to do. Fortunately, this time the wrench will be used to loosen the generator and slide the new belt easily over the pulley wheel.

"So, where are you guys headin' to?" he asks.

"Somewhere in Texas." replies David.

"Somewhere?"

"A place where we can do our work," says Paul.

The cowboy smiles and wipes his brow, "Important work?"

"We're on a mission to stop the war. We have to enlighten young people who haven't been told the truth about it," says Paul.

"Where have all the flowers gone, right?" replies the cowboy.

"Right," nods Paul.

Ten minutes later, the cowboy closes the engine hatch and takes the towel offered by David. He wipes his hands and face with great pleasure, then places it back in David's hands with a joyful smile, apparently elated by the interaction with fellow humans.

David beams back, "You saved our lives. How can we ever repay you?"

The cowboy points down the road in the direction of Texas. "Beyond is a wretched melancholy created by ignorance and greed. You are on the right path, my friends, which is one of verity and virtue. Someday a hand will reach out to you in need. That is how life unfolds."

The cowboy turns and ambles back to his Olds. He smiles when the big V-8 engine comes to life. He revs the motor a few times out of habit before pulling onto the highway, tipping his hat as he passes Paul and David. Alone, he grins with pleasure that the annoying voice from the back seat has gone silent. *Maybe his time in the wilderness is coming to an end.*

David and Paul watch the Olds until it reaches the rise of a distant hill before vanishing.

"That...was far out," says a stunned Paul. "Life unfolds?"

"I'm calling this experience, the miracle of the fan belt," says David. "A VW belt in the trunk of an Olds? And, verity and virtue? I don't even know what that means."

"I guess we'll be finding out," replies Paul. "I believe our verity and virtue. Someday a hand will reach out to you in need. That is how life unfolds."

The cowboy ambles back to his Olds and cranks up the big V-8 engine. He revs it up a few times out of habit then pulls out onto the highway, tipping his hat to David and Paul, grinning with then pulls back onto the lonely road, tips his hat to Paul and David, and sails onward, down the road toward whatever happens next.

Paul and David watch the Olds until it reaches the rise of a distant hill then vanishes beyond the crest.

"That was far out," says a stunned Paul. "Life unfolds?"

"A VW belt in the trunk of an Olds? If that wasn't a miracle, I don't know what is. And, verity and virtue? What does that mean?"

"I guess we'll be finding out," replies Paul. "Looks like our little road trip is going to be a lot more interesting than we thought."

Paul jumps behind the wheel and searches the radio for a decent signal. A Spanish language station playing a Mexican polka comes in clearly, as does a preacher babbling on about Jesus coming back to earth, both of which he can't change quickly enough. Next is a static-filled country and western station fading in and out, and finally, a clear signal from a station playing, "If You're Going to San Francisco" by Scott MacKenzie.

At that moment, David opens the door and jumps into the passenger seat and flinches when he hears the song. "Eeek!" he yelps. "Maybe going to Texas isn't that terrible an idea after all."

One hundred miles into the state of Texas, David and Paul enter a wide valley surrounded by large desert mountains and watch with interest as dark clouds begin forming in the distance.

While the storm races to them shooting out bolts of lightning on both sides of the road, a black spot suddenly appears in the middle of the highway. It grows larger with each passing moment and is on a collision course with the van. Paul is reminded of his military training and the signs of passing out. He was taught that he would experience traveling into a long black tunnel before losing consciousness, but this is just the opposite. No matter. While he searches his memory, the black spot is upon them—a large swarm of bumblebees is barreling down the middle of the highway playing a game of chicken and results in a frightening explosion of splattering bee bodies when they slam into the front of the van amid shattering glass.

Opening his eyes moments after the collision, Paul is happy to find the windshield still intact and the van's interior not filled with hundreds of angry bumblebees. Paul rubs his chest and feels his heart racing. He looks over to David and laughs because of the look of horror on his face.

Under
Siege

BEEVILLE, TEXAS 1935

The once isolated ranching community of Beeville, Texas, finds itself overwhelmed as the nearby naval airbase has swollen to house over five thousand men. The purpose of the base is training jet pilots for the war in Vietnam. The influx of Navy airmen has rocked the local ruling class and yanked them into a new world no longer resembling what used to be only a few years earlier. Young men have poured into Bee County from every state in the country and have flooded the town with their disposable income.

Beeville is in the midst an economic boom. The sailors have also brought psychedelic rock music, and liberal politics and behavior which the local young people have enthusiastically embraced,.

Under an umbrella-covered table, Gene, Harold, and Larry relax with sandwiches and beer after finishing up their round of golf in the sweltering heat of South Texas.

"Oh my God, Pete is gettin' ready to tee off," exclaims Gene, the owner of Alamo-Cola, the local soft drink bottling plant. He's a thin, high-strung fifty–year–old and sports a well-trimmed mustache. Swinging around in his seat he says, "Say Harold, could you please not razz poor old Pete for me?"

Gene's request is answered with a laugh. "Shit, that buzzard ain't gonna let a little razzin' throw his game off." Harold is a forty year-old, weathered rancher who looks at least ten years older than his age due to a life in the hot Texas sun chasing down strays on his ranch. He taps out an ash from his cigar and glances over to the first tee. "Especially seeing as how he ain't got one to begin with!"

On the first tee, Pete, a powerfully built forty year-old Texas Ranger pulls a driver out of his bag. The men watch as Pete places his ball and tee into position and focuses on his target down the lush, green fairway. He takes a couple of easy practice swings, then settles into his golf stance, waggling the club and loosening his shoulders before initiating his swing. He takes the club back slowly, but on his downswing he increases the velocity so greatly, that it forces him to lift his head, and falls backwards just before contact. The ball ends up spinning wildly down the fairway, bouncing along at a high rate of speed no more than two or three feet in the air.

Larry, throws his hands over his mouth and guffaws under his breath. "Oh Jesus, he should've used his practice swing!"

Harold yells out, "Peter! You better give yourself a ticket for that speedy-ass swing!"

Pete turns and glares at the group. He flips them the middle finger in quick-draw fashion, then slams his driver into his golf bag and plops down in the driver's seat of the golf cart. The gas engine coughs to a start and he sets off after his ball with a scowl and his face more red than usual.

"Harold, Pete's gonna' kick your ass someday!" laughs Larry.

"Shit. Say somethin' that'll scare me."

Harold turns back to the table and takes a deep swig from his beer, then leans in close to Gene. "Say Gene, I hear you got some trouble brewin' over at the plant. You gonna be able to deal with it?"

Gene strokes at his mustache nervously. "It's the God damn Mexicans! They're getting all uppity because of all the money the Navy is doling out right and left. It's got everything all screwed up these days."

"How many fuckin' boys they got out there nowadays?" asks Harold. "Five, six thousand? Shit, I remember when there wasn't more 'n couple hundred sailors doin' nothin' but keepin' the fuckin' weeds down. That, and those fuckin' jets scarin' my stock."

"The Navy is screwing up our economy," complains Gene. "Everyone wants to make federal wages, including the Mexicans!"

"God damn Navy," scoffs Larry. "A bunch of draft dodgers is what they are."

"Too fuckin' chicken-shit to join the Marines and help America kill fuckin' Charlie," says Harold.

"Can you say *fuckin' a* little more often, Harold?" complains Gene. "Jesus, learn another adjective."

Harold laughs, "What the hell are we fightin' commies for if it ain't for right to say what we want? And fuck you too while we're at it!"

Larry points to the golf course. "Calm down girls, looks like Pete is gonna hit his second shot."

The men all turn and watch as Pete approaches his ball, fifty yards from his tee shot. Once again, he takes two smooth practice swings before addressing the ball.

"Should've used one of those, Petey-boy!" laughs Harold.

Larry nudges Harold. "Betcha Pete nails it this time."

"Put your money on table, buddy, that'll be the easiest fuckin' money I'll make all week," laughs Harold.

The three men watch Pete study his target, the flag on the green three hundred yards away. Like most hackers, he makes the mistake of trying to reach his goal with one mighty strike, and, once again just before making contact with the ball, lifts his head and slices the ball into the next fairway.

"Oh Jesus! I can't look any more," yucks Harold. "This is just too damn painful to watch."

Gene waits for the laughter to quiet before tapping Harold on the shoulder. "Say Harold, is Congressman Buck going to be in town this weekend? Maybe he can give me a little labor advice."

"You think you got troubles? Ol' Buck is in the shitter because of that civil rights bill. His Houston buddies are gettin' ready to toss his ass back to Maine where he fuckin' belongs. So I doubt he's feeling much like huntin' these days."

"Buck has always been a good friend to the Beeville business community. I sure do hope he can make it," whines Gene.

"I'd love to see Buck's sorry ass, too, as long as he doesn't bring that idiot son of his with him," laughs Harold. "And I better start seein' some fuckin' birds, too. Little bastards must be gettin' smarter 'cause they're scarce as hell right now."

"Junior is okay," says Gene. "Did you know, he just graduated from Yale?"

Harold spits out, "Yale? Yale University? Shit, that dumb ass couldn't graduate high school if it wasn't for his big daddy pullin' strings. Why are you so interested in that Yankee fuck anyway?"

"I don't know, I like talking to him."

"That's right I forgot, he speaks fuckin' English."

Fucking
Texas

M ichael Blackwell is looking through the viewfinder of his camera at dark, threatening thunderheads looming over a rock–strewn mountain peak in a desolate West Texas valley. He snaps the photo and tells himself, "I might as well have photographic proof of who I am when my body is discovered."

He takes an exasperated breath as he sits on his seabag and rests his head in his hands. He stares off into the wilderness and thinks about the past year and what he could have done to avoid the draft, and the Navy—anything to avoid being stuck in the middle of desolation valley with a quart of water left in his canteen.

After fighting the draft for over a year, Michael found himself at the Los Angeles draft board center taking his final physical exam. It was his second exam within two months with the same result. He was healthy and had always been healthy.

At the last station, Michael confidently handed the examiner an identification card which showed that he was a member of the Worker's International Marxist-Leninist Party of Los Angeles— literally, a card-carrying communist. Although he is totally against the Vietnam War, Michael isn't really a communist, but his friend who got him the card is.

The examiner did a quick scan of the card with a scowl, then snarled at him in some weird southern accent. "A red, huh? Well, you're sure as hell gonna hate killing your little commie buddies now, ain't ya? Get yer fuckin' ass outta my face!"

Michael had been certain that being a communist would keep him out of the Army. After all, they are the enemy we're at war with. He was told to go home and wait for a notice from the Selective Service informing him when he should appear for a final examination before being carted off to war in a Greyhound bus.

With his physical exam concluded, he followed a slow moving

line of inductees out of the building and onto the sidewalk where he was greeted with the overpowering scent of marijuana. Booze and joints were being given to America's newest troops them by their friends who had shown up to wish them *bon voyage*. In a couple of hours these boys would begin the nightmarish experience of boot camp, then off to the more terrifying reality of war. Yet, they were behaving like they're going off to a Boy Scout Jamboree. Michael found the circus-like atmosphere overwhelmingly depressing.

Michael watched the line of boys march out of step toward the door of a bus. They lumbered to a clumsy halt after receiving their first order from an Army Sergeant who yelled out, "Halt, God damn it!" That command was immediately followed by the second order of, "Shut the fuck up and find a seat!" With that, the line of the future dead, or angry post-traumatic stress- suffering veterans stepped onto the bus in single file, one sad sack at a time.

That day was his last chance to avoid the draft. He had been certain the Army wouldn't accept a communist into their ranks, and now his choices were truly limited outside of escaping to Canada or going into hiding and becoming a wanted man—a felon who could spend up to ten years in a Federal prison if caught. His final option came three days later when a surfing buddy told him about an opening at a Naval Reserve unit. He would need to get signed up ASAP, and at the time it sounded like the most cowardly act he could imagine. With certain induction into the Army looming over his head, he needed to make a life-altering decision which seemed like a heavy burden for a nineteen year–old. His only goal six months earlier had been to save up enough money to travel to exotic tropical islands and spend his life surfing.

So, he signed away his freedom and reported to Navy boot camp in San Diego for a two year stint of active duty. His parents were glad he'd chosen to enlist in the Navy, it being the much safer alternative to the Army and Vietnam. More than anything, he was disappointed in his parents for giving up their son to war without much of a fight.

The faint sound of a car engine in the distance snaps Michael out of his daydreaming. He lifts his head and spots a pickup truck coming his way, and breathes a sigh of relief that this valley will not play a role in him being left to rot on the side of the road. He quickly jumps to his feet and flashes a beaming smile, and sticks out his thumb for a ride.

The truck approaches at a high rate of speed, then begins to slow as it nears. Michael's spirit's rise as he comes face to face the truck's occupants, two teenaged boys wearing cowboy hats and shit-eating grins. The driver lays on the horn and steps on the gas, while the other teen leans out the window and yells, "Suck on it, fuckin' queer!"

His heart drops and Michael offers the departing truck and its occupants an obligatory middle finger salute before grabbing his camera and taking a shot of it speeding away. When he prints up a black and white photo in a few days, it will feature a solitary pickup truck on a remote road heading toward dark, desolate mountains and a middle finger sticking out of the passenger side window.

The hooting and laughing fade away to silence.

"Fucking Texas," complains Michael.

The rancher who dropped him off here told him they didn't get many travelers on this old highway these days, especially since the new Interstate gave travelers a straighter shot at San Antonio.

"It's a might lonely, that's for sure," he said to Michael, "but that new road don't even compare in scenery to this old highway, don't you think?"

Michael can't fully appreciate the rancher's affection for the desolate beauty at the moment, but ten years from now when he's working on an art career, the photo he's just taken will pay for a down payment on a new Volvo station wagon. The rancher didn't tell him what his business was either, or how long he might be, but just before he drove off he laughed, "If you're still here when I finish up, I'll get you a bit closer to civilization."

Michael jumps to his feet when he spots a small white object a mile away, and it looks much like another vehicle heading his way. He holds his breath when the object pulls onto the shoulder of the road. "Oh shit, don't turn around!" he prays. "Please, don't turn around!"

Thankfully, the vehicle stops, and without further hesitation Michael lifts his seabag onto his shoulder with a grunt and begins walking at a very brisk pace toward his possible rescuers.

Paul pulls over to the side of the road and slides to a stop. He quickly jumps out to check the damage to his van which has him pretty upset. The van was the first big purchase he made after Vietnam and this would be the first of any damage to it. Fortunately they've only suffered a broken headlight, but the suicidal bumblebees splattered remains thickly cover the front of the van.

"Welcome to Texas," says David sarcastically.

"Fucking weird-ass state. I gotta piss somewhere," grumbles Paul. He slides down the gravel embankment and finds a small, lonely cactus and urinates on it.

"That poor little plant," jokes David.

"I'm helping him out. When was the last time this poor guy saw anything wet? I'm hungry, how about some lunch?"

David opens the van and pulls a loaf of bread and condiments out of the small ice box. As he concentrates on slicing an avocado and tomato for sandwiches, a voice calls out to them, "HELLO!"

David and Paul watch with interest as a clean-cut guy with a big smile, carrying a military duffle bag on his shoulder is walking toward them.

Michael drops his bag to the ground and places his hands on his knees to catch his breath from the long jog.

"What the hell!" exclaims Paul, "Where did you come from?"

"Sorry about surprising you like that. I've been stuck down the road for hours and I was afraid you might turn around and head off in the other direction."

"What are you doing out here?" asks David.

"My ride dropped me off and headed up into the mountains."

David asks Michael if he had seen a swarm bumblebees.

"A swarm of what?"

David thumbs back down the road and says, "Bumblebees. They slammed into us and nearly knocked us off the road."

"I didn't know they traveled in packs," replies Michael.

"That makes three of us," says Paul.

Paul sits down in the doorway and stares at Michael for a few moments, studying Michael's short hair and trimmed mustache. He wonders if he's in the FBI, sent out to arrest David for evading the draft or separate him from his "vacation" stash of LSD.

"What are you doing in Texas?" asks Paul.

"I'm stationed at a Navy air base."

"Why are you hitching, doesn't the Navy pay for your travel?"

"They do, but I spent my airfare partying with my friends. I barely had enough money left over for food and ended up with enough bus fare to get me as far as Las Cruces."

David extends his hand. "Live for today, right on. I'm David and this freak is Paul."

Michael extends a hand, "I'm Michael."

"So, where is this base located?"

"Beeville—about fifty miles from Corpus Christie."

David flinches. "Eek, more bees!"

"No shit. What's Beeville like?" asks Paul.

"Hot and humid and full of sailors and rednecks—mostly a bunch of cowboy shit."

Paul nods approvingly. "Sounds like just the kind of place we're looking for. Hopefully, you act like a soldier."

Michael is unsure of the comment. "What?"

Paul pulls a joint out of his shirt pocket and lights it. "You get high, right?"

"Hell yes! Where are you guys coming from?"

"San Francisco. We've come to dip our toes in the blue waters of the Gulf of Mexico," replies Paul jokingly.

"Sorry to disappoint you, but at its best, the gulf is the color of root beer."

"Great," moans Paul.

"Why on earth would you want to come to Texas?"

"To end the war. We're looking for a serious redneck town to start our work in."

"Well, Beeville would certainly fit that profile," says Michael.

"So, what do you do for the Navy anyway" asks David.

"I'm a photographer. It's total chaos on the base and they need evidence of the mess."

"Are there any young folks in Beeville we can turn on to fight the draft?" asks Paul.

"You'd be surprised. Thanks to the Navy base, the old folks have completely lost control over what the kids are up to."

"All right then, throw your bag in the van."

"Right on!" exclaims Michael gleefully. "Have you got a

place to stay yet? I've got a pretty cool little pad in town. You're welcome to crash there until you get settled."

"Thanks, man," replies Paul. "Let's see what happens."

"Meanwhile, tell us more about this city of bees," says David.

FELIX'S DINER

The glass door closes and leaves the unbearable heat outside as David, Paul, and Michael enter the air-conditioned diner which also services buses with a fast-food window. The interior is painted bright yellow with hundreds of Felix the Cat clocks on the walls with all of their tails wagging. None of them tell the same time. A narrow aisle separates a half dozen booths from the counter, although it feels more like a gauntlet as four rough-looking cowboys turn their heads in unison as the boys move past them to a roomy booth. The counter cowboys check them out with a bit of snarl mixed in with curiosity. As soon as they're seated, a friendly waitress with a sweet chirpy voice lays down menus and places a stack of silverware and paper napkins in the middle of the table.

"Can I get y'all something to start with—coffee?" she asks.

"Sounds good," says Paul.

Michael asks, "What kind of tea do you have?"

The waitress leans in close enough for Michael to get a whiff of the scented powder on her ample chest, "Lipton, honey-pie."

Michael asks, "Are you still serving breakfast?"

"All day long, darlin'."

"Can I get waffles and sausage?"

"You got it," she smiles. Turning to David, she asks," How about you, sweetie?"

"Hot chocolate and some toast. I like your clocks. How come none of them tell the same time?"

She turns around to the clocks and stares them with a studied look before laughing. "That's Felix, the owner of this little place. He says that time is all relative or something weird like that."

The waitress turns to the cowboys.

"Ain't that about right boys?"

One of the men, who appears to be the boss of this group, wears a pair of faded jeans, beat-up cowboy hat, and a faded work shirt. He swings around on his seat and sits spread-legged with his hands on his knees and his nose scrunched up.

"Felix has tested one too many nukes if you ask me. He's got some mathematical theories about reality being multi-dimensional or somethin' like that. It all sounds like crazy talk to me, but he sure as hell makes some damn good pancakes."

He lifts his chin and looks down his nose as he studies Paul's hippie attire of a Marine Corps jacket, Vietnam War insignias, and his last name stenciled over the breast pocket—all you're known by in the military. Paul had friends he fought with in the worst places on earth. Many of those guys never made it home. He knew about their girlfriends, their wives and children, and just about every detail of their lives back home. But he never knew their first names— Roberts, Barnes, Robles, Jeffries, who everyone called Jeff. Paul was known as Gill.

"Is that some kinda protest costume you wearin'?" asks the boss cowboy.

Paul chuckles, "You're the one with a cowboy hat and pointy boots. Now that's a costume."

The other men at the counter cough out laughing.

"Shit, you better quit while you're ahead!" says his friend.

Either out of hostility, ignorance, or maybe he's just trying to be helpful, the boss continues. "Y'all are in Texas. This is what we wear down here. There ain't no hippies in Texas."

A second cowboy swings around on his chair and asks, "Y'all sound like you're from California. You ain't draft dodgers, are ya?"

Paul stares at the man asking who or what he might be. "God damn Texans sure are nosy bunch of yahoos," he thinks.

"I wish I was a draft dodger," replies Paul. "I'm the dumb ass who ran out of my high school gym class and signed up for Vietnam after I got a brainwashing from a Marine recruiter. Nineteen sixty-four to nineteen sixty-six. Marksman, U.S. Marine Corps."

"He's got lots of medals, too," adds David.

The youngest cowboy of the group who appears to be in his early twenties, chimes in with enthusiasm. "Marines, huh? I was Brown Water Navy!"

Paul laughs out loud, "Are you the son of a bitch that left me hanging out to dry in that shit village on the Mekong?"

The young cowboy lets out a loud hoot and jerks back into his seat. "All right! Who were you with?"

"25th Infantry, Cu Chi, holding back the onslaught."

"No shit? You guys saw some action!"

"Way too much action," says Paul. "Besides everyone trying to kill us, the spiders were the worst. Damn things were the size of baseballs. They scared the hell out of me the first time I saw them."

The young cowboy nods his head in agreement.

"Yeah, you got that right. I was more afraid of falling off that crappy boat than getting tagged by rocket fire. The damn rivers were full of poisonous snakes and crocs!"

Boss cowboy leans in and says, "Well, thank you for your service, son, but you boys be careful down here. We got some big-ass bugs, and a lot of folk who don't take kindly toward hippies."

The waitress returns with the drinks and a plate of toast and jam. She turns to the boss and chastises him. "Now don't you be scarin' off my customers, you ol' rattlesnake. Anyway, who'd want to smoke that ol' maryjane when they can enjoy a nice big stack of Felix's waffles and sausage?"

The young cowboy thumbs at his friends and shakes his head.

"Don't worry about these miserable old dogs, they're just bent out of shape 'cause all the young chicks are into rock 'n roll and hippies. But I gotta tell ya, we do have a lot of mean, big-ass bugs in Texas."

Everyone stops what they're doing and looks out the large window as a loud rumble then rain suddenly comes out of nowhere. Most entertaining however, is the drenching of bus travelers who scramble for the safety, laughing and jostling one another as they all try to squeeze through the door of the bus at the same time.

They leave the diner with one headlight and both wipers furiously slapping copious amounts of rain off the windshield. In the few seconds it has taken them to get from the restaurant to inside the van, all are thoroughly soaked.

David laughs as he slams the door shut. "What in the hell is going on with this state?"

"Last year we got hit by a hurricane that dumped eighteen inches of rain in one day and everything went under water," says Michael. "I saw was a dead steer hanging in a tree with its head wedged between the branches. I swear it looked like it had been lynched. Man, I couldn't step on the gas fast enough."

Michael's House

A young man everyone calls JC is lying on the floor with his eyes closed, listening to a song on the record player. "Section 49," a long psychedelic instrumental by Country Joe and the Fish. Lying next to him is a pretty blond, blue-eyed, young woman named Nancy. Both are stretched out on their backs on a fake Persian rug sharing a joint. Various patterned print scarves are draped over the lamp shade. There are an overstuffed couch and chair, a wooden box is being used as a coffee table. Numerous psychedelic posters of rock shows cover the walls, including a large poster over the couch featuring a Texas rock group called The 13th Floor Elevators.

JC blinks open his eyes and stares at the ceiling before slowly pushing himself up to cross-legged. He glances at Nancy, whose eyes are closed, and shakes his head disapprovingly before crawling over to the record player and turning it off.

Nancy moans, "Awe, JC. Why did you turn it off?"

"Jesus Nancy, the same song has been playing for hours."

Nancy throws her arms over her head and takes a pleasantly languid stretch. Even under a baggy Navy work shirt, she exudes a seductive charm. The shirt has the name, Blackwell, stenciled over the breast pocket.

"I love that song," she says sleepily.

"Jesus, J. Edgar Hoover is right. Rock 'n roll has destroyed your brain."

"No, it's *Mad* magazine that destroyed my brain. I'm hungry, JC, you got anything to eat?"

"Oranges," replies JC.

Nancy rises and walks to the kitchen. She opens the refrigerator, looks inside and finds it empty except for two oranges and three small, shriveled peyote buttons on a shelf.

"You get all that free food at the base, JC. Why don't you

bring some home once in awhile?"

"The Navy is already screwing me over 'cause I'm a pothead. You're just too lazy to go to the store."

"I don't like getting hassled by everyone," whines Nancy.

"They're *your* people. Show 'em the light!"

Nancy stops at the screen door and stares out at the muddy alley and the potholes filled by today's rain. She peels the orange and complains, "It would take all the acid in the world to straighten out this stupid town. You know, if I did have a bunch, I could put it in the syrup at the Alamo-Cola plant."

"Yeah! Of course you'd have to get a job there."

"Naw, I could do it on a field trip."

"You're still going to school?"

"Sometimes."

Suddenly Nancy squeals. "Hey JC! Somebody just pulled up! Jesus, they've got California plates!"

JC rushes to the door nearly knocking Nancy aside and throws open the screen door which hits the house with a loud bang. They pile onto the small front porch and gawk at a VW van parked in the mud in front of the house with two long-haired guys smiling at them. When the van's side door opens and Michael jumps out, Nancy leaps off the porch and runs to him. She throws her arms around his neck and kisses him passionately on the lips.

"Did you miss me?" asks Michael jokingly.

"You jerk! You were gone so long, I thought you ditched me!"

"I'd never do that. What are you doing here? I thought you were going to summer school."

Nancy teases, "I'm ditching, dad, so I could hang out with JC and get stoned!"

Michael kisses her again and laughs, "Are you sure you're from Texas?"

David and Paul climb out of the van and wait patiently while Michael gets reacquainted with his girlfriend.

Prying himself away from Nancy's embrace, Michael begins introductions. "This is Paul and David who were kind enough to picked me up in Nowhere, Texas, moments before the buzzards showed up. Guys, this is Nancy and JC."

He returns to the van, pulls out his seabag and hands Nancy his tripod. "Is there anything to eat?" he asks.

Nancy shakes her head "no" with a frown.

"Sounds about right. Next stop then is a trip to Don's Dog House." Michael turns to David and Paul with a big smile and says, "You will not find a better taco in Texas."

Thanks to the rain, the air is filled with a chorus of "berrupt, berrupt," as hundreds of frogs sing along to the music coming from the little frame house. "Morning Dew" by the Grateful Dead plays softly in the darkened room lit by candles and a single table lamp. With full stomachs thanks to Don's tacos, Michael cradles Nancy to his chest as they recline on pillows and smoke a joint.

Michael asks JC, "What's been going on?"

Nancy answers quickly. "Oh, my God, I forgot to tell you! Janie married Danny!"

Michael almost chokes on the smoke. "Danny? The big rock and roll star?"

"Yep," answers Nancy matter-of-factly.

"What a trip!" he exclaims. "Jesus, I've only been gone thirty days! Your sister sure doesn't fuck around, does she?"

"What can I say? She's in love."

"Are you okay, JC?" asks Michael.

JC sighs and shakes his head no. "It's been a shitty year, but I'm cool now. First I get busted and am going off to the brig, then my girlfriend splits. I really loved her, too."

JC stares off into space looking melancholy while thinking about the his lost love.

Michael whispers to Nancy, "How long was that going on? Before I left on leave?"

Nancy cups her hand and whispers back, "It happened when JC got restricted to the base and was waiting for the court martial. Didn't you ever suspect it?"

"No, not at all."

Michael remembers Janie being pretty serious about JC for a long time. Even when he first showed up at the base last year, Janie and JC were a hot item. To find out that Janie was seeing someone else—it's too mind-blowing.

"I can't do the math while I'm high, Nancy," he says. "Hey, want to see what I brought?"

Michael gathers up his seabag lying near the door where he dropped it three hours earlier and heads into the small kitchen with Nancy eagerly following.

"Did you bring me a present?" she asks.

"Better," says Michael as he lifts the bag onto a wooden chair and opens it. He takes out a pair of neatly folded pants, a couple of shirts and underwear, and lays them on the table. He pauses for a moment before breaking into a big smile. "Ready?"

"What in the hell are you up to? Seriously, did you get me something super groovy in California?"

"Oh, yes, it's very super groovy."

"Please tell me you bought me, "Sergeant Pepper's Lonely Hearts Club Band!"

"Sorry, I'll get it for you if you want it that bad. This is way better than that over-produced record—this is more organic."

"Blasphemer!" laughs Nancy. "You just have to listen to it in the right frame of mind."

Michael reaches into the bag and pulls out a kilo of marijuana wrapped in red cellophane. He smiles, "This might make that album sound better?"

Nancy gasps. When Michael pulls out a second kilo of weed, she cries out, "Oh my God!"

It echoes throughout the house and has JC, Paul, and David running into the kitchen. They all crowd around the table and gawk at the pot.

"Here's the best part," beams Michael as he carefully opens a kilo. He takes a small pinch and holds it under Nancy's nose. "Have you ever smelled anything like it?"

"Ohhh, my God. It smells like a skunk. Is that a good thing?"

"It means it's very good. It's probably five or six times more powerful than anything we've ever smoked before."

JC shakes his head.

"I can't believe you thumbed all the way from California with a block of weed. Weren't you afraid of getting busted?"

"I'm proudly serving our country as a member of the U.S. Navy and I look like a cop. Who's going to hassle me? I wasn't really worried until I ran into these two freaks."

"This is an awful lot of weed, dude," says JC.

Michael agrees. "Yeah, but events came my way. What could I do but react like any normal red-blooded American."

"You bought this?" asks JC.

"No, it was free!"

"No way!"

"Yeah. My friend was in Vietnam with some gangsters from Detroit who were always complaining about no weed in Detroit. He told them they could score all the weed they needed when they got back to the States."

Michael hands JC a handful of pot and asks him to roll up some joints.

"When I went home on leave, everybody was freaking out because the connection was in jail. The gangsters had all this money fronted to them from even bigger gangsters back in Detroit, and nobody could find any weed."

Paul eyes Michael suspiciously. "But you could? You know, I'm from Detroit, and there are some seriously bad dudes you don't want anything to do with."

"So I've learned. But, the whole thing was hysterically funny and you should have seen these Detroit guys. My buddy took me to the gangsters' apartment in Hollywood, and after a couple of weeks in California, they had turned into hippies. They ditched their shiny suits and began wearing buckskin vests and suede bell bottoms. Like to them, L.A. was country, and I guess it is compared to Detroit. But, they were still nervous as hell and freaking out because they were living off the bigger gangster's money."

"So, how did you end up with all this?" asks JC.

"I ran into an old surfing friend and told him the story about the gangsters. First he laughed his ass off, then told me could get them all the weed they needed. So I set up a meeting."

Michael sweeps his hands across the table.

"This is my commission for introducing everyone. Cool, huh? It's super potent. I'm telling you, Texas will never be the same after they start smoking this."

After Paul takes a couple of hits he ends up standing in front of the 13th Floor Elevators poster staring at the swirling art. "I can't believe you know these guys. I saw them at the Avalon and it was the best concert ever. The dude blowing into those ceramic jugs really tripped me out. We couldn't believe they came out of Texas."

"Nancy's sister knows the drummer, and we always let him know when we've harvested buttons," says JC.

"What kind of buttons do you harvest?"

"Peyote!" squeals Nancy. "They grow wild all over the Rio Grande Valley—and it's legal too! That's why there are so many freaks and lost cowboys wandering the desert talking to God knows who."

"No shit. I think we met one when the van broke down. We'll need a peyote guide, then."

"Only if you want to find your way home," smiles Nancy.

"Hey man," exclaims Paul, suddenly becoming aware of the late hour. "We should get going. I need a shower and a bed. Have they got a good motel in this town?"

"There's a clean little motel out toward Skidmore."

"What the hell kind of a name is Skidmore?" laughs Paul.

"That's pretty tame for Texas. Have you ever heard of Ding Dong, or how about Dime Box?" says Nancy and begins to laugh uncontrollably, which makes Paul start laughing too.

"Obviously inspired by your peyote," laughs Paul. "So, are you from Beeville?"

"No," answers a laughing Nancy, "I'm from Pettus."

"Pet us?"

"Yes, we're very friendly."

Paul laughs, "That sounds like a good place to camp out at."

Nancy shakes her head. "There's nothing there but a gas station and my parent's chickens dropping eggs all over the place."

"What do you think, JC? Can they can stay here?" asks Michael.

"Sure," says JC. "You're going to need some cool company after I split."

JC turns to Paul and David and says,"The Navy sentenced me to six months at Portsmouth Naval Prison and gave me an undesirable discharge. I've only got a few more days of freedom."

"That's fucked up, man! Sorry to hear this," says Paul.

"The Captain wanted to make an example out of JC," says Michael. "Won't do shit. When I flood the base with my weed they'll forget all about dropping bombs on innocent villages."

"It could have been worse, but Michael saved my ass. If he hadn't warned me about the raid, they would have found a lot more weed stashed in my locker."

"Like I said, the Navy needs photographic evidence. Before the Shore Patrol picked me up to go on the bust, I gave JC a head's up," says Michael. He turns and wags his finger at JC, "and he was supposed to stash all his pot."

JC shrugs. "I had a lid in some old work shoes and forgot all about it."

"That is so messed up," says Paul. "Why not split?"

"I can do six months. Anyway, it's a cool little pad."

"It's up to you guys if you want to crash here," says Michael.

"Right on, man! What do you think, David?"

They leave the kitchen and return to the living room where they find a comfy spot propped up against the couch leaning on pillows. Nancy and Michael share the upholstered chair with their legs and arms entwined. David has been quiet all evening, spending most of it lying on the couch listening to the excellent record collection. He lifts his head with a sleepy grin and asks Michael, "Did I hear you say you had a surfing buddy? Do you surf?"

"It was all I used to do before the Navy found me," replies Michael.

"Far out, me too. Is there any surf down here?"

"Not really, mostly wind swell, but sometimes it gets good,

like when there's a hurricane spinning out in the Gulf."

JC laughs, "I don't think you'll be surfing or stopping the war if you smoke much of this weed. I could do prison easily if I could bring some of this shit with me. Nice score, Michael."

"Don't thank me, thank the weed growers in Michoacan."

"Speaking of stopping the war, we need to figure a way to do some anti-war counseling," says Paul. "Do you know anyone who might be interested?"

"Are you kidding?" exclaims Nancy. "They just built a new college outside of town. I know just about everyone. Also, do you guys need any acid? I've got a stash of it if you need some. It's really good—ever heard of Orange Sunshine?"

"No. Where did it come from?" asks Paul.

"My sister. She and her husband know all the freaks in Austin because of the band. I think some science students at the University started making it a couple of years ago."

Nancy snuggles up close to Michael, begins rubbing his neck affectionately and whispers, "How about sharing some of that weed with me, cool guy? I could use some extra spending money. How about a dozen ounces to get me going?"

Alamo-Cola

ene finds himself cornered by a group of angry Tejano workers. A dozen delivery trucks and their Anglo drivers sit idle in the lot because the men have chosen one of the busiest days of the week to complain about their pay and working conditions.

"Hell, I'm stuck in the middle!" pleads Gene. "My other guys aren't gonna be happy if the Mexicans get paid the same as them. You see what I mean, right?"

A young man with a powerful build, close cropped black hair, and tattooed forearms steps up face-to-face with Gene and thumbs to the drivers. "They don't look too upset to me," says Luis. "That's another thing, Gene, we're not God-damned Mexicans. My family was here when your people were still picking potatoes and cabbage in Ireland or wherever you come from. We're Texans, just like you!"

A middle-aged Tejano named Ruben, steps in front of Luis and crowds Gene. "We know our rights. It's not like back in the old days when you could treat us like shit and no one cared!"

Gene looks around the lot, first to his white drivers who stare back with blank looks, and then to the twenty brown-skin Tejanos encircling him and thinks maybe he should try a little harder to calm them.

"Haven't I always treated you people fairly?"

"No, not really, Gene," replies Ruben. "Out at the base they got civil rights and fair wages. That's what's happening these days, man. White, black and brown—we all get treated equally."

"I treat everyone the same. What are you talking about?"

Another Tejano man near the back of the crowd yells over Luis' shoulder. "I'm stuck on the loading dock getting paid half of what the white workers get. You hire new drivers and all of them are white—I'm never even asked."

"You know it's different for them," explains Gene. "For one

thing, they have higher living expenses than you do."

Luis jerks back in surprise. "What in the hell is that supposed to mean? Are you really that clueless?"

"It's all about a standard of living, Luis. Take housing for example—it's a lot more for the white workers than what you pay in Mexican Town."

Luis explodes in anger. "Are you fucking kidding me, Gene? You think we like living in those little shacks?"

"You know what I mean, Luis."

"No, I don't. You must think I'm ignorant."

"I don't think that," says Gene. "I've always respected you."

"Then let me have a chance to live in a good house, too! Pay me what I'm worth!"

"Come on, Luis. You guys get back to work and we'll try and settle this. I promise I'll figure something out."

Gene pulls out a pack of cigarettes and offers one to Luis who refuses. He sheepishly offers cigarettes to the other men who stare at Gene silently, refusing his offer. Gene nervously lights one for himself and takes a couple of quick, nervous puffs.

Ruben growls, "When Luis was fighting in Vietnam, everyone got the same pay. Nobody got more because they needed more for whores or cigarettes. This is bullshit, Gene!"

"Ruben, please calm down. We...we'll work something out," stutters Gene while slowly backing up to the rear entrance of the building.

Before Gene can make his escape, Ruben steps in and jabs at Gene's chest. "You wanna keep us from walking off the job, you gotta pay us the same as the white guys."

Gene looks to Luis for help, but he looks even angrier than Ruben. "Let's work together on this, please? Just give me a little time. I promise I'll see what I can do."

Gene eventually reaches the loading dock door and grabs the handle for security. Before he ducks inside, he pleads, "Please get back to work," but no one makes a move.

Once he's safely inside the factory, Gene makes a mental note to put an ad in the *Beeville Picayune* for new workers, starting with two to replace Ruben and Luis who are responsible for stirring up this trouble. The rest are simply following them like sheep. In the past, a call to City Hall would be all he needed to set things right. The area known as Mexican Town, is the realm of Benny, the city's Spanish-speaking, Mexican Sheriff. Usually a visit from him would keep things under control.

Gene thinks, "Maybe Benny can do something. Times haven't changed all that much, have they? "

Rancho
el Abejorro

Rancho el Abejorro, Spanish for Bumblebee Ranch, sits on ten thousand acres of rolling hills, wild meadows, oak forests, and prime grazing land for Harold's five thousand head of cattle. The ranch has long entertained the most powerful influence peddlers in Texas, from senators and governors, to a variety of power brokers who visit the Rancho to relax and do a little fishing or hunting.

Harold inherited the massive ranch from his father, who inherited it from his father and so on for four generations. The seven-thousand-square-foot adobe house features a large wood-paneled living room with open beam ceilings, and walls filled with framed paintings of vaqueros and cowboy life, Texas landscapes, and portraits of the Rancho's stud bulls.

Gene, Pete and Larry lounge on leather chairs smoking cigars and drinking aged whiskey from crystal tumblers. Larry exhales a line of smoke and admires his surroundings. "I sure could get used to this kind of living, Harold. This is one fine house."

Harold takes a glance around the room, scratches his beard stubble with his rough hands and replies, "Sure, if you like livin' in a fuckin' museum. Someday I'm gonna build my own place—modern, wood and glass, then I'll donate this mausoleum to the county and let them pay for the fuckin' upkeep."

He rubs the head of his dog sitting by his side and asks, "Say, did I ever tell you boys how I got Ol' Blackie, here?"

"Oh hell, is this another one of your tall tales?" moans Pete.

"Absolute fuckin' truth," replies Harold. "You see, Blackie's previous owner found himself on hard times and brought him over to show me his skills. So, we go out to the marsh and this guy sends Blackie out lookin' for birds. All of a sudden that crazy dog comes runnin' out of the fuckin' bushes, all excited and waggin' a big-ass stick in his mouth. Then, that crazy dog jumps up on my leg and start dry humpin' me! I asked his owner, 'what in the hell is wrong with this stupid-ass dog of yours, mister?'

He laughed and says, 'You're the one that's stupid. Blackie there is tryin' to tell ya that there's more fuckin' quail out there than you can shake a stick at!'"

Although Harold has told this tale many times, he's laughing so hard tears are rolling down his face. He scratches Blackies head and says, "This dog cost me three thousand dollars, but I wouldn't sell him for ten times that amount."

"Say, Harold," asks Pete, "what happened to your so-called, world's smartest hunting dog today? He didn't find shit."

"Don't blame the dog, Pete," replies Harold. "This has been one miserable year for birds."

Gene taps his cigar on a dark green glass ashtray sitting on a handmade, antique stand and lets out a phony laugh. "Hell, if that dog is so damn smart, why didn't he just tell us there weren't any birds out there to begin with?"

Blackie stares at Gene and growls quietly.

"Gene, that was just plain stupid," says an insulted Harold. "And speakin' of stupid, how's your little labor dispute goin'?"

"Don't ask," moans Gene. "It's that damn Navy base. They got five thousand sailors out there getting the kids high and smoking LSD and God knows what else. Even worse, they're all jacked up on that God damn hippie rock 'n roll. Hell, what ever happened to a nice melody with good lyrics you could dance to?"

While he concentrates on his highly polished, black cowboy boots looking for imperfections or dirt, Pete says, "Gene, the town has worked hard to get the base to expand, thanks to your buddy, Congressman Buck."

"It's a devil's bargain, Pete," replies Gene. "I do wish Buck could've made it today, though. You know, he might try helping out his friends more often instead of staying up in snooty Houston kissing big oil's ass."

Pete takes a handkerchief from his back pocket and rubs out an ash from Gene's cigar that has fallen on his boot. This done, he looks at Gene with a frown.

"Buck has his own problems right now with civil rights, and that's Federal level, Gene. If he votes the wrong way, he's toast in this state. Your little labor dispute isn't going to rank very high on his list right now."

"Serves him right," chimes in Harold. "Fuckin' Yankee carpetbagger. Look Gene, that base you're bellyachin' about has made us all a lot of money. We all have contracts with the Navy supplying them with all kinds of shit, including your soda pop."

"That's true. But now it's all this equality business. Damn that Johnson and his Civil Rights Act!"

"Its called evolution, Gene. Hell, I hardly recognize the town myself anymore," says Pete.

Harold lets out a loud hoot.

"Gene doesn't believe in evolution, Pete!"

Gene glares at a grinning Harold and says, "I don't give a rat's ass about the federal government and its civil rights. I've got fifty pissed-off Mexicans who are gonna walk off the job demanding I pay them more money!"

"Then pay 'em, you cheap bastard," laughs Harold. "That's one thing I don't fuck with. I pay everybody equally depending on their skills. Hell, if your Tejanos had more money, they could buy more crap from the rest of us!"

"Tejanos? Really, that's what you call them?" asks Pete.

"Mexicans live in Mexico, Pete, don't you know? Look, I'm just as big a fuckin' bigot as any of you guys, but if you don't treat folks right, they're gonna jump up and bite you in the ass."

"You do it your way, Harold, but I'm not going to have any workers telling me how to run my business! Why now? Everyone used to know their place. I tell you, it's that damn Navy base!"

"I think the fault lies with television," says Harold. "Television is a powerful medium that will change America to the core. It will end segregation, and if I'm right, will end the Vietnam War, too. I'm tellin' ya, California and New York already know what's happening in Texas before we do. Someday, we'll all become one big, happy homogenized America with every fuckin' town lookin' exactly the same as the next, with folks of all colors cheerfully spending their paychecks at stores selling the same shit to everyone."

"Damn, Harold, that is the most impressive statement I've ever heard you make. And you only said fuck once," jokes Pete.

"That's just down right depressing, Harold," says Larry. "But that ain't gonna happen here. This is Texas!"

"I'm just being observant," says Harold.

"Texas is goin' to hell," complains Pete. "We've got socialists teaching out at the college, and you should hear the crap Larry's got playin' out at the Barn."

"It's horrible racket, but we don't mind as long as it pays the bills," says Larry. "Ain't that right, boss?"

"Larry, that isn't the issue," replies Gene.

Harold pats Gene on the back.

"Shit, Gene, if Martin Luther King finds out about you and your Mexican labor problem he's gonna come down here and burn your little factory down!"

Gene angrily crushes out his cigar in the ashtray. "He comes down here, I guarantee you he won't be leaving. I can damn well promise you that!"

Stopping
the War

Paul turns at the corner just beyond the town square and spots the metal Quonset hut Michael described as the only German car mechanic in town. Pulling into the lot, they're greeted by a dozen trucks and cars in various states of repair. Dumbfounded stares from a group of tough-looking grease-rats hanging around the front of the shop.

"What do you think?" asks David.

"They look harmless enough, wouldn't you say?" laughs Paul.

Before they have a chance to find out, a large burly man with a thick German accent storms out through the bay doors. "What the hell are you knuckleheads gawking at? Get back to work!"

He stands with his hands on his hips and waits until the crew is back in the shop before turning around and cheerfully walking over to the van. "Can I help you boys?"

Paul steps out of the van and tells the man he needs some brake lining. "I should have checked them before we left California, but...?" he shrugs.

The man stares at Paul's fatigue jacket inquisitively. "Did you serve in the Marines, son?"

"I did," answers Paul politely. "Eighteen months before I got wounded."

"Son of a bitch!" growls the man. "Young men sent off to a war in a country we have no business in. It is bullshit!"

The man thrusts out his hand. "Otto," he states with confidence as he crushes Paul's hand.

"Paul," grimaces Paul.

"No one in this town listens to me and I know what it's like to be brainwashed. In World War II, the Nazis yanked me out of school when I was only fourteen and put me in charge of guarding what was left of Berlin!"

"You're lucky to be alive!" exclaims David.

"Alive? What I went through? A young boy should not experience the hell the Russians subjected me to when I was tossed into a prison with deviants and murderers. I would have rather been fighting in the trenches, it would have been safer. But, that was then and this is now, yah? All right, let's get this van serviced. We should change the oil too if you've not done it recently."

Otto turns to his crew and begins barking out orders.

Paul suspects he was a German officer by the way he's able to command his workers into action.

"This man has served our country honorably," says Otto, and points to an old farm truck being worked on. "Take that miserable creature off the lift," and abruptly does a snappy, military about-face and asks for the keys. "I would recommend the Bee City Diner across the street if you have not eaten. They have excellent Swedish pancakes and even better-looking waitresses. Your van will be ready in an hour."

As they walk to the diner, David laughs, "That was quite a Texas drawl Otto has there."

Otto is correct, the Bee City Diner does have some good-looking waitresses. One in particular, is a dark beauty who casts flirtatious glances at David every time she passes. He notices her, it would be difficult not to as she is drop-dead beautiful, but it's his first day in this town and there's always the possibility of a violent boyfriend lurking around the corner. He gives her a courteous smile before attacking the French toast which he claims are the best he's ever tasted.

Standing on the dusty sidewalk outside the diner, David pats his full belly and remarks, "Damn, that place sure knows how to make a great breakfast. I think we'll do all right in this town."

A blue Ford Falcon pulls up to the signal with a young family inside the car before Paul can answer. A well-dressed blond mom with her hair sprayed into a beehive stares at them through the passenger window with a frown. David smiles and flashes her a peace sign which sends her into a tizzy. Barely audible outside the confines of the car, David and Paul can hear her screaming, "Dirty fucking hippies!" as she pounds on the window with her tightly balled up fist with her middle finger sticking up. Fortunately for the poor beleaguered husband the light finally turns green and he can step on the gas and accelerate through the intersection. With his wife's meltdown ending in a cloud of dust, their two young girls in the back seat mimic mom, sticking out their tongues and flipping Paul and David off—only they're laughing hysterically.

"Sure. We'll do just fine," laughs Paul.

The van is not ready when they return to the garage.

"Give me another half hour," apologizes Otto. "Why don't you enjoy our beautiful town square across the street? It is a good waiting room."

Once again, Otto is correct. They find a bench under a large Linden tree and stare at the architecturally impressive courthouse overlooking the square's park-like setting.

"Must be a lot of money in this town to build a city hall like this. Did you see any oil wells anywhere?" asks David.

"I think it's cowboy money," replies Paul. "I noticed some pretty big cattle ranches on the way here."

David studies the large office windows and impressive ornate moulding. Although no one seems to be taking advantage of the view except for a guy on the third floor who looks like a Sheriff. David watches the man, arms crossed and seemingly lost in thought as he gazes off into the sky.

David wonders what the Sheriff is looking at, when without warning a fighter jet races overhead a thousand feet above the town making a terrifying screaming racket. "Wowee!" he exclaims. "So much for quiet country living!"

Two teenage boys stop in front of them and crane their necks skyward watching the jet. When it disappears over the horizon one of the boys asks, "Excuse me, mister, is that Army jacket for real? Were you in Vietnam?"

"It's a Marine fatigue jacket, and yes, I was."

"Cool," says the other boy. "I'm joining the Marines myself after I finish high school."

Although Paul would like to throw these two into a headlock and kick the shit out them, he stays cool and smiles. This could be his first advice as an anti-war counselor. The point of coming down here was to talk some sense into guys like this.

"You two got names?" he asks.

"I'm Bradley."

"Everyone calls me Bubba," says the other boy.

"I'm Paul. So, do why you want to join?"

Bubba replies, "'Cause I'll probably get drafted and the Army doesn't teach you shit. If I'm going to war, I wanna give myself a fighting chance!"

"Bubba, if that's why you want to be in the Marines rather than the Army, that's a good decision," says Paul.

Bradley chimes in, "We gotta stop the commies, right? Hell, I don't want the Chinese invading us. We should blow the shit out of them with an A-bomb before they attack!"

"We're not at war with China, Bradley. You should know that the Vietnamese hate the Chinese more than we do. You might have good reasons for wanting to protect America, but Vietnam isn't a fight we're going to win. It's a civil war and we're in the middle of it. I was just like you two—gung-ho and ready to kick ass, but the Vietnamese don't want us there because they see us as invaders. Any man, woman, and child can take you out, and many of them are doing just that. Old men are blowing up troop carriers and teenage girls are snipers. Do yourself a favor before you run off and get killed—read about Vietnam, and not from one of those dumb-ass Army recruiting pamphlets."

The two boys stare silently at the ground, confused, unsure of their own thoughts.

"Thanks, man," says Bubba before slowly walking away.

David turns to Paul. "That was a good start. You only have fifty thousand more to go."

Otto walks toward them shaking his head in disgust.

"The pads I have in stock are damaged. I have sent one of the boys to Karnes City for new ones. Should take about an hour."

After Otto returns to the shop, David stands and stretches.

"I don't think I can sit around any longer," he says. "I need to get a lay of the land and do some exploring. What do you want to do?"

"I'll hang out for awhile. If Otto comes back with another lame excuse, I'll head back to Michael's. We still don't know what these people are like and we've been warned about their opinion of hippies, so keep your eyes open."

For the next hour Paul smiles at the various passersby—some friendly, most confused or curious.

"Hey mister," says a voice.

Bubba has returned with three new friends and Paul wonders if he's brought backup to kick his ass back to California.

"Mister, my friends would like to hear what you were telling me about Vietnam. All of us are gonna have to register for the draft pretty soon, so we were thinking of joining. But, I think we might need some advice."

Paul studies the fresh-faced, country boys who barely shave and probably haven't even gotten laid, yet they're ready to throw their lives away like many of the guys he served with overseas.

"Take a seat. Like I told Bubba here, I simply want to clue you in about why and who you're gonna be fighting. Eighty percent of the South Vietnamese won't like you and will want you to go back to America. My question is—why are you buying the horseshit dished out to you by the recruiters who don't know their asses from a hole in the ground? The next time a recruiter approaches you, ask him if he's been to Vietnam, 'cause he wouldn't be promoting the war if he had. Most of those recruiters haven't been within a thousand miles of the place."

Another five boys stop and gather around Paul. The square begins filling with teenagers, most lounging on the grass in pairs or in small groups. He suspects this is a daily ritual but is curious why they're not more animated and vocal like most teenagers. As if to answer his question, a boy races into the square bragging to his friends about scoring a date with some girl named Wendy. He's promptly shushed by what is now Paul's audience.

"I encourage you guys to challenge opinions you'll hear about Vietnam by going to the library and reading about what happened over there after World War II. Vietnam veterans can tell America what is true and what isn't because we've been there. The idea of winning the war is being disputed by guys like me who have seen it first-hand. And we're telling America that our reasons for invading in the first place aren't true. Once I arrived home, I promised myself I would tell everyone I could the straight line—that what we're being told is all lies."

The crowd around Paul parts when a blond-haired, Beeville

Sheriff, who doesn't look much older than he is, patiently listens until Paul takes notice and nods recognition.

"Howdy friend," announces the Sheriff. "My name is Sheriff Donald Edwards, although most folks in town call me Donny. You've been sitting here for quite a spell. May I ask what your business is?"

Paul takes his time before answering. "I'm waiting for your local mechanic to repair my car."

Donny turns his head in the direction of the Quonset hut. "That would be at Otto's over there?"

"That's right."

"You just passin' through, then?"

"I'm visiting a friend stationed out at the Navy base."

"I see," says Donny. "Do you have identification?"

"Yes." Paul makes no effort to pull out his wallet.

"May I see it, please?"

Paul hands his license and military ID to the Sheriff. Donny studies them for a moment before handing them back to Paul.

"A Marine, huh? You fought in Vietnam, is that what I heard you tell the boys?" asks Donny.

"Wounded too; Song Cau Du. Did you serve?" asks Paul.

The question knocks Donny down a notch and Paul secretly enjoys the sight of authority figures melting when they're asked the simple question of, "Did you serve?"

"I surely wanted to," says Donny defensively, "but regulations don't allow security forces to be removed from the homeland. Just wanted to introduce myself. I suspect Otto has already told you all about Berlin and World War II. Interesting life old Otto has had. He usually leaves out about being in Hitler Youth and forced to defend Berlin after the Nazis killed themselves or went into hiding. It's most likely why he's so anti-war. Didn't mean to interrupt your little gathering. Enjoy your visit."

Mexican
Town

Racing through the dark night, two beams of light shine on a thin strip of a lonely country road. "Heat Wave," by Martha and The Vandellas, blasts from the car's radio as Carolina, a young Latina sings along with the chorus.

"Heat wave, taking' me higher, higher, higher, taking me higher! It's like a heat wave..."

"You should be in a group," says Luis. "You sing as good as anybody I've ever heard!"

Carolina slides across the black, naugahyde tuck and roll bench seat of the 1962 Chevy Impala and plants a kiss on Luis' cheek.

"Luis, you're so sweet, but girl groups don't sell many records these days. Everybody likes those pimply-faced English boys like the Rolling Stones."

"The uglier the better, huh?" laughs Luis. "Well, you still sing like a bird. Maybe you should sing country and western. You could be the brown Patsy Cline."

Carolina pictures herself in a cowboy hat and in one those shiny sequined shirts cowboy singers wear and she laughs to herself gazing out the window and seeing nothing but blackness.

"God Luis, I never thought I'd be afraid of the dark. Where in the hell are we going anyway?"

"Hey, you're with the baddest dude in Tejas, baby, you got nothing to be afraid of."

"I know, but where are we going?"

"I told Kiko I'd swing by and pick up some weed. You don't mind, do you?"

"Really, Luis? You couldn't find anything in town?"

"You think I want to be driving all the way out here just to get some shitty weed? Town is bone dry."

Carolina lets out a yelp when the headlights flash on a man

jumping out of the dark like a ghost on the side of the road. The spirit is holding its thumb out, hitch-hiking.

Luis slams on the brakes and slides on the dusty asphalt road before stopping. "What the hell!" he complains while looking in his rear view mirror for the hitch-hiker. It's too dark to see anything. He reaches past Carolina, rolls down the window, and hears the sounds of footsteps crunching the gravel.

David finally reaches the car, rests his hands on the door frame and catches his breath. He's surprised when he comes face to face with a dark girl with big eyes and a wide smile, and remembers her from the diner in town. Paul said she was flirting with him, but he didn't notice because the food was so good. Now he wishes he had been paying more attention to her. She's incredibly beautiful, and to his surprise, she's gazing at him with a sexual energy that fills the atmosphere.

Luis growls, "What in the hell are you doing out here, man? Damn, you scared the hell out of my girl!"

"Sorry about that. Could you give me a lift?"

"Where are you going?"

"I don't really know. I was checking out the countryside and got stuck out here when the sun went down."

"No shit," laughs Luis.

A moment of uncomfortable silence ensues as Luis takes his time studying David. He wonders what's up with this guy's long hair, loose-fitting Indian print shirt, and a definite California accent.

"You aren't from around here, are you?" asks Luis.

"That obvious, huh? I'm from California"

"*Califia?* I got some cousins in L.A.——you know Lincoln Heights? Happy Valley? City Terrace? I got family there."

"Yeah, small world, my dad was born in Lincoln Heights. Shit we might be cousins," laughs David.

Carolina stares at David's lips, then his amber eyes with long dark lashes before turning and whispering to Luis, "We should take him to the party. He's really cute, don't you think?"

Luis pulls back with a questioning frown.

"Me?"

"No, me! God, you're so weird."

Luis checks out David once more.

"Okay dude, this girl thinks you're okay. Get in."

Carolina scoots across the seat to make room and watches David's every move with her bright green eyes as he takes a seat.

David pulls the door shut and quickly rolls up the window.

"Your mosquitoes are pretty serious. Thanks for stopping."

Luis laughs, "Yeah, they've been known to carry off children and small dogs."

Carolina playfully punches Luis on the arm and teases, "God, Luis, you're so corny!"

Carolina turns to David and scoots close to him.

"I work at the Bee City Diner, do you remember me? I waited on you this morning. You wanted bananas and corn flakes on your French toast and I thought that was so funny."

"Carolina remembers your French toast but forgot to tell me about the party," jokes Luis.

Luis extends David a handshake across Carolina's breasts.

"My name's Luis. This little beauty here is Carolina."

David takes his hand and replies, "I'm David. David Macias." Then he looks at Carolina and says, "Of course I remember you. You were talking to another girl about a party."

"That's where I thought we were going," snaps Carolina.

"We'll get there party girl," says Luis. He asks David, "Do you speak Spanish? *Hablas Español?*"

"*Si, a veces*. I'm a Chicano mutt."

"Are you one of those hippies? You haven't turned your back on your people, have you?"

"Hell no," replies David. "Although my brother calls me a Chicano falso because in high school I became a surfer instead of joining his gang."

Luis and Carolina laugh in unison.

"I hope you're as funny as your brother. How about tonight you party with your own people, ese. We'll show you how we do it Tejano style."

Carolina studies David's profile and likes what she sees. She lays her hand softly on his thigh and looks into his eyes. "You don't know what you're missing until you've partied in Mexican Town."

"Mexican Town? Where's that?"

"It's every barrio in Texas," says Luis. "Texans are still pissed off about Davy Crockett getting his ass kicked at the Alamo, so they keep us corralled up in barrios—like we even want to live with them. Anyway, the pinche racists rule in case you don't already know."

"Don't get all political, Luis." Carolina ignores Luis' scowl and quickly asks David, "Do you know how to dance?"

"Yeah, my grandma was a Latin dance instructor and she taught me all kinds of dance steps. I think I still remember a few."

Carolina squeals with delight. "Finally, a boy who might have some moves!"

David gasps under his breath when Carolina lays her hand on his knee. He turns away thinking it might be an accident, but she keeps it there and squeezes a little tighter before moving her hand further up his leg and gently rubbing his upper thigh.

David thinks, "oh shit, this is all I need my first night out alone. God knows what these two are up to." He takes a sideways glance to Luis whose eyes are planted straight down the road, then back to Carolina who is beaming at him with a wide smile.

Shortly, they reach party which is at a small farm house on the outskirts of Mexican Town, lit up with paper lanterns, ribbons and balloons, with loud music echoing through the little community.

Luis, Carolina, and David enter a living room crowded with young Latino men and women dancing to, "Sweet Soul Music" by Arthur Conley, a fast-paced song blasting from the stereo.

They make their way through the crowd into the kitchen to a group of Tejano men crowded around an ice chest drinking beer from paper cups. A slim, dark-skinned man wearing elaborately-stitched cowboy boots and sporting a patch over his left eye, turns when they approach. "Luis!" he exclaims.

"*Orale vato*! Popeye!" replies an enthusiastic Luis.

Popeye gives him a big hug and exclaims, "*Mi primo*! What's happening?"

"Party time, *compañero*! Time to forget our troubles because the man has his foot on our throat."

Popeye reaches into the ice chest and pops open the beers with the opener built into the chest.

"Hell with 'em! Have a beer!"

"You know Carolina, right?" asks Luis.

Popeye nods and looks Carolina up and down. He pauses for a moment at her breasts, enthralled with the tight dress that shows off her cleavage and shapely hips.

"Look at you, cutie," he leers. "I like your hair."

Luis pulls David in with his other arm.

"This is David. He's a *chicano falso* from California."

Popeye raises his beer in a toast. "*Orale, falso*! Here's to the civilized world of *Califia*!"

The party grows in size and clamor, with guests nearly yelling over the sound of the stereo as one song after another keeps the guests dancing non-stop.

"So, how have you avoided the draft, David?" asks Luis.

"I'm on the run, moving around, changing my address."

Luis laughs. "And you end up in Beeville? Shit, I'd rather go to Vietnam than this God damn place. You against the war?"

"Very much."

"Right on," snarks Luis, raising his cup. "A toast to running away!"

Carolina hisses in Luis' ear, "Don't be an asshole, Luis. You said you were gonna behave."

"Like I said, no *chingasos*."

Luis turns back to David., "Sorry man, I was kidding. Shit, I wish I did what you're doing. Tell me, how you ended up in Beeville of all places?"

"It seemed as good a place as any to try and talk some sense into young guys still joining up for Vietnam. I take it you served?"

Luis stiffens and rattles off his battalion like a drill sergeant:, "Fourth Battalion, 9th Infantry assigned to the 25th!"

Carolina grabs Luis by the arm and says, "Jesus, Luis, come on. Don't start talking about the war. You told me you were gonna dance with me. Come on *loco*, let's dance!"

Carolina whispers in David's ear, "You're next handsome, so don't let that Popeye character give you anything weird."

Carolina swivels her hips suggestively as she drags Luis to the outdoor patio to where others are dancing. Men and women alike turn and gawk at Carolina when she walks onto the dance floor and begins swaying from side to side, grinding in close to Luis.

Suddenly, loud, arguing voices erupt from the living room. Everyone in the kitchen tightens up, and gets ready to throw down.

A young woman yells out, "Leave him alone!"

Yelling and cursing break out, drowning out the slow music. A lamp is knocked to the floor and a couple of girls scream when some of the boys start fighting.

Everyone outside stops dancing and races into the living room in time to see two non-local men kick open the screen door violently trying to escape four our locals who chase after them into the street.

The fight continues with the young men wildly swinging and kicking while the brawl travels around parked cars, the fighters cursing at each other in Spanish. One of the non-locals escapes to an older American car and starts the engine. He steps on the gas and spins out on the dirt, fishtailing down the street with his friend yelling at him to slow down so he can jump in. Two locals manage to kick the side of the car before the intruders distance themselves from the party. The last volley is a beer bottle thrown at the departing car that bounces off the trunk.

"*Maricon*! Chickenshit motherfuckers!" yell the locals. They playfully push and shove each other and laugh as if this was the most fun they've had all evening. As they head back into the house, a young woman confronts them, screaming into their faces. "What is wrong with you? Those were my friends!"

One of the locals lifts his chin in defiance and growls, "This is our barrio! Fuck those punks!"

"I hate you! All you do is fight!" cries the young woman.

David turns to Luis and asks, "What was that all about?"

Luis is still staring down the street at the escaping car as it makes a right turn onto the highway.

"I don't know, they looked like shitkickers from Refugio."

"Were they crashing the party?" asks David.

"They got their own parties—*pinche* wetbacks."

"They're our people too," says David.

"Hey, we were born here, man! Those farmers got a lot of nerve showing up where they don't belong."

The fight puts a damper on the festivities, and one by one, the guests filter off to other destinations. Luis, David, Carolina, and a few others end up in the back yard at a wooden picnic table. Luis pulls a baggie of weed out of his pocket and hands it to David.

"Roll us up one of those jumbo California joints you hippies like at the love-ins."

Before he has a chance to lick the paper, Carolina grabs him by the arm. "Wait a minute. Let's see what you can do before you get all goofy on me."

Tito Puente is on the turntable playing a fast-paced tune titled, "Mambo Gazon."

Carolina leads David out to the empty dance floor and faces him. He places his hand on her swaying hips, and swears to himself that he's never seen such a spectacular shape like hers before.

Carolina laughs with a twinkle in her eye and giggles, "Are you gonna make a move, handsome?"

They start the dance with a basic close hold to get a feel for each other, then quickly go to a Copa. David takes her right hand and turns her into his body for a hand drop, then he swings her into him ending up face to face. Carolina's eyes grow as big as saucers, surprised at his very professional moves.

"Oh my God, you have to marry me!" she laughs.

When the song ends, the remaining party guests give them a rousing cheer. Carolina hugs David tightly and kisses him on the cheek. She turns to Luis and laughs, "You're off the hook, baby, I think I found a new partner!"

David and Carolina return to the table holding hands and before they sit down, Luis asks Carolina, "Can we get high now?" David opens the bag of weed and sees it's filled with leaves, seeds and stems and closes it up.

"I've got some stuff you might like. Do you mind?"

"Head on, *vato*, let's see what they smoke in San Francisco," jokes Popeye.

David pulls out his own small stash of Michael's pot and carefully rolls a thin joint as Luis and Popeye watch him with interest.

"Don't be stingy, man, roll up a fat one!" laughs Luis. "We all want a taste."

"Trust me, this is all you'll need," smiles David. "Take a small hit and pass it on."

The joint gets passed around the table according to David's instruction, and by the time it gets back to David, Luis and Popeye are staring off into a star-filled sky.

"You ever think about goin' to the moon?" asks Popeye slowly. "I heard they're building a rocket."

Luis shakes his head. "Stupid-ass government wastes all that money on rockets to space when they can't even manage shit down here. They don't give a shit about the poor either, because we have no value to them."

"What's new?" replies Popeye. "We've been getting shit on us since that asshole Santa Ana lost this place to the white invader."

Shortly, the pot has Luis and Popeye laughing uncontrollably over who knows what. After a minute, Luis catches a breath and wipes away his tears.

"God, this shit is so good, although it might will kill me."

Carolina jokes, "At least we'll die laughing."

Luis offers a sober comment; "You know, our life can't remain like this. Things have to change."

Popeye nods in agreement. "It *is* the way it is, *compadre*. You try and change the way they run it and they'll kill you. They ain't gonna cave in to a bunch of Mexicans."

"Yeah, Mexicans—like we weren't here before them."

David quietly watches Luis and Popeye complain about their

lives for several minutes before he chimes in. "You know, the anti-war movement is starting to work because they got organized. The war will end someday because it's wrong, and everyone knows it. But it won't happen until enough people demand that it end."

David looks up and finds the entire table staring at him.

"It's the same at your work. It's wrong the way you're being treated, but until enough people fight back, it'll never change. With the civil rights movement growing, soon people like your boss won't be able to get away with what he's doing."

"How do we stop them? You can't kill them all," laughs Luis.

"If you're organized. There's a lot of power when everybody pulls together. That's our history. Even the most oppressed people, like the field workers in California, are pushing back against unfair working conditions and racism."

Luis shakes his head, "You wanna start a war? These white pricks run this place like they own it, which they mostly do."

David licks the glue on another joint. "Look at Martin Luther King or César Chavez. They've walked into some serious places, and now it's working for them."

"All I see are rich white college kids and colored people getting the shit kicked out them by Southern cops," replies Luis.

David lights the joint and takes a couple of shallow inhales before handing it to Carolina. "Look at where they were—Alabama and Mississippi. Years ago they would have been killed before they even started. They brought national attention to their cause, and because of that segregation will be a thing of the past. You've got twice as many workers as the whites and you do most of the work."

"Someone forgot to tell Texas there's no more segregation," laughs Luis. "But you're right, we do got plenty of people."

"You just need to find someone who is good at organizing workers and who can bring in others to support your cause."

"Is that why you came to Texas," asks Popeye, "to organize the *braceros*?"

"I don't know anything about labor unions. I came to Beeville to keep guys from joining the war. But, if you want something bad enough, you can make it happen."

Popeye leans back and laughs. "Aye, what a hippie! We've been wanting a change our whole lives, and nothing's happened. You want to keep kids from joining the Army to end the war in Vietnam? You saw those little *vatos* tonight. Those dumb asses think they can kick Charlie's ass. How are you going to convince them that they can't?"

Luis adds, "White kids have money and influence to avoid the draft. You're going to have a time of it figuring out a way for brown skin to stay out of that mess."

"Well, that's what I want to do. I don't see anyone else trying to talk sense into these kids," replies David.

"It won't be easy. For a lot of Tejanos, the military life is better than the one they got at home. They get free medical care, housing, and a steady paycheck."

David replies, "Yeah, if they don't get killed first."

Luis nods, "I agree, *ese*. I'm against the war on my people, too. But the Army is a way to escape poverty and to be treated as an equal. How about while you're figuring out how to stop the Vietnam War, you help us fight the war on Tejanos in Texas? Maybe help us get the white man to pay us some decent wages?"

Carolina takes David's hand in hers and gently rubs it. She looks deep into his eyes and says, "Like, you must have some ideas. Where do you think we should start?"

David looks down and studies her hand in his, the contrast between his olive skin, a mix of Mexican and European, against her pure Indio dark brown skin.

She asks again, "Why not help your people?"

David looks in to Carolina's large almond-shaped green eyes and thinks about the cowboy in the desert and remembers his words: *Someday a hand will reach out in need—this is how life unfolds.*

His decision to leave San Francisco makes more sense now than ever—to help those in need. It's a detour from coming to Texas to fight the draft, but what difference does it make which war he'll be fighting? David looks up from his pondering to a table of questioning brown faces, waiting for an answer. Finally he squeezes Carolina's hand and smiles, "Okay."

Carolina gasps with delight and plants a soft kiss on his lips. . .

The bright rays from the late morning sun are blocked by tightly-drawn curtains. The noisy swamp cooler is working overtime to keep it cool. Luis is stretched out on the couch daydreaming about last night's date, and how hey drove out of town, far away from prying eyes, and parked in a secluded spot by a meadow. After they removed their clothes they stood naked under the moon, gazing at each other hungrily for as long as they could before making love on the trunk of the car. Luis recalls the image of his lover's smooth skin, strong shoulders and the shapely back that tapered down to a narrow waist, and...

Someone is knocking at the door.

He groans as he lifts himself off the couch and slowly walks to the door mumbling a complaint. He peeks through the shade to find two hippies standing on the porch smiling at him. He cracks open the door and peeks out with an unfriendly scowl, then grunts, "Whaddaya want?"

"Hi, Luis. We met the other night. I was hitch-hiking and you and Carolina picked me up. We went to a party, remember?"

Luis stares at David for a moment, still spaced out from his interrupted daydream then replies, "Oh, yeah."

He looks past David to the long-haired hippie standing behind him and wonders, *who in the hell is that guy?*

The hot, humid air smacks him in the face and races in to destroy the cool he's been working so hard to keep in.

"Hurry up, get in!" he orders and rushes the guys into the house before slamming the door shut.

Rushed into the small unlit room, David and Paul spend an awkward moment adjusting their eyes to the dark, wondering if it was a such a good idea to make a surprise call like this.

"Damn, it's hot today! What's up?" asks Luis.

David extends his hand and says, "I didn't get your phone number. I apologize for surprising you like this, but you invited me over to talk about your work?"

"Yeah, yeah, I didn't forget. I'm spaced out because of this *pinche* heat. Make yourself at home. You want anything to drink, water, coffee, beer?"

"Yeah, a beer sounds good. Man, it is hot out today. How hot does it get in Texas?"

"Real fucking hot," laughs Luis.

"This is my friend Paul," says David.

As a Vietnam vet, Luis is immediately suspicious of David's friend, a hippie wearing a Marine Corps jacket. "Were you in Nam?"

Paul nods. "Got there in sixty-four and a bullet got me outta there in sixty-six."

Luis is fixated on Paul's jacket. "Is that right? You got drafted pretty early."

Paul knows from what David told him that Luis had a rough tour of duty and although he doesn't like talking about the war,

Luis' staring is creeping him out. "No, I joined. What's a dumb hick supposed to do when your country calls?"

"Nothing wrong with that."

"David tells me you served in Nam."

Luis stiffens. "That's right. Who'd you serve with?"

"25th Infantry—Cu Chi," answers Paul.

Luis steps back in shock. "Get the hell! I was 4th Battalion, 9th Infantry assigned to the 25th! Get over here, man!" exclaims Luis cheerfully as he yanks Paul to him and gives him a bear hug.

"Fucking Manchus!" laughs Paul. "You guys are legends!"

"Sit down, man, make yourself at home. Let me get us those beers! God damn, Cu Chi!"

Luis drops off the beers then rummages around in his bedroom and brings out a small cardboard box full of photographs from his time in Vietnam. For the next two hours, Luis and Paul reminisce about the war, sometimes laughing, occasionally not, like when Luis points to the guy in a photo sitting on an APC and got killed two weeks after the photo was taken.

Luis picks up another photo and stares at it. "This guy here? Baldwin, a really good dude from Oklahoma. One night we were sitting around camp getting' high and talking shit when he got up to take a piss. We heard a *pop, pop,* and that was it for Baldwin. Shitty-ass fuckin' war."

David finds it odd that although their stories are of miserable conditions and facing danger every waking minute, the photos show guys wearing sunglasses with their shirts off, flashing peace signs, toasting with a can of beer or a joint, and appearing to be having fun. Maybe when every day might be your last, you simply say, "Fuck it" and live for the moment. And if you're going to be living for the moment, you might as well get high and deal with it.

David is aware now that their experiences, still affecting

them with various physical and psychological issues, are clearly an exclusive club reserved for those who have survived the horrors of war.

Unlike Paul and Luis, David hasn't experienced anything remotely close to what they've gone through, and he wonders if what he's getting involved in might be more than he's capable of. He's aware that at some point in this venture, he might be forced to ask himself if he's willing to put his life on the line for those he's promised to help.

As if reading his mind, Luis asks, "How about that union we need? You're not backing out, are you?"

"That's what I'm here for," replies David. "I can start doing some research—find out how this kind of thing works."

"We can do it here," says Luis. "My house is your house— open for you anytime. Carolina would like having you around, too. You know she has a crush on you, don't you?"

David wonders why Luis would be telling him this about his girlfriend. Luis is a bad-ass Vietnam vet and he sure as hell didn't come all this way to be beaten by a jealous boyfriend.

THREE DAYS LATER

Thanks to Nancy and her library card, David was able to gather a decent amount of relevant material from the Bee County Public Library where it now fills Luis' kitchen table.

David picks up a book and turns to Carolina and Luis. "This sounds pretty simple. Step one is to clearly define our plan. They recommend we first present a list of demands to management signed by as many employees as possible."

Carolina rises from her chair and stands behind David. She rests her hands on his shoulders and begins massaging his neck.

"God, David your neck is tight."

He resists slightly, but she hits every spot in need of attention with the right amount of pressure; he relaxes his head and drops it to his chest.

"What else does it say?" asks Carolina.

"This is interesting. It says that the National Labor Relations Act of 1935 was a major turning point in American labor history, because it put the power of government behind the rights of workers to organize unions and bargain collectively with their employers about wages, hours, and working conditions."

"Does that mean we can go to court and sue Alamo-Cola for breaking the law?" asks Luis.

"It's probably not that easy. Plus, we'd have to hire a lawyer and who has the money for that? But it is illegal for management to ban the forming of a union. There's a category here that talks about "replacement costs," where it's illegal for the employer to fire everyone and replace them with cheaper labor just to save money."

"Even if we want more wages and benefits?" asks Luis.

"That's what it says."

"Screw Gene. If anyone tries to fill our spots we'll kick their asses. I don't think anyone even wants our jobs. Loading cases of cola in this heat? We got a lock on that shitty job and without us filling the trucks, nothing is going to roll."

"We have value even though management doesn't appreciate it. That's a strong bargaining position. First though, we need to find out how much support we have from the other workers."

"A few weeks ago, we had Gene surrounded. Ruben got us all together as a show of force," says Luis.

"Who's Ruben?" asks David.

"That's *mi Tio!*" squeals Carolina.

"Is he your leader?"

"No, we don't have a leader. Ruben was just sick and tired of getting shafted by that *pendejo*, Gene, and it turned out to be a spontaneous bitch session."

"Still, it's a start," says David. "You probably scared the crap out of Gene."

Luis laughs. "He was shaking in his boots. He couldn't even light his cigarette."

"Big deal, Luis," complains Carolina. "You scared an old man. You guys still didn't do anything."

Luis snaps back, "It's more than what you've done! You're still making fifty cents an hour at the diner."

Carolina angrily turns on Luis. "Hey, when you're done doing nothing at Alamo, come over to the restaurant and do nothing for us, too!"

A tense silence engulfs the kitchen as Luis and Carolina turn away from each other and silently boil and pout.

"Come on you two, let's not fight," pleads David. "We have to stay together on this. Let's draw up a list of demands and give them to this Gene character. Can you get those guys at work to sign a petition and back us up?"

"Hell yes. I'll beat the shit out of them if they don't."

Carolina wraps her arms around Luis' shoulders. "I'm sorry I yelled at you. When I get back, I'll make some coffee. You guys want some?"

"Sounds good," says David.

"Where are you going?" asks Luis.

"I gotta pee if you must know."

Luis turns to David and shrugs, "Women."

David shakes his head. "I have no idea. So, we have to have the numbers on our side or nothing will happen. We need to set up a meeting with everyone, and introduce me to Ruben. I'll start writing letters to some union people and tell them what we're dealing with down here. It would be nice to get some professional help."

"I'll call Ruben," says Luis.

"Good. I'll get some publicity, too."

"There's a few Spanish language papers in South Texas we can go to," says Luis. "Some of them are in cahoots with the rich businessmen and ranchers."

"I'll write them anyway, you never know."

Luis takes hold of David's wrist. His tone is serious. "Are you sure you want to do this? I appreciate you taking this on with us, but this is Texas, and what we're about to do is very dangerous."

"Yeah, you're probably right."

"No, I know I'm right. Have you heard about the recent strike down in Brownsville? The *braceros* got their asses kicked so bad, the governor had to send in the National Guard to protect them from the cops and the goons the farmers hired."

"I don't think this will end up that violent," replies David. "Gene's cola plant is small-time compared to the farms. It's only one bottling plant."

"Maybe. But our local Texas Ranger and his bigot buddies have a reputation for doing just that kind of shit. Hell, they were down there leading the charge."

"Violence is how they create fear to keep their power. We need to be smart and not engage them in any kind of confrontation. We simply present our demands for better working conditions. We don't trespass on Alamo's property or destroy any machinery. They can't beat us up for requesting better wages and benefits."

David puts down the book and says, "Luis, I need to ask you something important. It's kind of personal."

"Shoot, I got nothing to hide."

David fidgets. "No, it's about Carolina...don't get pissed."

"Spit it out, man. You're acting weird."

"You...you don't seem to mind Carolina touching me all the time, like that neck massage...she's sort of flirting with me."

"Oh, you finally noticed. So what, we're not married," laughs Luis. "She's an intelligent, beautiful woman with strong opinions, and I ain't getting on her wrong side either."

"I know, but she's your girlfriend."

"Girlfriend? She's more like a sister and she takes really good care of me. When I got back from Nam, all I wanted to do was fuck up anyone looking at me wrong, and everybody was looking at me wrong—dumb asses acting like everything was cool when we were doing awful shit and getting killed. If it hadn't been for Carolina, I was on my way to Huntsville State Prison for murdering someone, and I didn't give a shit if I did either. She saved me, man."

Luis looks over his shoulder to make sure Carolina is out of earshot and lowers his voice. "What we did to those Vietnamese? Paul has probably told you some of it, but it was messed up and I was pure *loco* when I got back home." He grins. "As far as her flirting with you, I'm surprised you haven't responded. I mean, she is beautiful, right? I'm beginning to wonder what's wrong with you. Carolina really likes you, but if you don't think it's cool, then don't get involved. But I know for a fact that she'd really like to get it on with you."

David stares at the papers in front of him and wonders what kind of strange Texas ménage á trois he's gotten himself into.

Carolina returns to the room shortly and stands next to David with her hands on her hips. "Why don't you just tell him, Luis, so he doesn't think we're perverts? I think this is a perfect time to let it out or you're gonna go nuts again."

"Hey, Carolina, cool it!" growls Luis.

"What's the problem?" asks a puzzled David. "You know,

you can tell me anything."

The room grows deathly quiet, so quiet in fact, that you can hear the house creaking in the afternoon wind. The friction between Carolina and Luis turns the atmosphere dark and tense as they glare at each other.

David pushes away from the table and stands. "Maybe this is a good time for me to leave. You guys obviously have things to discuss. I should go."

Luis ignores David. He stares blankly at the table with his fists tightly clenched.

Carolina goes to him and kisses him on his cheeks and hugs him. "Come on, baby," she says sweetly. "You know I love you—make it easy on yourself so we can all get on with our lives. I love you an awful lot. You know that, right?"

Luis mumbles, "Yeah, I know."

"Then, tell David. Do it for me, please?"

Luis takes a deep breath followed by a long slow exhale. He takes a few more deep breaths then regains his composure and says, "Okay, okay. But this doesn't leave the room, you have to promise me."

"I promise. So what's up?" replies David.

"I'm only telling you this because Carolina won't stop until I *do* go loco again. In case you hadn't noticed, I'm a homo, get it? A queer, gay, or whatever it is people are calling us these days."

Luis and Carolina watch anxiously for David's reaction.

David stares perplexed at Luis for a moment, then back to Carolina, standing next to him with her hands on Luis's shoulder. He chuckles, "No, I really hadn't noticed. But, it doesn't make any difference. I know a lot of gay men and women back home. I mean, no one has a claim on what's normal or decides who we choose to love. We are who we are and that's it. Someday, no one will give a shit about anyone's color or sexual preferences."

"That all sounds good," says Luis, "and I hope you're right. But, right now, being a queer in Texas is a death sentence. And you know how the Latino community views us—they're worse than the rednecks."

David agrees. "Yeah, it all comes from religion. They've made everyone screwed up about sex. The good thing is, I'm glad you two aren't as open-minded as I thought, because that was getting a little heavy for me to deal with. So, it's all cool, right, we got that out in the open?"

"Really, you were that uptight?" laughs Luis. "I thought you hippies were all into orgies and freelove."

"I don't think orgies are all that common, but you're right, there is a lot of sex going on back home," says David.

"And I wasn't bullshitting you about Carolina, either," kids Luis. "She really does want to fuck you."

Carolina punches Luis in the arm and squeals, "Jesus, Luis!" Then she turns and smiles sheepishly to David before laughing, "It is true, though."

David shakes his head. "You two are insane. Look, we need to quit horsing around and get these demands to Alamo-Cola as soon as possible. Let's get the guys on board and pay a visit to Gene."

"When word gets out who's behind this, you're gonna be the most unpopular hippie in town," jokes Luis.

David laughs, "I think any hippie would be unpopular in this town. But we have an advantage—the truth and the law."

"What about stopping the war? Isn't that why you came to Beeville?" asks Luis.

"How about we stop the war against Tejanos first?"

The Alamo-Cola receptionist snaps in a flat voice, "Gene will be with you shortly." It's obvious by her twitching head movements that she's uptight about them being at the counter, no more than three feet away. She looks over the silver-framed glasses perched on the end of her nose and instructs the men to, "Take a seat, please."

David, Ruben, and Luis do as they're told and sit down on a dark brown leather couch. While they wait they study attractively framed art of soft drink advertising posters from the turn-of-the-century. A number of photos show Gene with various dignitaries: a Houston Congressman standing over a pile of dead birds, an old Hollywood Western actor named Chill Wills, who has his big arms wrapped around Gene's shoulders, and Gene surrounded by school kids on a tour of the bottling plant.

"This is pretty strange after all these years," remarks Ruben. "Except for the time I picked up my employment application, I don't think I've ever been in the lobby."

Luis laughs, "It might be the last time, too."

The men are in the lobby of Alamo-Cola because Gene finally responded to a number of requests David and Ruben made to settle the dispute. In their last call to him, Gene spat into the phone that he was going to put an end to the strong-arming, as he described their demands, and agreed to this meeting to give them his decision.

The receptionist finally snaps "You may go up now."

They enter the office and stand before Gene patiently. He doesn't get up from his leather chair to greet them or to acknowledge their presence. Instead he chooses to remain seated behind his desk with a scowl on his face pretending to be absorbed in some kind of report. The men stand before him quietly for almost a minute, having agreed in advance not to speak to him first. They were expecting a cool greeting, so let him pout if he wants. Gene's secretary enters and takes a seat with a stenographer's pad on her lap.

Gene finally looks up from his reading material and grunts to David, "So, you're the guy behind all this trouble, right?"

"It seems you had trouble brewing long before I arrived," replies David.

Gene snorts, "You expect me to sit here wasting my time while your little union costs me tens of thousands of dollars?"

"That's up to you. The men are only asking for fair wages with benefits, and the union will simply protect those benefits. It's good for everyone. With more income in their pockets, everyone in town will benefit."

"Everyone but me. So you're an economist too, huh? Well, let me hear what you've got to say, but know this, I do not tolerate, nor do I give in to threats or strong-arm tactics."

"We've come in the spirit of fairness to present you with a list of demands signed by the men." David lays the paper on Gene's desk. "Please take the time to read this and then get back to us with your answer."

Gene grabs the list, but before he has a chance to respond, David turns to Ruben and Luis, and says, "Let's go." And with that, they leave the office.

Gene raises his hand to stop them, then he's stunned when the men close the door on him. He turns to his secretary and complains, "Did you see that? How disrespectful. Who in the hell do they think they are?"

He curses to himself for at least a minute before finally boiling over and sweeping his hand across the stack of mail on his desk, creating a paper storm of flying purchase orders and invoices. He jumps to his feet and kicks his office chair which slams against the paneled wall splintering the wood. Gene stares at it in disbelief.

His secretary gasps in shock and quietly slides off her chair and crouches defensively against the a cabinet. Gene stomps out from behind his desk shaking the list of demands and pages filled with signatures at her.

"Can you believe this? Look at this! Increased hourly wages, advancement opportunities, health benefits, disability...and, what the hell?" Gene stares unbelieving at the signatures in front of his face. "Some of these signatures are from my white guys! God damn it. Son-of-a-bitch!"

Gene rips at the demands but the stapled pages are too thick to tear. He attempts to wad them into a ball which doesn't work either. Frustrated, he finally throws the entire document across the office. It makes a direct hit into the wet bar and knocks an expensive crystal decanter to the floor. It shatters into a hundred diamond-like pieces and empties the contents onto his antique Persian rug.

Boycott!

The thousands of bats who inhabit the underground caves in the country surrounding Beeville have never before heard such a commotion in their neighborhood—animal or human. Inside the cavernous wood building known as the Big Red Barn, hundreds of young people have filled the huge dance floor rocking, bopping, twisting, and flailing wildly to music being played by a group of long-haired musicians on stage. The band rips through a hyperactive version of, "7 and 7 is" by the band Love. The lead singer is screaming lyrics into the microphone, battling amplified instruments, furious drumming and cymbal crashing which reverberate throughout the cavernous dance hall.

David watches Nancy and her sister Janie sail around the dance floor, braless and barefoot, dancing with complete abandon. To the local kids the girls look like witches with their long dresses tied with scarves flying about their waists. Most of the young crowd give them a wide berth and stare slack-jawed in wonder, but a dozen or more adventurous boys and girls have joined them in a twirling maelstrom of hair, scarves and free-form dance movements that resemble chasing butterflies.

Nancy makes an attempt to talk to her sister, literally yelling over the music. "Danny's band is really great!" she screams. "How are you doing?"

Janie cups her hands over her ear and yells back, "What? Yeah, this is really cool!"

David scans the building for Paul and Luis, and spots them with at least fifteen young boys at the rear of the dance hall—his growing anti-war entourage.

The extended guitar screeching and numerous drum rolls bring the song to an end much to the dismay of the kids who burst into cheering, clapping and whistling.

Danny, the lead guitarist, steps up to the microphone and

yells, "All right! Right on! Thank you, thank you very much. We're gonna take a short break. Hey, is everyone havin' a good time? Let me hear you say yeah!"

Hundreds of sweaty teenagers scream, "YEAH!"

"That's cool. We want everyone to rock their asses off," he yells. "That's what it's all about! Right?"

"Yeah!"

It's time to introduce the young folks to the poor treatment of Tejano workers at Alamo-Cola. Danny keeps the crowd occupied by mentioning future venues while motioning for David to quickly get up on stage before he loses his audience.

"Before y'all go running out to the parking lot, I'd like to introduce you to a friend of mine. I want everyone to give just one minute of your life, one little minute and listen to my buddy, David. Dig what he has to say 'cause it's important. You promise me that one minute and we'll give it back to you in spades in the second set! Whaddaya say?"

The crowds responds with a rousing, "Yeah!"

David walks to the center of the stage and patiently waits until the crowd quiets. The unsettled group is still buzzing from the electrifying music, but either out of curiosity or the pressure of not being cool by ditching Danny's request, they remain in the hall pretty much they were when the music stopped.

David steps up to the microphone and clears his throat.

"Thanks for your time, and I promise to keep it brief. You know, I'm glad we're all having a good time, but not everyone is as lucky as we are. There are a lot of folks in America who are not having a good time right now. We've got soldiers in Vietnam dying every day, and Latinos and Afro-Americans don't enjoy equal rights like we do, even though they're fighting in Vietnam. And right here in Beeville, our Tejano friends and neighbors are struggling for civil rights, too. Because they have brown skin, they're denied decent benefits and much of what we take for granted like decent housing and a living wage."

A guy at the rear of the dance hall yells out, "Go back to San Francisco!"

"Booo! Redneck!" yells someone in the crowd, followed by scattered laughter.

David laughs too, "Right on! Even knuckleheads get an opinion."

The crowd cheers and the heckler angrily pushes his way through the kids to the exit. He yells "fuck you," before stomping out of the dance hall.

David continues. "I'm here to tell you about friends of mine who need your help. They only want what most of us already enjoy—equality and fair treatment. Is bigotry and racism the kind of America you want to support?"

Nancy yells, "Fuck no!" It echoes through the hall and the crowd breaks out in laughter and clamorous cheering.

David continues, "All they asked was to be fairly treated with equal pay and benefits, and how did Alamo respond? Alamo fired every one of them and now our friends and neighbors are struggling to pay their bills and put food on the table. Alamo has left us no choice. I ask everyone to boycott all Alamo products until this issue is settled!"

A sea of young faces suddenly realize they are in the middle of something important taking place right before their eyes. The words sounding like stuff they've heard from Bob Dylan or Martin Luther King, and heard on television or records. And it's happening right in their home town.

Can we count on you to help us? We need your support. Boycott all Alamo products!"

Nancy and Janie begin chanting "Boycott! Boycott!" again and again. Soon the crowd joins in with them, screaming, "Boycott!"

David holds up a "Boycott Alamo-Cola," flyer over his head. "All right! Please take our flyers and pass them around town. Thanks for your time, and thanks for your support. And spread the word!"

David steps down from the stage and is immediately mobbed by young boys and girls voicing their support of the boycott.

"Right on, Man!"

"We're with you."

"How can we help?"

Danny steps up to the microphone and says, "We'll be right back, and don't forget, Remember the Alamo!" He hits the strings of the guitar with his fist that send feedback and machine-gun sounds screaming from the speakers.

Positioned near the exit of the Big Red Barn, Sheriff Donny stands with his arms crossed checking out the kids streaming past him into the warm evening. He nods a friendly greeting to many he recognizes and a few delinquents he remembers from whatever mayhem they might have been involved with in the past. Although most of the kids aren't eager to engage in conversation given their various states of alcohol or marijuana highs, some of them are comfortable enough to at least say, "Hi Donny, good to see ya!" as they race outside.

Larry, the manager of the Big Red Barn, approaches Donny and positions himself at his side. He points out a dozen small clusters of boys and girls hanging around their pick-up trucks and cars in the lot. "You hear that shit, Donny?" That's what's drivin' these kids nuts—hippy, psychedelic trash. And you can bet your ass they're out there blowin' pot too!"

Amused by Larry's take on what seems like a typical teenage

dance party, Donny laughs. "It ain't country, that's for sure. The place is full though, Gene's making money."

"Well, that rock band was paid to play music not stage some political rally. I tell Gene about this and they'll be lucky if he pays 'em. And what do you think about that agitator rilin' up the kids to side with the Mexicans?" asks Larry.

Donny shrugs. "Maybe it's about time. I played football with a lot of those guys and we sure as hell didn't mind cheerin' for them when they were scoring touchdowns or knocking the crap out of our opponents."

Larry is stunned. Donny's attitude is a bit out of step for a law enforcement officer and he backs away confused, slowly retreating into the dance hall. Adding to his displeasure are dozens of laughing teenagers who jostle him as they move past on their way outside.

Pressed up against the wall he calls back at Donny, "There's gonna be trouble, you can bet your ass on that!"

Donny mumbles, mostly to himself, "Most likely."

Larry turns away and bumps into David.

"Sorry man, my fault," smiles David.

"Humph," snarls Larry. He's forced up against the wall when Paul shoves past. He scowls at Paul, taking in his "hippie" bell-bottom jeans, suede boots, and well-worn military jacket with an embroidered peace sign over the breast pocket. Right behind the hippie is the even weirder rock band wearing clothing that makes them look like pirates or something out of Sherwood Forest. They cruise past without any acknowledgment, closely followed by the two witches who were creating a scene in front of the stage. Unable to take any more, Larry bulls his way through the swarm of exiting teenagers.

Donny watches all this with enjoyment and laughs out loud when Larry finally manages to shove his way through the onslaught to safety behind the bar.

Out of spite, Larry flips on the bright security lights to a loud groan of simultaneous complaints erupting from the parking lot.

"Turn off the lights, and, asshole!"

Janie passes Donny and is hurt when she smiles at him but he doesn't acknowledge her. She stops to say something, then has a change of mind. After a few steps toward the exit she turns around and walks back to him and stands before him to get his attention but Donny is looking off to the interior of the dance hall, deep in thought with a grin on his face.

Finally she says, "Hi Donny!"

It's the first time in years they've been close enough to look into each other's eyes. Janie has love and a warmth for him, yet all Donny can manage is a tight-lipped expression, though he remembers how he loved looking into her beautiful blue eyes when they slow danced at this same old dance hall a few years ago.

"How are you, Donny?"

"I'm okay, the same, you know."

"Really?"

"Yeah, I'm doing fine. Hey, the band sounds pretty good."

"You think so? Thanks, that means a lot to me."

"You know me, I like the old cowboy stuff. I hear you got married."

"I did. It's only been just a little while," she says.

"Well, congratulations."

Janie grabs his arm. "I just wanted to tell you how much you meant to me. You'll always have a special place in my heart, you need to know that. We shared so many great times, and you were always there for me when I needed you, comforting me when no one else could."

"Thanks, Janie. I'm glad you feel that way. It feels good

knowing you still think of me once in a while."

"Of course I do, Donny. We just headed off on different paths, that's all. It doesn't mean I didn't love you, because I did."

"Me too," says Donny. "Listen, I'd love to talk more, but I'm stuck on duty right now. You could do me a favor though, and talk to your sister. Maybe get her to stay in school or something. I worry about her gettin' into trouble, especially with all this hippie stuff goin' on."

"Sure, Donny. Thanks for the heads-up. You're such a hero. I mean it, truly."

Janie kisses Donny softly on the cheek before turning away.

Donny can't stand to watch her walk away from him. The memories of what they had ends quickly when he looks out to the parking lot and watches her join her rock star husband and kiss him on his lips. He'd like to arrest the whole bunch right now for some kind of drug possession, but the Olympic-sized torch he still holds in his heart for Janie keeps him from doing so.

Donny's reminiscing is interrupted by loud screaming coming from the parking lot. He pokes his head out the door and watches hundreds of bats attacking and eating the thousands of bugs who have been attracted to the bright security lights. He's nearly knocked aside as the horde of fleeing kids, pushing, shoving, and laughing hysterically as they crowd their way back inside the dance hall.

¡Huelga!

F our middle-aged Tejana women busy themselves making tamales on a sturdy table in the middle of a large farm-style kitchen. A small plastic radio sitting on the shelf is playing a song by Vincent Fernandez, titled, "El Remedio." It's about a confused lover who receives kisses but remains friends only with the love of his life. The women talk non-stop in Spanish about their children, events in town, or the proper ingredients for the tamales. It makes for a pleasant workplace.

Carolina's mother, affectionately known as, "Coco" because of her dark skin, stirs a large iron skillet filled with spicy chili Colorado, it's aroma fills the room. She takes the meat and ladles it into the center of flattened *masa* in a prepared corn husk. Then her friend folds the husk into a nice little package and hands it off to the next lady who stacks them with others in a steamer. Dozens of completed tamales wrapped in wax paper are piled on the counter waiting to be placed into a half dozen Coleman coolers being used as storage containers.

Coco dips a spoon into the pot and offers a taste of the filling to Carolina. She closes her eyes to savor the fragrance of the pungent spices. Upon tasting the meat she swoons, "*¿Cuándo me enseñarás esta receta?*" (When are you going to teach me this recipe?)

Coco shakes her head and laughs. "*Cuando te cases. Este fue un regalo para mí de parte de su abuela el día de mi boda.*" (When you marry. This was a gift to me from your grandmother on my wedding day.)

Ruben and Luis enter the kitchen and watch as the women begin loading the tamales. Luis hungrily grabs for a tamale and halted when Coco slaps him on the wrist with a ladle and wags her chubby dark finger at him.

"*Luis. ¡Sin tocar!*" (Luis. No touching!)

Luis laughs and rubs his wrist. "*¡Mamacita!* You're meaner than your daughter. How can I sell your product unless I know for sure it's any good?"

Luis playfully wraps his arms around Coco's waist and whispers to in her ear, "*Debes saber que sueño contigo.*" (You must know I dream about you.)

"Aye, Luis!" replies Coco shaking her head, making a pretense of disgust. She squirms away and chastises him. "*¡Le diré a mi hija que no eres más que un playboy!*" (I will tell my daughter you are nothing but a playboy!)

Ruben picks up the ice chest and motions for Luis to come with him. "Let's go, Hugh Hefner, time to sell your girlfriend's tamales."

"Ruben! *Eres tan malo*," squeals Coco. (You're so bad.)

Luis gives Coco a big kiss on the cheek before picking up an ice chest and following Ruben out the door.

A week later a dozen Alamo workers are crowded into Ruben's living room, filling all manner of chairs and patio benches brought in to seat them all. Luis stands lookout at the open front door. He warily over his shoulder out to the street in case Benny shows up with the goon squad to break up their gathering.

Ruben signals for everyone to get settled and quiet down.

"I want to thank all of you for coming today," he begins. "Before we get started, I want to remind everyone that this is a good time to begin looking out for each other. If the hair on the back of your neck stands up, man, that's primitive behavior telling you something is not right. This is a very dangerous time because we all know what can happen to us."

The workers silently nod in agreement.

"We all remember the Rio Grande Valley violence. Brown skin don't tell whites what to do—at least that is the way it used to be. Not any more! These people think we're satisfied with our position as lower class citizens. We have lived with this and that is fine! It's been our life and in many ways has benefitted us. We work hard, because we have had to. We don't have fancy homes and cars, but what we do have is more important than those things—we have each other. Family is the heart of our community."

"*¡Familia! Familia!*" shout the men and women.

"Times have changed all over the country," continues Ruben. "The racism of the past is slowly being eroded all throughout the county and Texas, I do mean slowly, but it is happening."

Ruben turns toward three white men standing at the rear of the crowd wearing Alamo-Cola shirts. "Joining us today are three brave friends who are supporting our efforts. Please give them your love and support for stepping up for us in these troubling times."

"*¡Di algo!*" shouts a guest. (Say something!)

One of the white workers steps forward and nods a greeting. "Thank you, *muchas gracias*," he says in stilted Spanish. "You guys have worked side by side with us at Alamo for many years, and I'm embarrassed to say that most of us have ignored the facts staring us in the face—that you guys were paid almost half the wages for doing the same work as we did. It ain't right. You may not believe this, but we're prisoners too. Just like you guys, racism controls our lives. Those in power can intimidate us or make us disappear if we speak out too loudly against them."

A second white worker stands and speaks. "We have added our signatures to the list of demands to show that we are in support of your goals and will do our best to help you out until Gene sits down and negotiates a fair work package for everyone."

The room erupts in celebration—so loud in fact, that even

Sheriff Benny, who has been parked down the street all morning, must have heard it.

When the group settles back down, Ruben motions for David to step forward. "If you haven't already met him, please welcome our friend, David Macias, who has been instrumental in getting us together to form this union."

David shakes each man's hand with a "*Muchas gracia.*"

He clears his throat. "Thank you so much for your support. *Si, familia*—the family. We all say we're family, and at this moment we are, but I don't see that unity out on the streets. Our people are as racist as the whites. We don't like Negroes—we curse farm workers from Mexico, and *Chicanos* from Corpus get their asses kicked when they want to party in Beeville because they're not from our barrio. It's the same all over—we blame the whites, but it's our own damn fault too because we're so fractured!"

The men are stunned. Shocked and confused, they lower their heads, embarrassed knowing that David's words to be true. A few clench their fists as their blood begins to boil. This is certainly not what they expected from the guy who started this. They didn't come here to be scolded like children, especially from a hippie outsider.

David senses the hostility which is what he feared might happen, but believes they need to face the truth before they can move forward. He continues. "The things that are happening in Beeville are alien to the whites. But you know what? They're alien to us, too. So, I suggest that before they figure out how to stop us from getting more organized, we start reaching out to the other Tejano communities, because we're all fighting the same enemy—poverty and racism! If we can do that, then this strike will succeed!"

Luis shouts, "*¡Por Vida! ¡Huelga! Por Vida! ¡Huelga!*"

All the seated working men stand and cheer repeatedly,

"*¡HUELGA! ¡POR VIDA!* (Strike! For Life!)

Emotions burst forth. The hard-working group of men hug one another, maybe the foot placed on their back is lifting, even if it's ever so slightly.

David shouts, "No going back!"

Carolina and Coco enter and call out for everyone to enjoy the feast prepared for them out back. The chairs and benches used for the assembly are carried out through the kitchen into the back yard, set with tables filled with pots of frijoles, tortillas, and plates of tamales. On the barbecue, billowing smoke fills the air with an aroma that comes from the seasoned meat cooking a backyard grill.

Luis takes a peek out the screen door as Sheriff Benny stops his car out front and stares at the house through his gold framed cop sunglasses, a reminder to Luis and the workers that this meeting will be reported to his superiors.

"Hey Benny!" yells Luis as he jumps off the steps and walks quickly to Benny's car. "Park your *coche* and join us! You still eat Mexican food, right *vato*?"

Not desiring a confrontation, Benny puts the car in gear and steps on the gas and leaves, fishtailing down the street.

David steps out of the house in time to see a police car leaving in a cloud of dust in its wake as it speeds off.

"Who was that?" asks David.

"A fucking *puto rata*," grumbles Luis.

Ruben, steps on to the porch and watches Benny speed off. He yells out. "Stand your ground like a man, you chicken shit!"

"Fuck him," laughs Luis.

Two days after the meeting, David, Luis, and Ruben enjoy a cold beer in front of Ruben's house on a pleasant, warm day.

Ruben's small but well cared for frame house sits in the middle of a large green lawn, shaded by a vast oak tree. Competing with the usual chatter of insects is the clicking of a rainbird sprinkler keeping the grass from burning.

Ruben's five-year-old son, Rafael, is sitting on his shoulders listening to the men talk, not about the union, but about Roberto Clemente, the great Latino baseball player.

Luis playfully slaps at his feet as Rafael giggles with delight trying but continually failing to avoid getting slapped.

"Rafael, you're so slow. Come on, faster!"

Rafael quickly moves his feet again, but in doing so, accidentally kicks Ruben on the side of his face.

"¡Hijo!" yells Ruben. "Both of you knock it off!

Ruben roughly pulls Rafael off his shoulders and angrily yells, "Rafy! Get into the house!" As he watches Rafael run into the house in tears, he instantly wishes he could take back his anger.

"Sorry man," apologizes Luis.

"No, I'm the one who's sorry," replies Ruben. "I've been uptight lately. I'm not used to sitting around like this doing nothing."

"Speaking of nothing, it's too quiet today," says Luis. "It makes me nervous."

David also notices the unusual silence, too, and says, "It's the calm before the storm."

Luis looks at David puzzled. "The what?"

"It's a saying. I think it has something to do with sailors in the old days noticing a change in the atmosphere before a storm."

Ruben laughs. "It's quiet because there are no women around. They're selling so many tamales, I think after all this is over they're gonna start a little restaurant."

Interrupting the peace is Sheriff Benny, slowly cruising down the dirt street before stopping in front of the men. He takes his time rolling down the passenger side window and gives the men a big toothy smile, which in the animal world would be taken as hostile behavior, and it is in this case, too. He slowly removes his sunglasses and leans over to peer out the window.

"Hey, why ain't you guys workin'?"

Luis laughs. "Haven't you heard, *vato*? If you really want to know, you should have got out of your car the other day 'cause' were taking back the Alamo. So tell me, Benny, what side are you gonna be on?"

Luis crosses his arms and glares menacingly at Benny.

"I'm on the law and order side, Luis. My job is to make sure no one starts any trouble if their little strike and boycott ain't working out like they wanted."

Luis moves toward Benny with his fists clenched, but Ruben steps forward and grabs his arm. He peers into the passenger side window and says to Benny, "Why don't you go ask Gene if our little boycott is working or not."

"You know, you could stop this if you wanted."

"No can do," responds Ruben.

Benny shakes his head. "You should have come to me if you had a gripe. Instead, you hired that hippie agitator who angered Gene with his demands. Now the old bastard has dug his heels in."

"Those were *our* demands," replies Ruben raising his voice.

Sheriff Benny grins. "Okay, okay, your demands."

Benny pulls out a handkerchief and wipes his sweating forehead and upper lip before saying, "People are wondering where you're getting your money to live on. You know, there's been a lot of *mota* floating around town lately and you guys ain't making any wages. I gotta put two and two together, you know what I mean?"

"Is that the excuse you and Ranger Pete are gonna use to start pushing us around like you guys did in Brownsville?"

"*Calma te,* Ruben, I'm just talking. Take it as a friendly warning. Just in case, you know?"

Luis chimes in. "If you really need some, I hear the base is crawling with lots of weed. Hey Benny, tell me you're happy getting paid half as much as the white Sheriffs."

Benny bristles at the remark. "Up your ass, Luis, and the same for your little slut girlfriend, too!"

Luis laughs at Benny, "You're just pissed off 'cause you were always begging her for a date and she never gave you the time of day. Ain't that right?"

Benny angrily spits out, "Like I ever wanted to date her. I don't do black, man."

"Look who's calling the kettle black, *pendejo*," laughs Luis.

Benny fumes and stares down the road momentarily: he was never good at cut-low sessions and changes the subject. He nods toward David. "Does the hippie know what he's getting into?"

David offers Benny a big smile and flashes him a peace sign.

"That's it then," shrugs Benny. "*Hasta luego, amigos.*"

Before Benny leaves Luis yells out, "When I tell Carolina you called her a slut, she's gonna beat your ass!"

Luis growls, "Chicken shit white boys send in their token Mexican to threaten us? Fuck those paddy assholes!"

Ruben spits at the ground as he watches Benny pull away. "Look at that asshole, he's not fooling anyone. Everybody knows he's a punk and a *pinche tio taco.*"

...Meanwhile

Tere is nothing better in Bee County when heat and high humidity is replaced by mild weather. Clear blue skies make the great panorama appear even more expansive than usual. On this glorious day, Gene, Ranger Pete, and Larry are hanging out at the country club where they are presently enjoying lunch at an outdoor table overlooking the golf course.

Gene waits for Larry to finish shuffling cards during their five-card draw poker game and offers Pete a cigar. Pete declines with a frown and watches with disgust as Gene goes through the elaborate process of trimming the tip, moistening the cigar by shoving it into his mouth and rolling it around on his lips before lighting it. Then he stokes the leaves hot by puffing away like a madman to keep it lit.

"That damn thing looks like a turd and smells even worse," complains Pete. "And all that sucking and licking is pretty damn queer, Gene, pretty damn queer."

Gene laughs, "Oh, once you get used to them cigars are very enjoyable. Did you know they can lower your blood pressure?"

"There's a whole lot more I'd rather enjoy, and that includes high blood pressure," replies Pete.

The guys pick up their cards and study them silently. Gene's frown tells Larry that he's not very pleased with what he's holding. "*No poker face whatsoever*" laughs Larry to himself.

"So, tell me, Gene, how are you doing?" asks Pete.

"I think you know, Pete. This boycott is killing me. Sales are off by seventy-five percent! God damn Mexicans aren't coming back to work like I thought they would."

"You fired them, what did you expect?" says Pete.

Gene huffs, "I expected them to come crawling back once they ran out of money and cooled down. What the hell are they living on anyway?"

Larry taps a long cigarette ash into the ashtray and watches the light wind blow most of it onto the table before turning to Gene. "The Mexicans got their relatives and friends in on it. I saw some little girls on the side of the road selling tamales on my way down to Corpus the other day."

Pete looks up from his cards and stares at Larry's goofball, shit-eating grin. "You bought one, didn't you?"

"Hell yes, I bought three! The damn things are delicious!"

"Jesus, thanks, Larry," whines Gene. "If that don't beat all. Last week, I got a visit from that hippie bastard and a few of the boys demanding I give in—bend over and take it in the ass. Some of my white drivers are asking me to cooperate with this crap, too!"

Gene throws down his cards on the table in disgust. "Fold! Dammit, Larry, you haven't given me a decent hand all day!"

"That's 'cause I'm a cheat."

"I bet you're not joking either," complains Gene.

Larry laughs, "How much?"

"Larry, you're such a prick," says Pete. "Gene, let's just calm down for a minute, okay? Jesus, you're scaring the golfers. Let's talk about this outsider that's got the Mexicans all worked up."

Larry swirls the last of his drink around the glass before downing it in one gulp. "I say let's round his ass up and straighten him out with a good beatin'."

"Larry, we've already given them a chance," says Pete. "Just the other day, I sent Benny over to give the Mexicans a friendly warning and they shut him down. And that wise-ass hippie outsider was with 'em, too, like it was all fun and games! So, that's that."

Pete take a glance around the clubhouse just in case anyone might be within earshot. He leans in with a deadly serious look on his face and whispers, "These Mexicans and that hippie communist agitator have cost Gene here a lot of money and I mean to show this wiseguy, who thinks he can just waltz into our town and mess with us, that it ain't going to happen without a fight. And that is a fight we always win."

Gene takes Pete's glass and refills it from a half empty bottle of whiskey on the table.

"What they don't know is that we've got our own agitator. Larry here is a pro at busting up this kind of labor dispute. You heard what he did in Mississippi, right?"

"Yes, I do recall that incident, but I don't want anything that drastic," says Gene. "Maybe Donny could arrest him for drugs or something."

"Donny is useless as hell," replies Pete. "I think he might even be going along with the Mexicans on this. Jesus Christ, first we got that damn Navy base turning all the kids into potheads and now this commie trash is riling up the Mexicans. We've gotta take a stand right now or say *adios* to our way of life forever!"

Larry tells Gene, "Don't you worry about a thing, Gene. This outside agitator? We'll take him out of the picture and watch what happens next. Their little strike will be yesterday's old news."

"You got that right, Larry," says Pete. "Mexicans do not have the ability to stay organized for long. You get rid of this hippie guy and they'll all go back to fighting and stabbing each other or some other shit. You'll see, they'll come crawling back on their hands and knees beggin' for you to take 'em back."

"Tell me what you need from me, Pete," asks Gene.

"You got two choices here. Larry and I will work up a plan to get rid of this guy, or you can give 'em what they want."

Gene nearly spits his cigar out of his mouth. "I'd rather shoot myself in the nuts than roll over to a bunch of communists. Just do what you have to do."

Satisfied with Gene's response, Pete leans back in his chair with a satisfied smile and crosses his arms. "I think you're making the right decision, Gene."

The soft click of a perfectly struck golf ball has Pete turning in his seat toward the fist tee. He watches the golfer's drive sail straight as an arrow over two hundred and fifty yards down the fairway and shakes his head in wonder. "How in the hell does he do that?" he asks.

"If you would only take a lesson, you could do that too. So, Pete, what are you planning?" asks Gene.

"Right now, the less you know the better. Larry and I will get something worked up—maybe beat the shit out of him and put him on a bus back to where he came from. If that don't work, we'll do what we have to do—something along those lines."

"This is the kind of work I know how to do," boasts Larry. "You don't need to worry about us not making this right for you and Alamo."

"Thanks guys. Whatever you have to do."

For the first time in weeks, Gene feels the tightness in his chest relax and his blood pressure drop. He leans back in his chair and takes in a deep breath of the clean country air before puffing on his cigar and exhaling a long stream of smoke on this fine day.

The Summer of Love

Last week's pleasant temperatures have been replaced by typical Summer weather—blistering heat and high humidity. David and Paul crowd into Michael's bedroom, the only room in the house with an air conditioner, listening to a stack of records cued up on the record player spindle.

Stretched out on the bed staring at the ceiling, Michael is thinking about an upsetting dream he had last night. The lab has been pushing him to learn to process color film on a new developer, and he thinks it may be why his dream involved being strangled by rolls of film.

"Hey, Michael, what about peyote and that place you were talking about?" asks Paul. "Don't you think it's time we got a taste of what Texas hippies have been hiding from the rest of the world? We've been working our asses off and I think we deserve a little break. What do you think, David?"

"Sounds like a good idea," replies David.

"How about you, Michael? Can you take time off?"

"As soon as this heat wave ends, sure. I gotta tell you a little about peyote though."

David and Paul ask in unison, "What's that?"

"On peyote you can go almost anywhere depending on your state of mind. You might discover another world, or talk to people who aren't there, or maybe they are there, and peyote just taps into another dimension."

"What kind of places are you talking about? You mean like inner dimensions and space?" asks David.

"Yeah, there's that and there's patterns and colors. You don't quite have control over your situation. All I know is that it comes from within—you're the director. Does any of that make sense? The worst part though is throwing up after eating the buttons. They're horrible tasting, but I've never heard of anyone freaking out or having a bad trip. But just in case, I'll be there and I won't be eating any. Well, maybe just a small one, but I'll be looking out for you while you trip."

MESCALITO

The sunset frames a rooster tail of dust that looks like fiery smoke being kicked up by a horse racing across the landscape. David has been watching the image for a few moments, but he's not certain whether the horse is real or not because he's blazing on peyote.

He closes his eyes, and atoms connecting him to the universe, linked together by electrical energy, begin radiating like a supernova before letting go and bursting into another realm. His entire being becomes pure white light, and if anyone asked him where his body was during his own personal big bang, he wouldn't be able to locate it. He expands into nothingness, and then slams back into himself. .

When he opens his eyes, the horse is now carrying a rider. It slides to a stop and rears up on its hind legs, and a slim Mexican man with long black hair woven with leather straps and polished turquoise beads, leaps from the saddle and walks over to David.

"*Buena noches, amigo,*" *says the man.*

David invites the man to sit down and offers him a drink of water from his *bota*. The man gracefully declines, then crosses his legs and seemingly floats to the ground in one smooth motion.

"What is your name?" David hears himself asking.

The man sits up straight and boasts in Spanish, "I am Juan Nepomuceno Cortina, a cavalry rider for General Mariano Aritisto. I fought bravely in the battles of Resca de Palma and Palo Alto against the invasion. I own this land, which is jealously coveted by the Americanos."

David stares into the kaleidoscope of Cortina's smiling face. His intense brown eyes brighten like glowing amber prisms when he speaks.

David's hands are in constant motion swatting at mosquitoes that are attracted by his campfire. He notices Juan Cortina is unaffected by the pests. "The mosquitoes don't seem to bother you," he remarks.

"They are bored with me," laughs Juan Cortina. "You are a new flavor to them."

"How long have you lived here?" asks David.

Juan Cortina looks across the land beyond the little campsite and tilts his head while he thinks about the last one hundred and fifty years.

"This land was settled by my family in 1812, and extended from Camargo, Tamaulipas, and north beyond the river to the lower Rio Grande Valley. It was ours until the Texans stole it from us after the war, then accused of cattle-rustling my own animals. It was only the high standing of my family that prevented me from being arrested outright and hanged.

In 1859, while I was on business in Brownsville, a Texas Ranger attacked one of my employees. Enraged, I shot the Ranger dead. It was then that I became a wanted man."

Juan Cortina smiles. "I must apologize if I am talking too much. It has been a long time since I held decent conversation with such an honest and spiritual man such as yourself."

David closes his eyes. "It's the peyote," he tells himself. "Relax and enjoy the trip."

David watches the air as it vibrates with colorful, pulsating, geometric patterns that encircle and smother him. The insects celebrate the setting sun with non-stop singing, a joyful music for a day ending so beautifully. The sky is bathed in a golden reddish glow before turning cobalt blue, then by blackness and a billion stars that stretch into infinity and quiver in rhythm with the song of the insects. A change in temperature creates an evening breeze that David thinks is the universe sighing in appreciation of its own magnificence. In his peyote state of mind, David believes for a moment that he's discovered the source of wind. Maybe he's right, but in the few seconds it takes to form into thought, the feeling passes.

David asks Juan Cortina, "Why are you here?"

> "A door opened. I miss my rancho and when someone calls to me I visit what used to be. Let me ask you the same question, How did you know to call me?"

"I did?" replies David.

> Juan Cortina holds out his hand and says, "Please, take hold of it."

When David takes Juan's hand, he finds himself in a colorful meadow filled with wildflowers facing Juan Cortina. A bright, blue sky dotted with clouds that contracts and expands, breathing like the stars and crickets.

> A melancholy fills Juan Cortina as he takes a few moments to gaze at the colorful sky and meadow.
> "Many years ago my land looked much like this field before it was taken by the white devils who trample everything to dust. There is only so much humiliation a person can take before fighting back. When one has been left with little choice, or has nothing left to lose,

there is no need of fear. Your objective, as you have seen, has been to chastise the villainy of our enemies, which, until this day, has gone unpunished. These people have connived with each other, and have formed a deceitful, duplicitous claims to persecute and rob us. This has been allowed for no other crime on our part than of being Mexican origin, considering us destitute of those gifts which they themselves do not possess. Remember this my friend, you are the one on a righteous path, not them."

Juan Cortina releases his grip and night closes in like a blanket, blocking out the stars and surrounding landscape.

"Do not be sidetracked from your goal. More importantly, be fearless when facing death, as that certainty will bring you victory."

Juan Cortina disappears and David discovers himself alone in the blackness. Disoriented, he scans the valley and wonders how he could have traveled so far without noticing. He focuses on the small bright glow of the campfire, and begins the slow walk back to camp far away in the distance.

PAUL: BORN AGAIN

Like a switch suddenly clicked to off, night arrives. To illuminate the traveler's path, peyote plants that cover the valley floor begin a slow dance in swirling geometric patterns. It's such a stunning display, and overwhelms Paul so greatly, that he gasps and drops to his knees before falling face-first in the dirt. Warm grains of sand come to life and surround him like a dry psychedelic bath.

"Immerse yourself in the *Isimayo!*" commands a voice

coming outside his body.

Weeping uncontrollably, he frantically scoops away enough *Isimayo* to form a shallow grave. He takes handfuls of sand and covers himself in it, believing this will cleanse away the pain he's been carrying for the past year for killing another human.

> The voice tells, him, "*Isimayo* is a good flaking dirt used by the ancient people who inhabit this sacred land to heal and soothe. *Isimayo* is held in high esteem, and will bring you solace."

Paul climbs into his grave and covers his body with *Isimayo* until only his head remains uncovered. The sacred dirt patiently waits for his tears to stop flowing, then covers his face. There is a moment of anxiety, but it passes quickly when the bright glow of a million spinning lights encircle him to form a powerful beam of light that pushes him deep below the surface.

The bean of light takes Paul into a jello-like, three-dimensional world that presses in on him, which reminds him of his experiences in Vietnam with opium. There are inhabitants in this world who glide past him toward a glowing destination far in the distance. A few of them glance in his direction, but most ignore him. Others float above the crowd, fighting the current. Paul isn't certain. One such inhabitant, is a handsome man wearing a checkered shirt. He has small bright lights circling his neck, blinking like a Christmas decoration. He waves his arms, trying to communicate with Paul, but is pushed away by an unknown force. He continues to claw his way forward repeatedly, until finally unable to fight the current, he's swept back into the distance.

Paul wonders what the man was attempting to tell him: it must have been very important. As he waits for the man to appear once more, a hand comes to rest on his shoulder. It belongs to a young Vietnamese man dressed in embroidered, silk pajamas is standing next to him. When Paul last saw him, he was dying from a bullet wound in a rice paddy.

The man smiles and says, "*If you can hear me and feel my touch, then you will know why Isimayo brought you here.*"

"Am I dead? Who are those people?" asks Paul.

"We are Travelers. But, no, your time has not come. "

"I'm sorry that I killed you," gasps Paul, then nearly bursts into tears. "Please forgive me."

"I cannot forgive you because I hold no grudge against you."

Before the Vietnamese man steps into the river of humanity, he tells Paul, "Remember your last wish before you died. Go home, American, go home."

The underground city fades to blackness. Paul feels his grave begin to tighten its grip and smother him. When he accepts his fate, which must be death, pain and sadness escape as a fountain of despair, It vomits up from deep within and violently pushes him from the darkness and tosses him to the ground. Gasping for air, Paul draws in a deep breath and rolls onto his back, howling uncontrollably. A blast of warm air smacks him in the face, and his entire being is filled with absolute joy. Paul promises himself to embrace life, to love, and most of all, to try and give up smoking and appreciate breathing instead.

David groans and pulls the thin blanket over his head when the late afternoon sun hits him squarely in the eyes. He rolls away from the light onto his side, but it's too late, he's wide awake. From a hammock inside the VW camper he stares at Michael lying below in the foldout bed.

"Are you awake?" he asks Michael.

"I am now," replies a yawning Michael.

David shakes his head. "I don't remember how I got here."

"I kept an eye on you. You didn't wander too far away."

David stretches his arms over his head. "Really? I didn't see you anywhere. I was like miles away from the camp!"

Bright light fills the van as Paul throws open the side door. He's covered in dust with a wild look in his eyes, and looks like a mad man.

Grinning from ear to ear, Paul exclaims, "Did you know that peyote is laid out in a huge geometric pattern, and that there's a magical underworld right below us?"

David laughs, "I thought my trip was mind blowing. Look at yourself: how did you get so filthy?"

Paul looks down at his dirt-covered shirt and laughs. "Rebirth is messy!" He steps away from the van and brushes away the dust from his clothes. "Thank you, Michael. I really needed this."

Michael nods. "Now you know why the natives embrace it with such enthusiasm. We should get some food in us pretty soon though. Peyote is a little tough on the stomach, but if we hurry, I can take us to a great place to eat."

"How was your trip, David?" asks Paul.

"Insane and beyond explanation. I met an ancient Mexican man who told me he used to own all this land. I don't think I've seen the last of him either. He told me I needed to be courageous."

"That's wise advice, considering your work with Alamo," says Michael.

"Man, I could really use a bath," laughs Paul. "But first, I need to sacrifice something. An offering to the peyote gods."

"I'll toast my draft card," says David.

Paul takes off his jacket, then steps away from the van to

knock all the dust off. "This needs to go."

Michael and David watch as Paul sets fire to dried mesquite branches formed into a funeral pyre. He steps back and watches the flames as they grow to a height he deems worthy of a proper sacrifice then tosses the jacket into it. He patiently watches his jacket turn to ash before quietly saying, "Thank you for your service."

Staring out the window as the highway crosses through the King Ranch, the country's largest cattle ranch, Michael strains his eyes and mind looking for geometric patterns but to no avail. It doesn't mean they're not there. Maybe they only dance at night he laughs to himself, but that's peyote for you.

They cross over the Rio Grande River, little more than a drainage ditch, having been sucked dry by Colorado, New Mexico, Texas and Mexico on its two-thousand-mile journey from the Rockies to the Gulf of Mexico.

"Look at what we're doing to that poor thing," says David, "the killing off a perfectly good river."

In Nuevo Laredo, Mexico, which is a pretty colonial city on the border, they treat themselves to showers and a steam bath. The baths are followed by massages given to them by friendly middle-aged women with strong brown hands and cheerful banter. In the early evening they step out of the Cadillac Bar and Cantina, thoroughly stuffed from an excellent dinner of *chile rellenos* and *carne asada*.

Michael takes them to the walled-in district known as, "Boy's Town," a red light district formally named *Zona de Tolerancia*. It was created by General John J. Pershing while chasing Pancho Villa around Northern Mexico, as a way to keep troop morale high.

Behind the walls are restaurants, small single-room studios for independent prostitutes, and two cool nightclubs. Michael chooses *El Papagayo*, which he says features rocking bands, an authentic 1930's Art Deco interior and a huge dance floor. The girls who work there are young and pretty and just as happy to dance with you as take you into one of their garden court rooms.

At the entrance, Paul pulls a out cigarette and immediately, the bouncer dressed in a black suit with a pink tie flicks open his lighter and lights it. "*Que la pases bien* (Have a good time)," he smiles.

As they step through the entryway, the boys find a centrally located table close to the dance floor where a Mexican Beatles cover band is ripping through a version of, "Hold Me Tight." On the dance floor are a half dozen patrons, mostly Americans of various ages, who shake their asses and shuffle their feet while the girls offer them friendly smiles, even though they've done this all before many times.

A waitress leans in and asks, "Something to drink?"

"*Tres cervezas por favor*," requests Michael.

The waitress returns in less than a minute with three very small bottles of Victoria Beer and says, "*Seis dollares*, American."

Paul lets out a hoot while pulling six dollars out of his wallet. After the waitress departs he complains, "Oh my God, two dollars for a shitty little beer! What is the attraction, again?"

Michael laughs. "Look around, man. Have you *ever* seen so many beautiful girls in one place? It probably isn't cool, but I'm a lame-ass sailor in the Navy, against my will I might add, and I'm in crappy Texas. I just need to have a little fun."

"Okay, okay, I'm not judging." Paul raises his beer up for a toast. "Here's to two dollars! *Salude, amigos!*"

A young woman stops at the table and asks Paul to light the cigarette dangling from her mouth. Paul unconsciously pats the pocket for a lighter in a jacket that is no longer there—offered to the Gods. He fumbles around in his pant pockets and comes up empty. He smiles at her apologetically and shrugs, "I'm sorry, I don't have any matches," and offers her his lit cigarette.

Insulted, she steps back and hisses, "*¡Pinche bastardo!*" and stomps off in a huff back to the bar.

A red-faced Paul asks, "What just happened?"

"You fucked up, that's what," says Michael. "Go apologize to her or they'll run us out of here before we even get to finish our two dollar beers! And they sure as hell aren't going to dance with us either."

Paul glances at the bar filled with young women standing at the counter. They glare at him, listening to the unlit cigarette girl as she complaints in Spanish while pointing him out.

"Oh shit," moans Paul.

"Go apologize!"

Paul scoots his chair back and sheepishly walks over to the offended girl with the bad vibes increasing the closer he gets. They're all sneering at him, and a couple of the girls have their arms crossed, looking angry enough to toss him out of the club without the help of the bouncer. Paul faces the cigarette girl and says, "I'm sorry, I think I accidentally insulted you."

She turns away with a click of her tongue.

Paul looks to the other girls for help, asking, "Do any of you girls speak English? *Habla English?*"

The girls continue glaring at him with disdain as he continues asking with no luck.

"*Habla English?* Does anyone speak English?"

"I do," says a quiet voice. "I speak English."

Paul turns around and nearly gasps in surprise when he faces the girl standing before him. She's not wearing any makeup and her large, light amber eyes, contrasts with her black hair and caramel-color skin. There's a sadness in her eyes which confuses him, but strangely, he wants to find out more about her.

Paul composes himself and asks her, "Could you help me? I think I'm in trouble. All the girls are mad at me."

The girl asks the mad girl, "¿Rita, por qué estás enojado con él? (Rita, why are you mad at him?)

Rita answers with a scowl on her face, "¡Ni siquiera soy lo suficientemente bueno para que él encienda mi cigarrillo! (I'm not even good enough for him to light my cigarette!)

The girl asks Paul, "Do you think Rita is not good enough for you to even give her a light for her cigarette?"

"That wasn't it!" sputters Paul. "I burned up my jacket out in the desert, and I guess accidentally burned my lighter, too. That's why I offered her a cigarette. I didn't know she would take it as an insult! Tell her I'm sorry, please?"

The girl lets his apology hang in the air while she studies his face and wonders about him. He is very handsome of course, a sort of rugged good looks, and maybe he will be kind to her if he asks to go to a room. Finally, she turns to the insulted girl and her friends and laughs, "Él no estaba insultando. No tiene ningún partidos para usted cigarrillo." (He was not insulting you, He doesn't have any matches for your cigarette.)

Paul listens to the girl explain his behavior, and whatever she said seems to have broken the ice. The other girls laugh and tease Rita, and even Rita laughs along with them.

"Thank you for helping me out. I've never been to Mexico before and I guess it shows. May I ask your name?"

"Ramona," she says, immediately pleased by the courtesy.

Paul offers his hand.

"Paul," and takes her outstretched hand, which is small, soft, and he thinks is the perfect temperature.

"It is a beautiful name," smiles Ramona. "Did you know that it means, humble?"

"That seems appropriate at the moment," he laughs.

Ramona glances over to Paul's table and notices Michael and David staring at them.

"Are your friends in a hurry to leave?"

"No. They're just checking us out. I think they're waiting for me to put my foot in my mouth again."

Ramona leans over to two girls standing nearby and points to Michael and David. "¿Podrías pedirle a esos chicos que bailen?" (Could you ask those guys to dance?)

They happily comply and grab David and Michael from their chairs and soon have them dancing to another fast-paced version of a Beatles cover, "Devil in Her Heart."

Paul notices the bartender staring at Ramona with a sneer on his face and suggests, "Maybe I should buy some more drinks, or would you like to dance? I think your boss is getting uptight."

"He's only a spy for the bosses," beams Ramona. "Do you know how to dance slow?"

"Isn't this song is too fast-paced for that?" asks Paul.

Ramona steps close to him, and says with a smile, "It is up to us, don't you think?"

Why do people fall in love? A pheromone, according to scientists, is a chemical we produce which they describe as a behavior-altering agent that impacts the response from another person. If one is lucky enough to meet the right person, it is a two-way street. Something takes place between Paul and Ramona, and without another word he takes her by the hand and leads her to the dance floor where they hold each other tight and move to their own slow rhythm.

Ramona looks at David and watches him perform some very

respectable swing moves. "Did you know your friend could dance like that?"

"Not until now," laughs Paul. "I think I'll have to ask him for some lessons."

When the song ends they remain on the dance floor, holding each other tight, and Ramona realizes she is not the only one who is in need of a warm, caring embrace.

"Would you like to go outside and get away from the noise?" asks Ramona.

Ramona takes Paul by the hand and leads him through a side door into a lush courtyard, a garden of eden existing within a whorehouse. Flowering plants, a koi pond and a dozen single-story apartments line one side of the building. After a quiet walk under a bougainvillea–covered archway they stop in front of a thick wooden door. Ramona knocks twice before opening it. Once inside the small tidy room, Ramona sits on the edge of the bed and pats the mattress, inviting Paul to sit next to her.

"How did your jacket burn up?" she asks. "Did you have an accident?"

Paul searches for the right words. How can he explain why he kept it so close to his heart for so long? Finally he says, "It was an offering. Does that sound silly?"

Ramona smiles, "I don't know—was it a religious offering?"

"Sort of. It was a war relic I've been wearing since I got home from Vietnam. I fought alongside boys who were just like me and I loved those guys. Many didn't make it home, so I suppose I wore it to honor them—to remind me of that episode in my life."

"Why did you burn it, if it was so important?"

"It was also a crutch. I learned you have to leave the past behind in order to live in the present. I was taught this from a man I killed in Vietnam who came to me in a dream and repeated his last words before he died. He told me to go home."

Paul thinks about interconnected events over the past few days. His peyote vision allowed him to destroy the jacket and his lighter, all of which lead him to this beautiful girl.

Life unfolds.

Paul looks into Ramona's large bright eyes and asks, "Do you mind if we just lie here?"

"No. That would be nice."

She asks Paul to remove his shoes and to lie next to her. Side-by-side, she takes hold of his hand and they quietly stare at the ceiling, both lost in thought. Ramona snuggles against him and wraps her arms over Paul's chest. Maybe she's projecting too much into this moment, but she has a feeling that her life is not over. Not yet, at least.

After the exhausting night of peyote, within a few moments, Paul drifts off to sleep, leaving Ramona to wonder if a time will ever come when a young man like the one lying next to her will be doing so out of love.

She reminisces about a day she spent with her Popi as they walked on the pathway of a large stone fortress overlooking the Pacific Ocean. They watched large ocean swells explode over a rock reef and peel up the coast. Ramona remembers what her father said to her at that moment, but had never given it the importance it deserved.

"We must remember this moment, always, because life is fleeting. I'm afraid I am a dreamer and dreams are short-lived."

"Are you worried about your new job in America?"

"No, my sweet. It will be a challenging opportunity, and I will certainly miss the ocean. My only concern is that our new life will only make you happy."

Ramona took his hand and said, "I promise you then: I will

always remain happy, no matter what happens."

At that moment a surfer began paddling with all his might for a large wave. The surfer made the long drop to the trough of the wave, leaned into his turn and propelled the surfboard onto the wave's face just under the curling lip that chased him more than fifty yards to the beach. When the surfer ended his ride with a graceful kickout, her father jumped to his feet and cupped his hands over his mouth and yelled, "Bravo! Bravo!"

She smiles as she remembers this, and how she slapped her knees with joy watching her father dance with excitement.

Her father's disappearance three months ago sent her life into a tailspin, but there was little time for despair. The bills began piling up and there was no money for food. She found work in a printing shop taking orders and pasting type into layouts. She left their comfortable house and moved into a small apartment. The owners of the shop liked her drawings and even paid her to use one of them for the cover of a restaurant menu. Then a month ago a man in a black suit approached her on the street asking about her father. He said her father had borrowed two thousand dollars from him and he wanted to know when he was going to pay it back.

"I don't know what you are talking about," she replied and quickly turned away.

He grabbed her by the arm and pushed her up against the side of a building and growled that he wanted the loan repaid, and quickly, too, because the men who had fronted him the money had run out of patience.

She was terrified, and pleaded with him. "I have a job. I can give you some money every week."

"I know where you work, but it won't be enough to satisfy them. They don't trust you and want me to keep an eye on you, just in case you decide to run away."

The man softened his voice and said, "I can help you out, *chica*. My friends own a very popular nightclub in La Zona. If you work hard, you can pay off this debt in no time."

Ramona didn't know anything about nightclubs, but he told her she no choice in the matter. He said she was smart and pretty, and would learn the ropes in no time at all.

"Listen," he said. "You go to my friend, Rodrigo, who runs *El Papagayo*. Tell him who you are and that you are a friend of Arturo, and that you need to work."

Earlier this evening, before she entered the club, she paused to take a deep breath, remembering what she promised her father a long time ago, "Think only of good things and always be happy." She hoped that, maybe, there will be a nice boy who won't make her feel like trash, like what happened last night, her first night of being forced by the club owner to engage in prostitution.

She had taken a sailor to a room and he cursed her after having sex. "You're the deadest fuck I ever had," he yelled before tossing a twenty dollar bill onto the bed and angrily stomping out of the room. She held the crumpled bill and stared at the beautiful engraving of an old American President. Anyone else might have been brought to tears, ashamed and humiliated, but she had to agree with the sailor because that was exactly how she felt—dead.

She smiles to herself, thinking about the young *Americano* named Paul, who is now lying beside her. He was at a table with two friends when she watched Rita curse him and stomp off to the bar in a huff. Paul's friends laughed at him, and now she chuckles too, remembering how sheepishly he walked to the bar and asked, "Does anyone speak English?"

Paul opens his eyes to find Ramona's beautiful face looking at him with a sweet smile.

"You've been sleeping for twenty minutes," she says quietly. "You were so at peace, I didn't want to wake you up. You looked like a sleeping baby and I wished I could have been there with you."

"That would be a sweet dream. Really? I've been asleep for twenty minutes? Maybe we should get back to the club, I don't want you to get into any trouble."

"Don't worry, we're okay," sighs Ramona. "It would be nice if we could stay just like this."

Paul nods. "I would like that very much."

"Promise me then, you'll come back to me."

"As if she needs to ask," thinks Paul. "Of course I will."

Paul pulls Ramona to him and holds her, taking in the scent of her skin and hair, which reminds him of a fresh sea breeze, and prays for this memory to last.

"This is embarrassing," he says, "but how much do I owe?"

"Just pay for the room."

"Are you sure?" asks Paul.

"Yes, I'm sure."

"How much is it?"

Ramona smiles, "Two dollars."

Ramona kisses him gently. Her lips are soft and cool on his, and it surprises him because it's so incredibly sensual.

Paradise

Naked, hot-pink neon tubes spell out "Paradise Bar" in cursive script glimmers against a white stucco wall with a patina of caked-on dirt and suicidal bugs. The failing transformer buzzes, struggling to power the sign as loud voices and a muffled guitar and accordion inside the building keeps a beat for the heavenly journey of moths seeking the light.

With one too many shots of whiskey in his belly, Ruben concentrates on finishing his drink and getting out of the noisy bar. He can't even hear the music because the men are all arguing about the labor problems at Alamo-Cola. Finally he looks up and yells, *"¡Cállate, estoy tratando de concentrarme!* (Shut the hell up, I'm trying to concentrate!)

The men are celebrating after getting their ten dollar weekly stipend from the union this afternoon. Tonight there's a little extra drinking money and maybe a friendly supporter of the strike who can be counted on to buy a round. Most of the talk is good-humored, but occasionally tempers have flared, then quickly laughed off with another round of drinks.

Music blasts out into the night when the heavy wooden front door of the bar violently swings out and hits the door stop with a loud thump. Ruben steps onto the sidewalk and takes a cautious look up and down the street before pulling up his jacket collar and stuffing his hands into his pockets. The door is slow to close behind him, and, when it does the night grows quiet—*maybe a little too quiet,* thinks Ruben. It's like the old saying goes, the calm before the storm.

Texas Ranger Pete is feeling pretty satisfied with life as he cruises the empty streets of Beeville. All has been peaceful tonight, as it should be, with no trashy bullshit behavior like drunk sailors fighting drunk cowboys. Tonight, everyone has returned to their respective homes or back to the base without any trouble. And if there are any wild-ass yahoos looking to create a little mayhem, they're staying out of sight.

Pete's bright headlights spot what appears to be a Mexican man up ahead walking on the side of the road, out too late to be merely going for an evening stroll. And in Pete's opinion, he's also too far away from where he should be—in Mexican Town.

Ruben does not like the long dark shadow he's casting from the bright headlights of a car slowing down behind him. He looks over his shoulder and shields his eyes from the glare before noticing the silhouette of a cop car. He picks up his pace but so does the car, finally pulling over and blocking his path.

"Fuck me," he says under his breath and slowly turns to face the music. He approaches the well-appointed police vehicle with side and roof spotlights and the silhouette of a shotgun on the gun rack. Although his view of the occupant is blocked by the glare of the lights, he knows it has got be Texas Ranger Pete, the only cop in town gung-ho enough to be out this late looking for action.

Pete breaks into a wide grin as he recognizes this Mexican to be one of the troublemakers at Alamo. He slides the power window down and asks in an over-friendly manner, "You on your way to Mexican Town, partner?"

"Yes, sir," answers Ruben.

"You're kind of a long way from home. Where's your car?"

"Didn't want to drive 'cause I was gonna be drinking."

Pete studies Ruben unhurriedly. "That's mighty law-abiding of you. Well then, get in, I'll give you a lift."

"That's okay, I need to walk off the booze."

Ruben hears the back door unlock with a click.

"I ain't asking," insists Pete.

Ruben opens the door and slides onto the back seat. "What's up with the ride?"

Pete shrugs his shoulders. "Just tryin' to be friendly."

Pete steps on the gas and accelerates until the dashed white lines on the road become a blur. (*Another tension-filled ride with a redneck cop and a brown skinned man*). Ruben suspects there will not be a good outcome for him.

It's a quiet ride until Pete smirks, "you and your friends sure as hell started a shit-storm with your boycott of Alamo-Cola."

Ruben knows to keep his mouth shut and let the white man run his mouth.

"Can't figure out how you all got so unified. That ain't like you people pulling together like that. I guess it's like that folk song about the times are changing."

"Guess so," replies Ruben.

"Don't say much, do you?"

A mile down the road Pete swerves into a dirt parking lot and slides to a stop. He shuts off the engine and walks slowly around the front of the car, the bright headlights highlight a malevolent grin on his face. He opens the door and motions for Ruben to step out.

"Safely home, just like I promised."

Ruben exits cautiously, watching Pete in case he reaches for his gun, and is slow to respond when Pete grabs his arm and throws him to the ground, then delivers a solid kick to his side.

"You think you got it bad, you ungrateful asshole? Go back to goddamn Mexico and see how they do civil rights down there!"

Ruben groans and rolls onto his side holding his ribs as Pete continues screaming at him. "You greasers better knock this shit off or you will find yourself way out of luck. Do you *comprende, pendejo*?"

Ruben rises to his hands and knees gasping for air as Pete

delivers another hard kick, this time to his stomach, which sends him face-first into the dirt.

"I'll send you and that hippie bastard you brought in straight to hell, and nobody's gonna give a shit about it!"

Ruben pushes himself up just as Pete steps in to kick him in the face. This time Ruben blocks him with his forearm and almost knocks Pete over. He jumps to his feet unsteadily and takes a step toward Pete with his fists clenched, ready to beat this cop to death if at all possible.

In the midst of nearly stumbling to the ground, Pete quickly pulls his pistol out of the holster and steadies his stance. He raises the gun up and aims directly at Ruben's chest and motions with it for Ruben to come closer. "There ya go, Pancho. You're one bad-ass ain't ya? Come on now, give me your best shot."

Ruben takes a step back in fear and holds up his hands in surrender. "Wait! Wait! Don't shoot!"

"Good decision, Pancho," sneers Pete.

Pete waves his gun in the direction of Mexican Town.

"Now don't make me out to be a liar. I said I'd get you home safely. Go on now, get on home!"

Ruben backs away holding his ribs, glad to be alive and quietly curses to himself, "*Por favor Dios, envía a alguien a matar a ese bastardo asesino.*" (Please god, send someone to kill that murderous bastard.) Before he disappears into the dark streets of Mexican Town, he hears Pete yell, "Don't forget to spread the word, *amigo!*"

Donating
to the War

Ramona, come closer, Shut softly your watery eyes
The pangs of your sadness will pass as your senses will rise
The flowers of the city, though breathlike, get deathlike at times
And there's no use in tryin', To deal with the dyin'
Though I cannot explain that in lines

P aul strums the guitar, singing Bob Dylan's, "To Ramona" on the front porch steps with a stethoscope taped to the back of the guitar, using it like a headphone. David and Michael come through the screen door eating watermelon. They sit down on the steps and bury their faces in the sweet juicy watermelon, spitting seeds to the dirt, quietly listening until the song ends.

"That sounded pretty good," says Michael. "Ramona, huh? Are you in love?"

Paul removes the stethoscope ear pieces.

"I can't stop thinking about her. Is that weird? I mean, we've only spent an hour together, but I feel something is pulling at me, telling me to go back to her. I remember what Sasha said and I'm beginning to think she really was a witch.

"Do you plan on going back to see her?" asks David.

"I'm splitting tonight because it's too damn hot to go during the day. The poor van might melt. You wanna go too?"

David shakes his head, no. "Sorry, you're going to have to be in love all by yourself. Anyway, I have to be here, especially after what happened to Ruben. I can't believe that Ranger can get away with shit like that."

"What did you expect?" says Michael. "The ruling class have run Beeville like feudal lords since Texas became a state. Now their grip on power is being threatened, by you, I might add. They've no choice but to strike back."

David laughs. "Did you just say ruling class? I had no idea you were a communist."

Michael spits out a seed with a click of his tongue and replies, "Communism sucks. It couldn't even keep me from getting drafted."

"David, this *is* beginning to get ugly," says Paul. "Maybe you should come with me. I don't want to see you give up, but they might be coming after you next."

"The hell with that," says David firmly. "I'm prepared to deal with it."

"Deal with it? What is that supposed to mean?"

"I've given this a lot of thought. Look, these guys rule by fear and I'm not afraid of them, and that makes me free to do whatever has to be done."

"That's a nice philosophy," says Paul, "but I don't think these assholes know shit about philosophy."

"I just know that I have to be courageous. I was a surfer in an East L.A. barrio—I know how intimidation works. You have to stand your ground or you get your ass kicked. It's that simple. No one helped you in Vietnam. You knew that running away and shitting your pants was more dangerous than fighting. Right?"

"Yeah, I fought back, but I got lucky. This union work doesn't have to be a death sentence."

"I'm not going to let these rednecks keep me from helping my friends when they need me the most. Shit has happened to us that is unexplainable. Whatever happened in the Rio Grande Valley changed you too—I can see it."

"I agree, but could you at least proceed with caution?"

David leans back against the stairs and looks up into the blue sky, closes his eyes and ignores Paul, who is waiting for an answer.

Paul gives up and mumbles to himself before finger-picking, "Tennessee Stud."

Except for the sound of Michael spitting watermelon seeds, an uncomfortable silence descends on the dusty little alley despite Paul's pretty version of the country/bluegrass classic. But he's not just mindlessly spitting seeds. Michael is also thinking about how the two of them risked so much in leaving San Francisco. He remembers when he first met Nancy; she had remarked, "You don't seem very far out to me." It wasn't the response he was hoping for because he was asking her out on a date. Thankfully she went out with him anyway. But it gave him pause, especially with his safe duty as a Navy photographer, while his friends and thousands of others were slopping their way through Vietnamese jungles with bullets flying all around. Maybe he should have run off to San Francisco and joined in the anti-war movement. So why hadn't he? "*What are you going to do about it?*" he finally asks himself.

Michael answers his own question when he asks David, "How are your people getting by?"

"Carolina and the other women are working," replies David. "They've had cake and tamale sales which have brought in some money, at least enough to give everyone a few bucks every week. Shit, if I knew what I was doing, I would have raised more money to begin with before everyone got fired."

"The boycott's working though, right? That's why Alamo is freaking out. You're affecting his business,"

"Oh yeah, he's had to lay off pretty much everyone."

Michael squats down in front of David. "It sounds like you're really close to winning, so let me do something."

David smiles appreciatively and replies, "Come on, the Navy isn't going to let you get involved in some local labor war."

Michael sneers, "I don't give a shit about the Navy, especially after those boozers sent JC to the brig. Seriously, I have a ton of money from all my freelance work. All those fucking weddings and officer portraits. I'm rolling in cash!"

"That's your money. We'll find other ways to raise funding."

"Seriously, I have to help out in some way. I shouldn't even be here. Why didn't I at least try and do what you did, or go to Canada? I didn't do shit to avoid the draft except join the dumb-ass Naval Reserve. I feel like such a chickenshit! Let me do one thing to help. At least give me a reason why I ended up here in the first place. It certainly wasn't to be a photographer."

Paul stops playing. He jumps off the porch and embraces Michael with a big hug and exclaims, "I know *exactly* what you're going through and I'm a much bigger fuck-up than you'll ever be! I *joined* the Marines because I *bought* all their patriotic bullshit!"

"Don't be hard on yourself, Michael," says David.

"I'm not, but I would *enjoy even* more donating to a worthy cause, especially if it will help fight the creep treating our friends like shit. If it pays someone's rent or utilities, or puts food on the table, then I want in. I need to help."

"If you're serious, I can't tell you how much we'll appreciate it. We'll be forever in your debt."

"Thanks, but you guys don't owe me anything. You and the workers are on the right side of a good cause, and you shouldn't fail because you lack money. Someday this strike will end and the war will be over, and I want to look back on this time with a certain pride at what was accomplished, and that I played some part in it."

"Right on, Michael!" says David. "I sometimes forget that we came down here to enlighten these Texans, and that's what we're going to do. Fuck 'em if they don't like it!"

Navy Life

Three squadron Commanders file into the Captain's office, a spacious wood-paneled room, and snap to attention. Ignoring them is Captain Woods, ensconced behind his large wooden desk staring at a photograph. He carefully lays it on the desk then takes another 8x10" black–and–white photograph lying in front of him. After a few moments, he huffs out a frustrated breath, lays that one down and grabs another one. He shakes his head in disgust and clears his throat, then slams his hand down hard on the desktop and directs his anger squarely at the officers.

"Son-of-a-bitch! I can't have this! Do you understand me? These are your boys, God damn it! Commander Able, could you please tell me what in the hell is going on?"

Squadron VT-26 leader Commander Able is confused by the images he's seeing on the desk.

"This has caught us completely by surprise, sir. I thought the men were doing an outstanding job."

Captain Woods explodes.

"An outstanding job? High as a kite on drugs? Are you telling me that my pilots are supposed to feel confident going up in aircraft worked on by marijuana addicts?"

Lt. John O'Neill, the Naval Intelligence officer in attendance, is a savvy inspector specializing in espionage and stolen military equipment. He points to one of the photos on the desk.

"Commander Able, this photo here shows acid rock posters covering the walls and slovenly living spaces. In some of the rooms, the American flag itself is hung upside down in protest or plastered with peace sign decals. We believe that some very powerful marijuana has suddenly shown up on the base. It's...uh... possible some of the men are abusing marijuana."

"What do you mean, abusing marijuana?" complains Captain

Woods. "Any marijuana use is abuse and completely unacceptable. Do you all understand me?"

The officers return the question with a chorus of, "Yes sir!"

Captain Woods throws the photo down onto the desk and watches it slide off the glossy surface and sail onto the floor. He stares at it tight lipped, and his face bright red in anger.

"I want those miserable barracks searched from top to bottom do you hear me? Clear this shit out now before it gets totally out of control. And inform those pothead sailors who might have lost their focus that we're engaged in a bitter struggle against the enemies of the United States. In case anyone has forgotten, we're in the middle of a goddam war! If any sailor isn't giving me their complete and undivided attention, I will take them out on the tarmac and shoot them myself! Is that clear? Son of a bitch! Zero tolerance! "

Following the tense meeting in the Captains's office, word quickly spread about upcoming searches and surprise inspections— thanks to a warning from Lt. John O'Neill's favorite photographer who accompanies him on almost every investigation.

Enlisted personnel were ordered to square away their rooms and clear out offensive anti-war posters, but no one was found to have any of the pot O'Neill had mentioned.

Days after the Captain's meltdown, Michael and O'Neill are heading out to investigate and photograph a damaged jet parked on the end of the runway after missing the arresting gear cable when O'Neill asks, "Have you heard from JC lately?"

"Yeah, he's getting out next month."

"Really? I thought he got six months?"

"I guess the Navy needs their prison cells for actual criminals."

O'Neil laughs. "Hey, did you know JC gave me the recipe for

peyote tea? My wife and I want to try it. Do you know where I can score some peyote buttons?"

"No, sir," replies Michael emphatically.

"Come on, I'm not interested in busting anyone for weed, and that included JC. That was gung-ho Shore Patrol looking for brownie points from Captain Woods."

"Go to Austin, sir. You might not actually get anyone to turn you on because you look like a cop. Oh, wait a minute, you are a cop! So, I think you might have a tough time finding anyone who would sell you anything."

"Don't be so uptight, Michael. You're telling me you've never taken any peyote and you don't smoke pot? I really find that hard to believe."

"I'm taking the Fifth on this conversation, sir."

"I'll tell you what. You bring me some buttons and I'll stop snooping around the base looking for pot that's got the Captain all puckered up. Shit, I didn't join Naval Intelligence to bust potheads. I'm only interested in stolen government equipment, sabotage from commie spies and the like. What do you say, huh?"

Michael likes O'Neill, and, a Naval Intelligence Officer who likes peyote is a far out concept. Plus, O'Neill not busting anyone he gave pot to would ease his paranoia about getting ratted out. He assesses his risky relationship and finally has to say the hell with it—he'll use the peyote to blackmail O'Neill if he turns on him in the future.

"All right," replies Michael. "I've got a small bag of buttons I can give you. But from now on, you have to start harvesting them on your own. I will tell you where you can find them though."

The Summer
of Love

Part II

Jimi Hendrix plays on the record player while Nancy relaxes on the front porch steps peeling an orange. When a Beeville Sheriff's car rounds the corner she turns her head and keeps her eyes on it as it slowly approaches the house, bouncing over the ruts before coming to a stop.

Sheriff Donny rolls down the window and smiles, cocks his head to one side and listens to the music with feigned interest before removing his sunglasses. "Howdy kiddo! That sounds pretty good," he says cheerfully.

Nancy stares at him with her nose scrunched up and wonders if he's putting her on.

"Do you mind turning it down a bit? I got something I wanna talk to you about."

Nancy looks away and grumbles, "Wait 'til the songs over."

Donny shrugs, "Okay." He leans back in his seat and bops his head in time to the beat, and watches out of the corner of his eye as Nancy gobbles up the juicy orange and wipes her mouth with her shirt sleeve. When the song ends she goes into the house and turns off the record player.

Returning to the porch, she sits down and asks, "You really like Hendrix or are you puttin' me on?"

"Is that who that was? Yeah, it sounded pretty good. I mean, I'd rather be listening to Buddy Holly or Hank Williams, but that was kinda interesting."

"Yeah, I like those guys, too. So, what have you been doing lately? I saw you talking to Janie at the Big Barn dance."

"Just catchin' up."

"You still have a big crush on her, don't you?" smiles Nancy.

"Always will. That's just how I am."

"You should have gone to California with her when you had the chance instead of joining the cops."

"That was her thing. I'm a Texas boy, you know that. I might ask you the same question, why are you still in Beeville? This town ain't right for you, just like it wasn't right for Janie."

"You can say that again. As soon as I can figure something out, count on me getting out of this dump."

"It's always good to have plans. So, how is Janie—really?"

"She's doing great, Donny."

"You think she's happy, married to a rock 'n roll dude from Corpus? Where's the future in that?"

"Well, that's the difference between you and her. I thought she looked radiant."

"She looked tired and poor to me. So, you hanging out with hippies these days?"

"Michael is a photographer in the Navy!"

"Yeah, I know, which is why I haven't arrested him yet. I mean, who needs the Navy on your ass, right? But I pretty much know everything that goes on in town ... more than you might think. For starters, I know your boyfriend here is livin' with a couple of hippie potheads, and his old roommate got sent to the Naval prison for possession. Hell, I bet that if I walked into that little shack of his right now, I'd find something prison-worthy."

Watching Nancy tighten up, Donny is glad to have her full attention, and his cheerful demeanor takes on a more serious tone.

"Word is out that those hippies got a bunch of dope they're selling to the kids out at the college."

"Whoever told you that is full of shit," replies Nancy. "David and Paul have been helping out the workers at Alamo-Cola and the poor guys gettin' fucked over by the draft. So I don't think they have much time to be standing on the corner selling drugs to kids. I think even *you* might like them."

"What were their names again?" asks Donny.

"I thought you knew everything?"

"It don't matter little sister. Just inform your friends *we* know something is going on. There's been a lot of marijuana use out at the high school and college lately."

Nancy shrugs, "So?"

The police radio begins squawking. Donny reaches over and lowers the volume before turning back to Nancy with a dark look on his face.

"So? So, I don't give a shit about the weed. Hell, cowboys and Mexicans have been smokin' weed for a hundred years, and we got, lost-their-minds cosmic peyote cowboys all over the damn state long before any hippies showed up. But now we got students tripping on some really weird shit out at the school, and it sure as hell didn't come from Mexican Town."

Nancy clenches her jaw and stares at the ground.

Donny, on the other hand, is enjoying Nancy's discomfort.

"Hell Nancy, if you *ever* went to school, you'd know what the hell's been going on out there. The whole place has turned into a hippie-dippy hell hole. Shit, some of the kids are even protesting in front of the Army Recruiting Office. Town has gotten totally out of control and folks are gettin' a bit fed up with it."

Nancy throws her orange peel into the tall weedy grass next to the house as Donny continues.

"I'm telling you this because I believe I can draw a straight line from all the shit going on lately, directly to the moment those two hippies showed up in this little house you're hanging out at. I know one of them is stirring up trouble at Alamo-Cola, which is just fine with me 'cause Gene is a greedy dumb shit, and his buddy has been trying to keep local boys from signing up for the draft. That there is a different kind of trouble, 'cause it's downright unpatriotic. Anyone caught marching down Main Street protesting the war or burning their draft cards is gonna get a serious ass-kicking, and I may not be able to keep it from happening."

"So far, it sounds like they're doin' some pretty good stuff," replies Nancy.

"Jesus, Nancy, why are you such a hard-ass? I've come here to give you and your friends a warning 'cause I don't want to see you gettin' into any trouble. You tell them I'm giving them a chance to behave themselves like decent folk, which means for own their health, they should clear out and take their act somewhere else. You understand me?"

Donny begins to roll up his window then hesitates. "Nancy, you tell your friends about our local law enforcement officers and how they would just love to round them up and beat the devil out of 'em before dumping them in Huntsville State Prison for five or ten years. If they want, they will find drugs somewhere, trust me."

Tight lipped and pissed, Nancy wraps her arms around her knees and pulls them close to her chest.

"Next time you see Janie, tell her hi for me."

Donny puts the car in gear and gives Nancy a warm smile and a tip of his hat as he leaves. Nancy watches the police car buck and bounce down the alley, and feels a brief moment of pleasure watching Donny's head bobble about like one of those dashboard dolls. She keeps an eye on him until he turns at the corner and disappears onto the paved street beyond.

"Shit," she curses.

A full moon lights the alley as David places his belongings in the back of Michael's VW bug. A warm humid breeze blows in his face and it's not comforting, but in fact, is a troubling wind. It strikes him that what the Cowboy said about Texas is correct—there is a sadness permeating this atmosphere. Maybe it's the heat and high humidity which *is* oppressive, but he's got a feeling that people are not truly happy with life. He laughs to himself when he thinks it's probably why they brag so much about Texas.

Nancy gives him many kisses on the cheek before he opens the squeaky passenger door and plops down onto the seat.

She steps back from the car with her arms crossed and sighs, "Well, that was fun while it lasted."

The engine takes its time starting. A half-dozen quick pumps on the gas pedal and it finally coughs to life. Nancy watches the car back out into the alley, hears Michael grind a gear putting in first, and makes no effort to stop the tears from flowing when David sticks his arm out the window and waves bye.

Michael stops the car in front of Luis' house on one of Mexican Town's few roads with a street light. The illumination is a welcome sign for thousands of bugs to dance all night under the yellow beam. David drops his box of belongings on the ground then reaches over the seat for his backpack.

"Thanks for everything," says David.

"Watch your step with these cowboys, okay? You're safe in Mexican Town, but don't be hitchhiking around. If you need a ride or want to borrow my car, call me at the photo lab."

"Will do."

"I'm serious, David. Don't be walking around by yourself."

David nods "okay" and lifts his backpack over his shoulder and picks up his cardboard box before slowly walking to the house He laughs as he dances and dodges the hundreds of crawling and flying insects under the glow of the street light.

Inside the bedroom, David lays his box on the floor and sits on the edge of the bed lost in thought. It takes him a few seconds to grow accustomed to the dark before noticing Carolina sitting on an overstuffed chair next to the open window, observing him, waiting for a reaction. His smile is her invitation and she slowly pulls her light cotton sweatshirt over her head. Either to entice him or simply because the warm breeze feels so good on her bare skin, she pauses. The moon highlights the curvature of her breasts, and turns her brown skin lavender. Carolina lays her sweatshirt on the floor and sits unmoving with her hands on her lap waiting for him.

David removes his shirt and holds out his hand to her. When she takes it, he pulls her close and presses her warm naked breasts against his chest, and kisses her softly.

Hours later, Carolina rolls onto her back and gazes out the window lost in thought.

"Maybe you should take the Sheriff's warning; you don't know these people like I do. They're animals."

David sighs, "We're so close to succeeding. I can't leave now even if I wanted too, which I don't."

Carolina takes David's hand and kisses it softly.

"I worry that something terrible might happen. When you're a brown-skin in Texas, it usually does."

David sighs a breath before drifting off.

"I'm not afraid. This time, we're going to win."

> Standing at the foot of the bed, Juan Cortina has his hands on his hips, patiently waiting for David to snap out of sleep."Wake up, *cabron*! The shit is hitting the fan, and all you can think of at this historical moment is *pinoche*?"

David asks himself, "Am I dreaming?"

"Why am I here is what you should be asking. I have great news, *amigo*. Mescalito is coming to your aid. But, you have to end this nonsense with the *chica*. Oh, I don't blame you, *amigo*—my God, what a beautiful *negrita*. But you must send her back to her other lovers before you lose focus. I told you to be fearless, and I wasn't just whistling through my ass. Your enemies are gathering and they mean to end this by any means necessary. Pay attention!"

Carolina is propped up on her elbow, staring at David before kissing him on the lips.

"I love watching you sleep," she says. "You must have been dreaming. Who were you talking to?"

"My guardian angel."

"You're so funny. I'll be sad when you have to leave."

David sits up.

"What are you talking about? You and I are just beginning. Last night was more than just sex."

"It certainly was, and it was beautiful, as I expected. But you'll still be hated by the whites when this is all over at Alamo. This little town is not for you, you know that."

"Come with me, then."

"That is very tempting, but my family and friends are here, and I want to help the women like you did for the men. No one cares about us, including our own people. The women have supported the men by working hard with little pay and even less respect. I've learned a lot these past few months."

David pulls her to his chest and strokes her hair, kissing her softly. "I will always be here for you."

Carolina hugs him tight.

"Thank you, but you need to focus on your own affairs right now. I know these town leaders and the cops. They'll do anything to keep us from getting organized and gaining any power. I don't want to be a distraction when so much is at stake."

David wonders why this sounds like the same conversation he was having with Juan Cortina. Is it possible Carolina is able to her Juan speaking to him?

"Where is this coming from?" asks David,

"Listen to me carefully. I want to make love to you until the minute you leave. But don't go falling in love with me, okay? Just love me."

Carolina runs her fingers through David's long hair and kisses him on the neck and whispers, "I do care for you very much, you must know that."

"I do," replies David, "and whatever happens to us, there's one thing I will never forget as long as I live."

"What is that?" she asks.

David pulls Carolina close and kisses her on the forehead.

"The image of you, naked in the moonlight. I swear to God it took my breath away."

To Ramona

After a long midnight drive, then camping in his van on the American side of the border, Paul stumbles through the swinging doors at El Papagayo. It's early afternoon and the club is empty except for Rita, sitting at the bar browsing through a fashion magazine. She glances up and casts a dismissive sneer at Paul before returning to flipping through the pages.

"Remember me?" he asks with a weak smile.

"*No habla inglés.*"

Paul wonders why she wouldn't remember him apologizing to her only three nights ago, especially after the big fuss she made out the damn lighter. He's beginning to wonder if maybe it was a mistake coming back to see Ramona. Paul decides to wait and takes a chair. He sits quietly for an hour before finally giving up and sauntering over to Rita whose face is still buried in the magazine. She makes him wait before lifting her eyes and snarling,

"*¿Qué deseas?*" (What do you want?)

"Could you tell Ramona I was looking for her?"

Rita returns to her magazine without answering, glancing up only when she hears Paul curse as he stomps off in a huff.

"*Estupido* hippie," she growls to herself.

Leaving Nuevo Laredo, Paul crosses the International Bridge separating his world from Ramona's and berates himself for being such a rube. What was he thinking? A single meeting would be remembered by a girl who must meet three or four men every night?

His retreat lasts only as far as crossing the Rio Grande into Texas. A few blocks from the border, a "vacancy" sign draws him to the parking lot of a motel. Exhausted from the long drive, he barely remembers accepting the room key before going to his room and falling asleep fully clothed. He wakes up hours later wondering why he hadn't noticed what a dump he rented.

After a shower and breakfast at an American diner on the

US side of the border, Paul returns to El Papagayo and waits for Ramona. He spends the day watching the cleanup crew mop the floors and clean table tops. Once again it looks like his venture is a bust. Head bowed in defeat, he slowly pushes back his chair just as Ramona steps through the entryway. Her eyes brighten in surprise when she sees him and she runs to his open arms exclaiming, "I've been thinking about you for days! I thought when you left you would never return. But you came back!"

"I take it Rita didn't tell you I was here yesterday looking for you. I thought I had made a big mistake."

"You were here? That bitch! She didn't say anything to me."

"I don't think she likes me," says Paul.

"She doesn't like anyone. But you're here. I am so happy!"

"Me too. Can I take you to lunch or something?"

"I have to work on an art commission. Could you stay with me while I sketch a building?"

"You're an artist?" asks a surprised Paul.

"I'm still learning, but yes, I guess I am." Ramona opens up her oversize purse and reveals its contents—pencils, charcoal sticks and a pad of drawing paper.

"Do you live at Papagayo?"

Ramona smiles with delight at his naivete.

"My God, Pablo, who would want to live in a whorehouse? You were lucky to find me. I never come here during the day unless I want to draw something."

"I'm sorry, I just thought…I'm sorry, this is all so different for me," he mumbles.

"It is for me, too. But, I'm so happy you returned."

"I'm still wondering why you picked me."

"Did I pick you? Well, you are very handsome for one thing. But more than that, I sensed a good soul the moment I first saw you. My emotion pushed me toward you, and I had no control over it. Does that make any sense? But you're the one who returned to Mexico. I have to ask you the same question: Why me?"

"Simple. I turned around and was stunned by your beauty. Then, once we began talking, and I held you in our dance, everything seemed … I don't know, there's a familiarity I can't explain."

Ramona nods. "Me too. Let's get out of this place."

Ramona takes his hand and leads him out of the club into the streets of Nuevo Laredo toward the central plaza. They take a bench and Ramona pulls out a drawing pad and some charcoal sticks. Paul is fascinated watching her as she expertly draws a fountain and an old building in the background.

He's curious how this remarkable girl next to him could end up working in a brothel disguised as a night club. He wants to ask but feels it would be an invasion of her privacy, as this is only their first day together. He decides he should let her tell him when the time is right.

While she sketches, Ramona thinks about telling him about how she came to be working at the nightclub. But she's worried he might leave her and never return. Still, he needs to be told, and if he can't handle it, then she will be sad. But lately, she's used to being sad.

"You're probably wondering why I work at El Papagayo."

"It doesn't make any difference to me unless it's something really terrible. You don't have to tell me."

Ramona focuses on her drawing until a few tears drop onto the paper. She stares at the wet pool of charcoal, and unable to control emotions that have been bottled up for months, she cups her hands over face and begins crying.

Paul pulls her to him and puts his arm around her shoulders, waiting for her to calm. She stops crying shortly and wipes away the tears with her shirt sleeve.

"Please forgive my outburst," she sniffles. "It isn't like me to be so emotional, especially in public."

Paul says softly, "Please, tell me what's going on."

It takes Ramona a few moments to compose herself before telling Paul, "Me and my father came to this town when he began work as a labor consultant on the big farms across the border. What he found were poor workers who were being abused and exploited by the growers. The ranchers who were his employers, were very cruel and he eventually quit working for them."

"I know a little something about this. My friend is involved with Texas workers trying to form a union."

"Then he should be very careful. My father became involved with union organizers because he was very troubled by what he saw. To help them, my father spent every dollar he had, and when he ran out of money, he borrowed from some very bad people. Then one day, he never came home. He simply vanished from the face of the earth. After he disappeared I was told by those men that I was responsible for his debt and they forced me to go to work at El Papagayo."

"That doesn't sound right. Did you go to the cops and report him?" asks Paul.

"That is not how it works in Mexico. These men pay large bribes to the police who let them do what they want."

Paul stares at Ramona in disbelief.

Ramona continues.

"They organized a large protest, and the growers hired thugs who came in and beat them up until the American Army came in and stopped it. But my father never came home. For weeks I asked everyone if they had seen him, but no one knew anything. Some offered to take me in, but they are so poor, I would be too much of a burden for them. My father knew their attempts to unionize had become dangerous, but he wanted so much to help them. You don't know what it's like to be so alone!"

Paul hugs her tightly. "I found you and that's all that matters. But you're wrong, I do know what it's like to be alone. The loneliest place on earth is lying in the mud ten thousand miles from home with a bullet in your leg. It seems we both know something about being trapped in a nightmare."

Ramona huffs out a breath, "I'm sorry, I'm afraid I have to get ready for work."

Paul flinches at the thought of her having sex with strangers to pay off her father's debt. She senses his discomfort and takes his hand in hers. "Please don't be upset. I wasn't making enough money for them as a cocktail waitress. They threatened me and told me I would need to prostitute myself. I know this is no comfort to you, but so far I have only taken one boy into the room, and he was very disappointed. I do want to see you again and I hope you feel the same."

"Of course I do. Can I at least walk you home?"

"Give some thought to what I have told you. If you still want to see me, meet me tomorrow at this bench at noon."

Ramona packs up her sketch pad and kisses Paul on the cheek before turning away and walking across the plaza with her large bag of art supplies. When she gets to the main boulevard, she waves to him then disappears into the crowd.

Paul checks out of his dingy motel room the next morning and arrives in the plaza before noon, securing the same bench. For the next half hour he watches the pigeons swooping down from the palm trees surrounding the plaza for bits of any edible litter— abandoned ice cream cones, bread crumbs or peanut shells.

Paul lifts his eyes when he hears Ramona's sweet voice.

"Would you like to see where I live?"

They leave the park and walk through the business district, mostly commenting on the insane amount of goods packed into the small shops: silver jewelry hanging in the windows, or the tantalizing aroma of chickens roasting over a spit in a restaurant. They enter a colorful working-class neighborhood of brightly painted small homes on narrow lots with windows barricaded by wrought iron bars. After a short distance, Ramona stops and points to a yellow house with white trim, "My home."

A dozen small birds take flight from a bird feeder when she rattles her keys to unlock the gate. She ushers him into a small yard and unlocks a pink wooden door surrounded by a climbing rose bush, potted flowering cactus and geraniums.

"This is nice" remarks Paul.

"I moved here after Popi disappeared. My new neighbors are very nice and look out for me. I'll make us some tea."

Once inside the home, Paul does a quick survey of her tidy but small apartment. Her double bed takes up most of the living space and he's not surprised to find professional-looking watercolor paintings and pencil drawings taped on the walls. He takes his time viewing them while Ramona places a kettle of water on a small stove.

"These are all yours, right? They're beautiful."

Ramona smiles proudly.

"Thank you, Paul. Even though I have two jobs, it doesn't keep me from my art."

Paul carefully studies each painting or drawing, traveling from one to the next before stopping before a framed photograph of a smiling, handsome man who looks very familiar. When he remembers why: the sad floating man from his peyote dream who tried to tell him something before being swept away, he is shocked beyond belief. He blinks back tears and takes a deep breath trying to shake his mind back to reality.

"Who … who is this man in the photo?" he stutters.

"That's Popi. Isn't he handsome? It breaks my heart he's not here. He would like you very much."

But Paul baffled. On peyote, he experienced another world, but that was just tripping on peyote, like the barnacles who sang to him on his acid trip. This is reality, and he's left speechless. He motions for Ramona to come to him.

"Are you okay, Paul? You look like you've just seen a ghost."

"I'm a little overwhelmed by everything, I guess," he replies lamely.

"The tea will help. Warm tea is very soothing on a hot day."

For the next fifteen minutes they sit quietly on the bed and sip their tea while Ramona tells Paul about some of the women in her paintings.

One of the subjects is working as a call girl because her father had a car accident and rather than have him sentenced to jail, she was paying off the injured family.

Murder and madness, or maybe it's only the chirping of birds, but in the quiet of a small cottage in Nuevo Laredo, Mexico, two people begin to fall in love.

Paul lays his tea on the table and kisses Ramona.

"I want you to stay with me Paul, I really do, but I'm afraid I have to get ready for work."

"Work? But it's early."

Ramona laughs, "Sweet Paul. I still work at the print shop."

"Oh, sorry, I forgot."

Paul sits on the edge of the bed watching Ramona as she brushes her hair in front of a mirror. He catches her smiling at him in the reflection and wonders how long he can keep his secret of meeting her father in a peyote trance, or keep his mouth shut about her working in a cathouse.

"How long are you planning on staying?" asks Ramona.

"I don't know. How long would you like me to?"

Ramona turns around and hugs him. "You want to stay?"

Paul feels like he's in the midst of a nervous breakdown with thoughts like, *"crazy about you,"* or *"insanely in love."* He laughs out of the blue and, as if reading his mind, Ramona says, "I feel the same way, too. It's a mental sickness."

They kiss and embrace but there is still so much doubt pulling them apart. Ramona worries this might be too good to last given her recent history, and Paul wonders if he can handle her night job, even as much as she hates it. Finally Ramona gently pushes him away and straightens out her dress, and takes a deep breath out of frustration.

"Will you walk me to work?"

"I wish I didn't have to," he replies, and immediately regrets saying it. "I meant that someday, maybe we ... maybe we might ..." Paul can't explain his heart but wishes he could.

"Paul?" asks a waiting Ramona.

"You know I care for you," he finally blurts out.

Ramona teases his hair and laughs.

"Look at yourself. You want to tell me something, but you're afraid I'll think you're being foolish. Is that what has your tongue all tied up?"

"I don't know what to say," he mumbles. "I have to go back to Texas soon, and I'm afraid if I'm gone too long you'll forget all about me. Does that sound pathetic?"

Ramona smiles and rubs his neck.

"Maybe a little, but no, I understand."

Paul opens his wallet and counts out five, twenty dollar bills. "Please, take this—for your other job."

Ramona hesitates but he forces it into her hands anyway.

"You are the one I care for and it breaks my heart that you're under the weight of that debt which isn't even yours."

Ramona hugs Paul and takes the money and wraps her arm through his and leads him to the door. "Now, will you please walk me to work?"

"Can I meet you tomorrow? In the park?"

Ramona smiles and hugs him tight. "Pick me up from the print shop after work. I get off at seven."

Paul spends the next five hours on the streets of downtown Laredo mindlessly poking around the hundreds of shops looking for gifts. At a liquor store selling mostly Tequila, Paul discovers a dust-covered, black ceramic jug with crude, hand-painted lettering buried deep behind the commercially made brands on the shelf.

"The finest Mescal in all of *Mechico*. It is made by the Serrano Indians in Oaxaca and it is very rare," the salesman explains with a sly grin. "But for you, *amigo*, thirty American dollars."

Paul stops in front of Ramona's workplace, and as much as he wants to see her, taking her to El Papagayo is not something he's looking forward to.

The door to the print shop opens and the moment Ramona spots Paul she enthusiastically races to the van and slides across the bench seat to give him heart-felt, passionate kiss. Paul returns the favor enthusiastically and eventually they end up lying on the seat making out without a care in the world, or a thought as to who might be walking by. Finally Ramona sits up and straightens out her clothing.

"I can't go back to that club, could you take me home, please?" she says.

Once the door is closed to the living room, they immediately begin caressing and kissing each other in a mad dance across the room removing articles of clothing before falling onto the bed. With their warm naked bodies pressed against each other, neither one is surprised to discover how perfectly they fit together, as if a final piece of a puzzle effortlessly falls into place.

Ramona absorbs every physical and emotional sensation of this remarkable joining—nothing like the fumbling awkward sex she had with a boy at a beach party when she was a teenager, or the horrible experience at El Papagayo. For the first time in her life she discovers what making love is when you're in love. Hours later, exhausted from their lovemaking, they eventually fall asleep while still embracing each other.

In the morning Ramona climbs out of bed and prepares Paul a uniquely flavored pink tea made from loquat leaves picked from a tree in the neighborhood. "Not many know just how good these leaves are for you. Plus, they're free and they taste delicious!"

Ramona places the cups of tea on the night stand and crawls next to Paul under the thin sheet covering him and says quietly, "I'm sorry I've been so pathetic. Mexicans are famous for our sad stories." She takes Paul's hand and kisses it. "Now, I've told you of Popi's mysterious disappearance and his daughter's tale of woe. Tell me Pablo, what is your story?"

Paul thinks about his life and wonders where to begin. His story compared to Ramona's is fairly uneventful except for his time in Vietnam. He tells her about his middle-class childhood growing up just outside Detroit with birthdays, 4th of July celebrations, and his pride in being a Boy Scout with a sash full of merit badges. She discovers that he was an All-Star Little League second baseman and ran track and field in high school. It wasn't until signing up for the war that he discovered the real world, emerging from his protective suburban cocoon and finding a world as foreign to him as the moon. His parents' support of the war has driven a wedge between them. Since he returned from the war, he's found it impossible to reconcile their differences.

"My father is gung-ho about everything America and my anti-war stance makes it difficult for us to be around each other."

Paul laughs and says, "Besides that, not much else except I'm trying to get my life back together after being in Vietnam. Before I made it home, my parents planned a big party to welcome me back—the war hero, which was the exact opposite of what I wanted."

"They were proud of you, that's all," says Ramona.

"I know. I told them I appreciated their efforts, but I was no longer the kid who joined the Marines to fight communism. The war changed me and that's what they didn't get. My father thinks Vietnam is like World War II, which he fought in. But it's completely different, and I didn't want anyone thanking me for the horrible shit we are doing to those poor people."

"What happened when you refused them?"

"My dad said I was an ungrateful, unpatriotic, baby-boomer shithead. I couldn't believe it. After I had volunteered to go to Nam and was wounded. How could he turn on me and be such a hard-ass? He basically chased me away."

"How long ago was that?"

"About a year and a half."

"That is truly sad. I don't know how a parent could abandon their child because of politics. I don't mean to judge your father but to me, it is shameful. Not knowing where my Popi is, I would give anything to have him with me. Politics would never divide us."

"I agree completely," mumbles Paul.

"You still have him in spite of all that. I think it might be good for you to call him and try again."

"My mother will … would … love you," he stumbles.

His unconscious mistake isn't missed by Ramona. She takes his hand and rubs it softly with a twinkle in her eye.

"Maybe you should call her first. Women know how to soften up their men." She scoots close and lays her head on Paul's chest, runs her hands over his stomach and touches the deep bullet wound on his upper thigh, feeling the indentation before pausing.

"Was it painful?" she asks.

"Not at first, because I was in shock, but yes, it was so horrible that it went beyond pain. I think I might have even laughed. What about you? Any bullet holes or scars?"

Ramona laughs and shows him her left foot. She points to a good-sized scar on her instep, turned white by time. "I stepped on a broken beer bottle on the beach. I thought I was going to bleed to death but my Popi got me to the hospital."

Paul holds her foot and remarks that it is quite a scar, then he notices what a beautiful foot it is. He's never thought about feet before, but now he jokes to himself that from now on he will.

"It breaks my heart that you were in Vietnam. What bothers me are the wealthy and powerful sending young men and women to war to make themselves even richer."

"I had no idea you were a socialist."

Ramona chuckles.

"You you seemed so mysterious to me when I first saw you. Maybe that's why I was drawn to you. I sensed that something had happened, and it changed you. I could see it."

"Life is way more complex than anyone can imagine," replies a surprised Paul. "Something did happen only hours before we met.

It's why I didn't have a light for Rita's cigarette."

"I am glad it did. Do you think you and I have met before in another life? That sounds crazy, doesn't it?"

Paul laughs. "Nothing sounds crazy to me any more."

Paul turns to Ramona, and for the next hour they fall into an intense lovemaking session, exploring of every square inch of each other's bodies. Finally exhausted, they fall asleep in each other's arms.

A bright sun that shines through a crack in the curtain informs them it's about noon. Paul props himself up and tells Ramona, "I really don't want to, but I have to check up on David. He's put himself in a situation similar to your father's and I'm worried."

"I understand completely, Paul. If anything happens to him you will never forgive yourself. Before you go, let me tell you how I feel so you can stop worrying about me."

She kisses him and looks deep into his eyes. "I want you to come to me every minute of the day. I know your heart, so don't feel obligated to say anything more, okay?"

Paul might be mad at his father, but the old guy invested his hazardous duty pay in the stock market and it is now worth twenty times its original value. When his dad presented the stock certificates to him on their last visit, he told Paul not to piss it away on drugs and whores. Paul laughs at the thought, and wonders how his dad will respond to Ramona when, or if, they finally meet.

It's true he and Ramona barely know each other, but some force of nature, a chemical reaction, or even a past life, drove them into each other's arms. The biggest mistake either of them could make would be to ignore it. With her dad gone, who else was there to protect and take care of her if it isn't him?

Instead of driving straight back to Beeville, Paul found a bank in Laredo, Texas, who arranged a quick sale of some of his stock certificates.

"Thank you for your service, son" said the broker with a chuckle. "Being conveniently located, we're often asked to assist individuals needing cash for an expeditious skedaddle across the border."

The sound of a Volkswagon engine has Ramona dropping her drawing pad and falling into Paul's arms at the doorway. They make it to the bed fully clothed with their arms tightly wrapped around each other, and stay that way for several minutes before Ramona asks him about David. "He must be very brave to go against those people. My father tried and it cost him his life."

Paul replies, "And I'm so sorry. But I'm not concerned for David at the moment, it's you I worry about."

Ramona buries her face in his chest and holds him tight.

They listen to a street vendor calling out for afternoon treats with jingling bells on his cart and listen to the squealing of happy children as they order watermelon, ice *frescas* and chocolate treats. Ramona sighs, thinking that it wasn't very long ago that she was just like one of those carefree children.

"I'm starving," says Paul. "Is there a place we can get some decent food?"

They walk to a nearby open-air restaurant whose owners fill the table with bowls of frijoles, tortillas, and a ceramic jug of water before placing a menu on the table. After lunch, they walk to the plaza and Paul orders two ice cream cones being sold by an elderly man with a cart featuring colorful balloons that bounce against the wind chimes. They find an empty bench, and when the ice cream is gone, Paul cradles Ramona in his arms. A gentle, soothing breeze begins to blow, and within a few moments they are lulled to sleep.

When they wake, they laugh at each other having taken a siesta like an old married couple. Paul thinks this is the right time to bring up settling her outstanding debt.

Ramona won't hear of it. "I love that you want to protect me, but I never want to be in debt again, especially if it means putting your life in danger for me."

Her words hurt and throw him into a slow burn. He can't be mad at her desire to be independent, but he also can't hang around the border and watch her go off to work in a cathouse to pay off the debt. In spite of what he told Ramona, David is in danger, and it won't be long before Alamo-Cola hires the same thugs who broke up the Brownsville strike and hit back. It's probably what happened to Ramona's father.

"This is not about ownership," replies Paul. "I want to be your companion, your friend and lover. But mostly, I want you to be free of those gangsters."

Ramona drops her head. "Try to understand. I don't think they will let me go so easily. They could hurt you, which would break my heart. Even now, I worry because they have spies everywhere to keep girls from fleeing."

Paul looks around the plaza. "Point one out to me and I'll kick his ass right now."

"There is a man in my neighborhood, a very bad man who loaned my father the money."

"Is he watching us now?" asks Paul.

"I haven't seen him today. But he could have told them about me seeing you."

Ramona looks around the park and points to the ice cream vendor. "That man sells drugs from his cart. I've seen him. The ice cream business is just a front."

"God-damn Mexico," grumbles Paul.

Everything right now is an annoyance—Texas and its racism, men blowing off steam with the whores in Boy's Town. Any one of the girls could be just like Ramona, forced into the sex business because of poverty. Paul swears to himself that she will never suffer that kind of humiliation again. He has to force the issue—*it's for her own safety.* His thoughts have him balled up and angry, fuming as he sits in silence. Ramona tries to calm him with a gentle touch but he flinches instead.

"Don't be mad at me, please?" she pleads. " I don't like going there either. You know I love you. You know that, don't you?"

Paul nods. "Then what are we going to do? How much do you owe the gangsters?"

"Paul, please. I don't want you to...."

Paul cuts her off abruptly.

"How much do you still owe those bastards?"

Ramona slowly whistles out a breath. "Almost two thousand American dollars. But with the interest, it might even be more."

Paul pulls out his wallet stuffed with hundred dollar bills and counts out twenty of them.

"Here is two thousand dollars. Let's gather up your paintings and drop the cash off at the club. If those thugs don't think it's enough then they'll have to catch us before we make it across the border."

Ramona's eyes grow large staring at the bills. "Why do you have so much money? I know people who have that much cash sell drugs. You don't you sell drugs, do you?"

Paul shakes his head. "No, I sent most of my hazardous duty pay home for safekeeping and my father invested it in the stock market. The smart son-of-a-bitch made me a ton of money!"

"Thank goodness! I don't know what I would do if you were

ever arrested and sent to prison. The people who hold me captive in the club sell drugs and I don't want you to be anything like them."

"Don't worry, I'm not," says Paul sincerely. "I promise you I would never do that. After I cashed in some stock, I drove straight to you."

Paul takes her by the arms and looks directly into her eyes. "I know this is a big step for you, because I know what it's like to be institutionalized—that's what war did to me. I was brainwashed into believing that killing another human was the patriotic thing to do, and I lost who I used to be until I met you. When I came back, it took months to get over Vietnam where I had grown comfortable as a hired killer. It's no different than the prison you've been forced to work in, because like me, you are strong and will do what it takes in order to survive, but it takes its toll, trust me. Give this money to your boss, then let's get the hell out of here!"

"I'm afraid he will find an excuse to keep me here."

"Then I'll give him the damn money," he replies forcefully. "I think he will get a sense of who I am and what lengths I would go through for you."

"Please Paul, don't put your life in danger for me."

"That is exactly why I have to do this. If I can't protect you, what good am I? Tell me his name."

Ramona takes a long thoughtful look around the picturesque plaza—the children, the pigeons crowding the walkways begging for food, and the vendors selling everything from frozen ice cones to steamed corn on the cob. She thinks to herself, "this is not my home, what reason do I have to linger in this sad place any longer? The man I love is sitting right next to me, so why am I hesitating?"

Finally she smiles and says, "Rodrigo."

Paul hugs her. "I swear you will not regret this. Once we pay the debt we'll figure out a way to get you across the border."

"It won't be a problem, I have a passport. Popi got me one before we left Mazatlan."

Ramona makes the call and sets up a meeting. Ten minutes later Paul walks through the swinging doors of the club and looks around for Rodrigo. A well-dressed man sitting at the bar looks up and waves him over with a flip of his head. "Firecrackers, marijuana, reds? Tell me what you want."

"Rodrigo?" asks Paul.

"Oh, you must be the little girls's friend. She said you got the money she owes me."

Paul stares at Rodrigo for a moment, wondering if Rodrigo can sense that he's dealing with someone who has killed before. As he lays twenty hundred dollar bills on the bar, Paul stares into Rodrigo's eyes and tells him, "Her name is Ramona. This should cover her debt."

Rodrigo snorts out a huff. But he picks up the money, then childishly begins counting it out verbally, laying each bill down, one at a time. When he slaps the last bill on the bar top, he gives Paul an inquisitive look and asks, "Why so much?"

"Her father borrowed two thousand dollars from you."

Rodrigo laughs out loud and turns to the bartender standing behind the bar with his hands hidden under the counter.

Paul thinks the bartender has his hands on a gun.

"¡Qué tonto!" (What a fool!) She only owes me one thousand dollars, killer!" laughs Rodrigo before asking the bartender. "¿Estoy en lo correcto?" (Am I right?)

The bartender nods, "Si, jefe." (Yes, boss)

"Your little chica, she made a couple of pesos, too. But, thank you for this generous settlement. I hope she's worth it, because from what I heard, Ella no era muy buena en el saco. (She was not very good in the sack.) Pero, you two have a nice quiet life, okay?

Now get out of my club."

As Paul leaves, he hears Rodrigo and the bartender laughing and joking in Spanish, either about him, or a guy named, Arturo.

At her apartment, Ramona asks him about the meeting and if it's safe to leave. Paul tells her, "You never know with guys like that, but I think we're okay. He said something in Spanish but I didn't understand it. Do you know an Arturo?"

"Yes! He's the man who loaned the money to my Popi. Do you think Rodrigo is going to send him out to get me back?"

Paul shakes his head. "I don't know. Those were some pretty rough-looking guys, so how about we get the hell out of town as soon as possible."

Paul stands watch out front while Ramona fills the van with her paintings and clothes. Before leaving, she writes a thank you note to her landlord, and places the key in an envelope, then closes the gate.

"I need to let my boss know what's going on," says Ramona. "Can we stop by the print shop?"

"A kiss for luck?" asks Paul.

Ramona leans in and kisses him softly on the lips.

As they near the border, a motorcyclist suddenly sails out of a side street and ends up on their tail, zig-zagging from one side of the lane to other.

"Shit!" complains Paul. "I think we're being followed."

Ramona swings around in her seat and watches the biker for a moment. "It might be Arturo. He has a motorcycle."

"Is it him?" asks Paul.

"I can't tell, he's wearing a helmet."

Paul waits for the cyclist to make a move ands plans to run

him off the road if he comes too close. Fortunately the cyclist turns off at the next intersection, but replacing him almost immediately is a large truck who cuts off a car when it abruptly jams in back of them from another lane. Paul hears a horn blast from the offended driver, which causes Ramona to let out a surprised yelp.

Paul glances over to Ramona and laughs when he sees she has a tight grip on large wrench, prepared to use it if necessary.

On the American side of the bridge, a Border Patrol Officer waves them through with barely a glance. Looking through the rear window they let out a sigh of relief when the same officer steps in front of the truck and waves it over to the inspection station.

"We're free!" exclaims Paul.

"Do you think they were sent to stop us?" asks Ramona.

Paul shakes his head. "I don't know, maybe we just imagined the whole thing."

Ramona begins giggling realizing the chase might have only been in her mind. Paul reaches over and turns on the radio. "Born to be Wild," by Steppenwolf, starts playing and Ramona's first three minutes of freedom is spent laughing and singing along with the radio, heading as far away from Mexico as possible.

Get your motor runnin'
Head out on the highway
Lookin' for adventure, and whatever comes our way
Born to be wild!

"I'm surprised you know that song," says Paul.

"Pablo, rock and roll doesn't end at the border. It looks like we have a lot to learn about each other, don't we?"

Paul smiles at the thought. "I'm looking forward to it."

A few miles from the border, they pull off the highway into a gas station and park next to a phone booth.

"I've got to call David."

After getting a large amount of change from the service station, Paul opens the glass doors of the booth and is baptized by a blast of scorching hot air. He deposits a dime into the slot and waits for an operator.

"Please deposit two dollars and seventy-five cents, please," says an operator with a serious Texas drawl.

Paul deposits the proper amount of quarters.

"Thank you for using Southwestern Bell."

After a few rings, Luis picks up the phone.

"Luis, it's Paul."

"My bother! Howzit hanging?"

"Thanks to good fortune, they still are!"

"That's good to hear," laughs Luis. "You looking for David?"

"Yeah, is he around?"

Seconds later David gets on the line and asks, "Paul, what's happening? Is everything okay?"

"Couldn't be better, man. How are things with the cowboys?"

"Pretty cool so far. Alamo is getting feisty, but we're being careful. Are you on your way back?"

Paul would love to tell him about stealing Ramona from the gangsters, but would also like to surprise the shit of him.

"If you need me, I can be there tomorrow, but I was thinking about checking out the Gulf. You know in all these months we have yet to see the damn thing."

David chuckles. "I guess we got a little sidetracked. Take your time, I'm in good hands. What about Ramona?"

"I'll tell you all about her later. I'm on a pay phone and my time is almost up."

"Paul jumps in the van and asks Ramona, "No regrets?"

Ramona takes a deep breath, "Ready, no regrets."

They stare at a half-opened bathroom door on the side of the station and Paul takes Ramona's hand and with the sink as their only witness, he promises to love and cherish her for better or worse, and what could be worse than her losing her father and being forced to work in a whorehouse? When he's finished, Ramona kisses him and promises to always love him, even after death does them part.

On a narrow strip of asphalt highway that stretches straight and flat all the way to the horizon, Ramona can't stop her tears from flowing.

"What's wrong?" asks Paul. "Are you sad?"

"You misunderstand, these are tears of joy. I thought my life was over when I was forced to work in that place. But thanks to you and whatever brought us together, I am happy and free of that life."

Staring out the desolate landscape, Ramona wonders why so many had fought and died to gain control of this land.

As if reading her mind, Paul remarks, "It gets better, you'll see. Tomorrow we'll go to the Gulf of Mexico and lie on the beach. But tonight, how about we find a seafood shanty and have crab legs, how does that sound?"

"Delicious. I can almost picture the seagulls and the sounds of waves lapping against the wharf."

After two hours of staring at the yellow dashed lines on the monotonous road, the Gulf or a seafood shanty fail to come their way. Finally they spot a restaurant which is also the office to a motel located next door under some large oak trees.

"Restaurant is closed buddy, sorry," says the desk clerk. "But I can get you some chips and beers to hold you over 'til mornin'. We got clean bathrooms and showers for y'all if ya need a room."

By the glow of a full moon Paul and Ramona hold each other

in a tight embrace and simply enjoy the body heat keeping them warm under the blankets before slowly beginning another night of lovemaking. After an hour or more, Ramona whispers in Paul's ear, "We could really use a shower."

Late the next morning, they enter the motel's nearly empty restaurant to be greeted by the warm aroma of coffee and bacon. The waitress immediately offers them coffee and a complimentary homemade bear claw before they even order. "We're very proud of these babies and I hate to see any go to waste," she says.

The scent of salty air announces that they are nearing the Gulf of Mexico. After crossing a bridge over an inland waterway, they reach the crest of a large sand dune stretching for miles down the coast. Unfortunately, their first glimpse of the Gulf is a considerable letdown. The water is not the color of root beer as Michael described, but instead is the color of a brown mushroom. The beach is packed with families, sunbathers, and clam diggers, but the biggest surprise is finding a dozen surfers riding some well-shaped waves. The romantic image they held in their minds about lying on the beach evaporates quickly when they're forced to drive a half-mile along a hard, flat sandy beach looking for a parking space.

Paul finally backs the van into a spot and turns off the engine. Silence ensues as he and Ramona stare out to the water in a mild state of shock. Sensing disappointment, Paul asks Ramona, "How about we dip our toes in the water? At least we can say we did it."

Ramona sighs, "Paul, what are we doing?"

He knows she's not asking about sitting in a sandy parking lot staring out at a depressing ocean.

"I don't have an immediate plan if that's what you're asking. All I know is I wanted you safely out of Mexico. Now I need to see if David is in any danger, then we can get the hell out of Texas and head anywhere we want. How does that sound?"

Ramona stares out at the water lost in thought.

"What? You'd love California!" exclaims Paul.

Ramona takes Paul's hand in hers.

"Just when I had given up hope of ever having a decent life again, a beautiful, gentle person came to me and we fell in love. You saved my life. But I worry that some of your friends might think I'm not a good person because I worked in that club."

"It was against your will! Anyone who thinks that way about you will have me as an enemy. You'll fight me on this because you want to be independent. But I have enough money for both of us to go to school, too. Why are you hesitating about leaving Texas? You don't want go back to Mexico."

"Never! But I have to find out what happened to my father. I'm pretty sure he was killed by the growers."

"You think he's dead?" asks Paul.

"I don't know. The workers told me that the *Americanos* took him, but nobody knows where."

"Then we need to find out, and we won't give up until we know the truth about his disappearance. I don't care how long it takes, either. Now, let's get our feet wet."

They climb out of the van and stand at the water's edge. Paul rolls up his pant legs and Ramona lifts her skirt. They enter the water holding hands, slowly and cautiously through a murky sea that is as warm as the hot, humid air. More than fifty yards from shore, small, gentle waves are still lapping at their knees.

"I think we could walk to Florida," says an amused Ramona.

Ramona's first view of Beeville is nearly as depressing as her first look at the Gulf. Just over the railroad tracks is a funky-looking drive-in restaurant named, "Don's Dog House."

"This place makes the best tacos you've ever tasted."

Ramona lets out a hoot. "I'm sure you're right, Pablo, but I should be the judge of what is a good taco, don't you think? "

The looks of the little town improves as they pass through the main drag of small businesses in old Victorian buildings filling both sides of the street. Paul slows the van as they drive past Alamo-Cola. The noisy bottling lines one used hear from the street are now quiet, and behind the locked gate are a dozen delivery trucks sitting idle in the parking lot.

"It looks like the boycott is working. David must be pretty stoked about this!" exclaims Paul.

"Stoked?" asks Ramona. "What does that mean?"

"Excited," replies Paul. "California surfers use it to describe the feeling they get after riding a good wave."

"Oh, yes, I used to watch those surfers. They looked like they were having so much fun."

David is a surfer and so is our friend Michael."

"I'll be stoked to meet them," laughs Ramona.

Leaving the main business district they pass the cattle auction house, then rows of equipment rentals, used auto parts and repair shops, and a cocktail lounge with pink neon letters over the door. Finally, they come to an aging strip mall—a one-story building with a market, laundromat, a barber and a beauty shop. Paul makes a turn onto a dirt street that takes them into a neighborhood of small frame homes on large lots. Many have vegetable gardens, chickens in the yard, and clothes hanging on lines.

Ramona thinks about being a Mexican in the United States, which is known for its racism, and even how *Tejanos* will treat her.

A half a mile down the street, Paul and Ramona spot David stumbling off the porch of Luis's house and waving his arms as he runs out to the street to greet them.

Good News

David shoves a healthy portion of *chorizo* and scrambled eggs into his mouth with a tortilla and takes the dish towel on his lap and wipes away sweat beading up on his cheeks from the spicy sausage. He tears off another piece of tortilla and uses it like a spoon to scoop up more off the plate.

Carolina enters the kitchen wearing a loose-fitting man's shirt hanging to her thighs and humming a sweet Mexican ballad. David stops eating and watches her all the way to the sink. When she leans over to wash out a cup he stares at her shapely brown legs that demand attention. He swivels around in his chair and hugs her tightly from behind, reaches up under her shirt and rubs her firm thighs.

"David, I thought you were hungry," she laughs.

"I am, but why do I have to choose between *chorizo* and your beautiful body? Where's Luis?"

"He's deep in sleep. I couldn't even get him up for breakfast, and he's never refused my mom's *chorizo*. He must have been out partying late last night."

"Out with a new boyfriend?" jokes David.

Carolina grabs him by the hair and pulls him in close. She whispers in David's ear, "Luis told me to give you a kiss."

"Luis wants to kiss me?"

Carolina shrugs with a wicked smile.

David glances toward Luis' bedroom then says with a shrug, "Okay, give it to me."

She offers him a juicy French kiss, expertly rolling her tongue around his before pulling away and moaning, "Umm, my *chorizo* tastes good!"

David pulls her onto his lap and returns her kiss with an equal amount of passion.

Carolina laughs, "Jesus, David! What's got into you?"

"I don't know, but Luis is a really good kisser."

"Oh my God! You're sick!"

Someone is knocking on the front door, but Carolina and David pay no attention to it and continue their lovemaking until the bedroom door flies open. Luis stomps across the living room to the front door. "Mother fuck!" he screams.

Carolina cries out, "Don't open the door!"

Startled, Luis snaps out of his mad trance and stops short of the door. He spins around and gasps when he's greeted by Carolina's legs wrapped around David.

"Didn't you hear that banging on the door? Put some clothes on for Christ sakes!"

Luis waits for Carolina to leave the kitchen before opening the front door violently and frightening two Latino men wearing cowboy hats and dark suits who leap back in surprise, puzzling Luis, who thinks, "They must be fucking Jehovah's Witnesses."

"I don't give a shit about your God damn 'Watchtower,'" he hisses before slamming the door in their face.

He steps back into the living room, but they start knocking on the door again. This time Luis clenches his fists, preparing to punch the shit out of these Christian morons if they don't stop bugging him. He yanks the door open. "Whadaya fuckin' want?"

The men hold their ground this time. "*Buenos dias, compadre.* I hope we are not interrupting you so early in the day."

"Well, you are!"

"Please forgive us. We have important news regarding your labor issues. Your associate, Ruben Gonzales, told us that David Macias works at this address."

"Ruben said that, huh? Okay, who are you?"

The man pulls out a business card and hands it to Luis who studies it suspiciously.

"My name is Ramon Martinez, and I'm field officer for the American Federation of Labor and the Congress of Industrial Organizations. We are the largest federation of unions in the United States."

Ramon turns to his partner. "*Mi compadre* Rosalio Muños, one of the founders of the Mexican American Youth Organization, also known as MAYO. They have over thirty chapters throughout the state committed to *La Raza*. David Macias wrote to us about your struggle with Alamo-Cola and we've come to assist you in your efforts."

Luis opens the screen door and steps onto his small porch. He looks up and down the street before asking, "No shit? You have any problems getting here?"

Ramon and Rosalio turn and survey the street with him, but the neighborhood is quiet with only a few cars parked haphazardly in front of small frame houses.

"That bad, huh?" asks Ramon. "There was a Sheriff's car parked up by the highway. A Tejano cop—*un policia negro?*"

"Yeah, the white man's errand boy. He's a black-hearted rat for the *bastardos ricos*. We better get inside."

Luis blocks Ramon and Rosalio with his arm and says, "Wait a minute." He turns away and orders David to clean off the table. "We got guests."

"You caught me by surprise, I was asleep," says Luis as he leans into the room while David rattles dishes and straightens up the kitchen. After a few minutes, Carolina walks out of her bedroom dressed in jeans and a long-sleeve shirt.

"Okay!" Luis graciously holds the screen door open for them and waves them into the living room.

"Smells good," smiles Rosalio.

"Carolina's homemade *chorizo. Hace que los hombres se*

vuelvan locos. (It makes men go crazy)," grins Luis. "You guys want some coffee?"

"Yes, thank you," replies Ramon.

Ramon lays his briefcase on the coffee table and removes a number of legal-looking contracts. "As you know, the whites and their stooges consider Tejanos and those south of the border as the same—unorganized, uneducated lower class people who fight too much and drink too much. What they don't realize is that the times are changing. The union and others are succeeding throughout the state organizing workers in the fields and in the factories. There are thousands of us working to protect our rights as equal citizens, using our strength in numbers, demanding to be treated fairly with liveable wages, benefits, and the same treatment the white workers receive."

Luis lightly punches David in the arm. "Do you hear that, man, thousands!"

Ramon continues. "We have been concentrating our efforts in the state's urban areas where a greater number of workers and more violations of civil rights are happening, and I am sorry to say, that we have left you guys here in the country at the mercy of these bastards. *Perdone,* Carolina."

"You can't embarrass her, Ramon, she has a mouth like a sailor!" laughs Luis.

"Alamo-Cola?" Ramon continues. "They shouldn't have let it get this far, especially firing employees like they did. A boycott is usually a last resort, and then only after all negotiations have come to an impasse."

Ramon pauses for a sip of coffee and continues. "This guy, Gene? He shows a complete disdain towards his Tejano employees, and that practice is going to end immediately." He takes out a folder and removes a dozen pages with columns of text and holds it up for all to see. "These are bottling companies where we now represent workers. There are Alamo bottling plants all over the state, Alamo-Cola is just a franchise—one of many. If he doesn't listen to your demands like a civilized manager, we'll pressure his association to force him to cooperate with us. He has no choice."

Ramon softens with a wide grin. "How does that sound?"

"Great!" exclaims Luis. "What do we do now?"

Ramon asks Rosalio to speak.

"To start with," begins Rosalio, "we've got to change the way we treat our brown brothers throughout the state. No more barrio mentality. We need every worker in every Mexican Town in South Texas to join us in our fight. And be very careful, getting fired is just the beginning. What we know from previous run-ins with your local Ranger is that you've got one of the most dangerous cops in the state. When guys like this have their backs against the wall, they can resort to some really desperate behavior."

"That's the truth," says Luis. "Man, this feels good. It's like the door is finally opening for us."

"We'll still have to kick it in," says Ramon. "But that racist shit is on its way out."

Ramon takes David's hand and holds it as he tells him. "You should be proud, David. You guys took on this town and organized your brothers in a dangerous climate. The boycott is a powerful weapon and news of your struggle has spread throughout the state, inspiring others to join the fight. You did an extraordinary job. You've got some *cajones*, especially in this part of the state. When this is over, you should join us and continue the struggle throughout Texas. We need more young men and women to help us bring an end to this nonsense. What do you say to that?"

Carolina looks at David with joyful tears. "Look at what you started. I knew you were special—the first time I saw you, I knew it."

David sits on the front porch steps staring at a line of red ants scurrying across the step below his feet carrying what appears to be termite larvae. Fierce-looking ants stand guard on the perimeter protecting the workers, much like what he's just learned from Ramon and Rosalio—strength in numbers with support from those willing to do battle with those seeking to harm the troops.

Looking up from his meditation, he spots Paul's van turning the corner from the highway and nearly stumbles in surprise when he jumps off the porch and races to the street. He eagerly waits in the street as the van slowly makes its way toward him and when it finally stops, he nearly pulls Paul out trying to hug him.

"Hey, did you miss me?" laughs Paul.

"I really did. So much has happened, you won't believe it."

"You're not the only one with a surprise."

Paul sweeps his hand over to Ramona who smiles sweetly and quietly says, "Hi, David. Paul has told me so much about you."

David flinches before whispering to Paul.

"Jesus, she's more beautiful than I remember."

Paul smiles.

"Inside and out, brother."

Paul pulls off the street and begins telling David of the events leading up to Ramona's flight from Mexico. He removes a black ceramic bottle from a brightly-colored woven bag and tells David, "This is the finest Mescal in all of Mexico. It produces almost the same effect as the peyote buttons Paul told me you guys have eaten. I can only guess this tastes so much better."

David studies the crude-looking bottle, turning it on its side looking for any alcohol content or writing, and says, "It might, but it sure looks a lot more dangerous."

"It's hand made by Indians in the mountains of Oaxaca. It's pretty mysterious, don't you think?" says Paul.

"It's amazing, thank you. I wish you were here earlier," says David. "You just missed the guys from the AFL-CIO, who invited us to join their union. We now have the entire state behind us. We're going to win this battle."

Paul gives David an enthusiastic bear hug.

"Congratulations, man! It looks like you've done your duty and served your country honorably. What are your plans then?"

David stares at his feet and hesitates to answer. "I was afraid you'd want me to split back to California with you, but Alamo-Cola is just a start. Texas is filled with poor workers needing someone to represent them and the Teamsters want me to work with them in San Antonio."

"Guess what, we're not leaving either."

"Really? I'm glad to hear it, but why?"

Paul turns to Ramona and pulls her to him. "I told you a little about Ramona's dad, right? We think he was killed on this side of the border, and we're not leaving until we find out what happened."

David takes Ramona's hand. "I am so sorry, Ramona. If there is anything I can do to help, I'm here for you guys."

All eyes turn to the house when the front door opens with a squeak and Carolina steps out into the bright sun wearing shorts and a man's T-shirt.

Ramona chuckles to David, "I see it's not only work keeping you here."

"Is it that obvious?" he replies. "Yeah, I'm pretty sure I'm in love."

It is the Summer of Love," says Ramona. "What else can we do but celebrate our good fortune!"

"Right on!" says David enthusiastically. "So, where are you

guys planning on staying? You can park the van here and camp out if you want. I'm sure Luis wouldn't mind."

"Michael offered us a bedroom. I think we'll be safe from Beeville's finest for a day or two before splitting to Austin and check out the schools. Oh yeah. We saw some good surf."

"It'll be nice to score some waves someday—maybe rent a board if they have any," replies David.

"For all the work you've been doing, I'll buy you a board," laughs Paul.

Carolina takes Ramona by the arm and says, "Let's get out of this heat. I'll make us some iced tea."

David watches Carolina and Ramona walk up the steps arm in arm, laughing and speaking in Spanish. It's clear to him that life really does unfold. When he left San Francisco just a few months ago, he would have never imagined this scenario. He asks Paul, "Tell me more about you and Ramona."

"Seriously, she has been through some shit. That nightclub in Laredo? She was forced to work there to pay off a debt because her father borrowed a bunch of money from some gangsters. She doesn't know what the hell happened to him, but she thinks some Texas cops and ranchers had something to do with it. How about that for messed up? People just don't disappear into thin air."

David shakes his head. "It sure is easy to get into trouble with these cowboys, isn't it? Austin sounds like a good choice, though."

"Yeah. Maybe I'll study law and Ramona can work on an art degree. She's a great artist and you're going to need a good lawyer if I know you. But, please be careful. I *will* go to war with anyone who fucks with you."

David gives Paul a hug. "How about we forget about Texas shit for a few hours and concentrate on that strange-looking bottle of Mescal?"

A Day Off

Ramona and Paul left for Austin early the next morning, while Carolina and Luis took off for a cousin's baptism in Corpus Christi. The baptism sounded like fun, but he was tired and needed a break. David couldn't even remember the last time he'd had a quiet morning all to himself and was looking forward to finishing a science fiction book he'd brought with him when he left San Francisco.

A few pages into the book the phone begins ringing. David stares at it for a moment not wanting to be bothered, then slowly picks it up. "Hello?"

"Am I speaking to David Macias?"

"Yes. Who is this?"

"My name is Dr. Neal Goltra. I teach at Coastal Hills College. Your friend, Paul Gill, told me about your work a few weeks ago. I hope I'm not disturbing you, but I want to ask if you have some time for an interview?"

"Sure. When would you like to meet?" asks David.

"I know it's a weekend, but is it possible to do it today? Could you meet me at the school? My wife has the car until late, so I'm trapped here all day."

"I don't think that's a problem, but why the rush?"

"I'm speaking at a conference in Austin next week and the work you're doing will fit perfectly into the theme of my speech."

"What's it about?"

"How does this sound: "The Second American Revolution— The Struggle for Civil Rights." If all goes well, I'd also like to set up a date when you could address my class, too."

"Count me in. I'll be out there as soon as possible."

David phones Michael's house and receives a ringing phone and nothing else. He calls the photo lab at the base and the sailor tells him that Michael split to Austin to see his girlfriend.

"He should be in tomorrow," says the sailor.

It's a long bus ride from Mexican Town out to the college, but two hours later, three transfers, and a bit of sneaking around to avoid cops friendly with Alamo, David finds himself becoming a chapter in a course Dr. Goltra is creating.

David learned that Dr. Goltra has been instructing his students about Vietnam, and how the war has less to do with communist infiltration and more about keeping American influence and capital wealth alive in Southeast Asia. David wishes he and Dr. Goltra had met months ago, but is encouraged to discover someone in South Texas presenting a counterpoint to the patriotic fiction being spoon-fed to students by their parents, schools, and government.

The morning passed too quickly and David lost track of time. Sprinting across the campus after the meeting, he ended up one hundred yards away from a departing bus. David caught his breath and laughed to himself—maybe one shorter answer to Dr. Goltra's many questions might have gotten him to the bus on time. He studied the bus schedule and as luck would have it, that was the last bus into town. His only choice was to walk or hitchhike to town and catch a bus that would take him to Mexican Town.

In a sweltering free-standing telephone booth in front of a gas station, Larry puffs away on a cigarette with the handset pressed to his ear while swatting mosquitos and other odd flying insects. He smacks a large bug that lands on his bright green shirt and watches it bounce off the glass with a complaint, then attack him before quickly exiting through the accordion-style doors. Larry wonders if bugs are capable of feeling emotions such as anger.

"Humph, God-damned stupid-ass bugs," he says to himself.

More bothersome is the plumber on the other end of the line—the third call to him in less than an hour

"Where is your clog located?" asks the plumber.

"Under the sink at the bar."

The line grows quiet for a moment until the plumber asks, "How many sinks ya got out there?"

A lump of phlegm finds its way into Larry's throat and he coughs in surprise as David walks right past the booth no more than fifteen feet away.

"Son-of-a-bitch!" he coughs.

"What did you say, partner? Did you just call me a son of a bitch?" demands the plumber.

"Look, there's only one bar with one sink, and that sink is clogged! Just fix the damn thing!" He slams the handset onto the cradle and stares slack-jawed when David stops a short distance away and sticks out his thumb. "Jesus Christ, he's hitchhiking! Right in front of me like he doesn't know or give a shit that he is a wanted man in this town."

After two or three cars zip past without slowing, David turns around and continues walking down the highway toward town.

Larry leans out the door for a better look, holding on to the door handle protectively as if someone might cut in and keep him from his next call. He flicks his cigarette out to the street and fumbles around his pocket for more change, then places a dime in the slot.

"Texas Ranger Services, Alice Jensen speaking."

"Hey Alice, is Pete in?"

"Oh, hi Larry," replies Alice seductively. "Haven't seen you in awhile. What's goin' on big guy? I was hopin' you might be callin' me instead of that grouchy ol' Pete."

"Could you please not horse around, Alice? Just get me Pete, okay? I got something important going on."

"My goodness, Larry, you certainly are in a bad mood. Hold on then, I'll put you through. Have a nice day, *Lawrence!*"

After a lengthy pause, Pete answers.

"You hurt poor Alice's feelings. What the hell's wrong with you, Larry, you got a burr under your saddle?"

"Fuckin' Christ, I'll buy her some flowers," snaps Larry.

"You should be nice to her, Larry. She's a beautiful woman who enjoys a good time with a powerful man, much like yourself, for instance."

"Pete, I don't want to hear about Alice's sexual appetite, we got more important issues. That hippie son-of-a-bitch is in my sight! He walked right past me, hitchhiking!"

"Good lord! Well, that is pretty careless of him."

"Yeah or just stupid. Like where's his Mexican friends now, huh? How about I grab this guy?"

"Do it. Then meet me out at El Abejorro in an hour."

"I can take care of it in less time than that," replies Larry.

"I've got to round up Gene first."

"Why? What good is he?' asks Larry.

"He's our insurance policy, Larry."

Larry shrugs and hangs up the phone. He quicksteps to the gas pumps where the young gas jockey has just finished filling up his car. "You check the oil, too?" asks Larry.

"Yes sir," replies the attendant.

"Tires? You check the air?"

"They are good to go, sir."

Larry hands the attendant a ten dollar bill.

Gas jockey shakes his head. "Got to pay inside, sir."

"You shitin' me? I don't have time for this!"

Larry looks down at his money, then back down the road to

David, who so far hasn't had any luck scoring a ride. Larry pulls out another two dollars."

"Here ya go, keep the change."

"No can do, sir. I'm not supposed to handle any money. Boss said he'd fire me if I did."

"Oh, God damn it to hell," cusses Larry. "My lucky day to run into you." He stomps across the pavement and holds his breath as a large cattle truck passes by and prays that it doesn't stop, and when it doesn't, lets out a sigh of relief.

A cattle bell clangs loudly overhead when he enters the air-conditioned little office and convenience store, startling Larry and causing him to drop his car keys onto the dusty floor.

"Shit-ass, miserable fucking gas station," he grumbles as he bends down to retrieve them.

Larry approaches the counter and is met by the back of a bald head who Larry assumes is the "Boss," sitting on an old overstuffed chair watching a black–and–white television set beaming a bright image of Richard Nixon standing in front of a dozen microphones.

Larry taps the counter with his keys to get some attention or at least get this guy to get his scrawny ass off the chair and take his money so he can get the hell out of this shithole.

"Here's for the fill-up, buddy."

Boss waves him off. "Hold on there just a second."

Larry walks to the door to check on David and is relieved to find him still waiting for a ride. He returns to the counter and watches candidate, Richard Nixon, speaking at a press conference.

Sporting his usual five o'clock shadow, Nixon begins speaking to the press. "Vice-President Humphrey is so anxious for a settlement of the war to enhance his election chances, that he would endanger our troops and embolden the Viet Cong enemy by promising large cutbacks of U.S. combat forces."

Boss grunts loudly as he pushes himself over to the television when Nixon's speech is interrupted by a question. He turns back to Larry, shaking his head in disgust.

"God damn Johnson is a Texas boy, too. It's embarrassing is what it is. Christ, the most powerful army on the planet can't even kick the shit out of a few barefoot coolies. So, how much was your gas, mister?"

"Ten bucks. Gimme a pack of Lucky Strikes while you're at it, too."

Boss reaches over to a cigarette display covering most of the back wall and flips the pack onto the counter in one swift move. He opens a drawer, grabs a book of matches and with a flip of his wrist, lands it directly on top of the pack of cigarettes. Without missing a beat in his well-practiced, choreographed display, he rings up the cash register.

"That's ten dollars and thirty-five cents," he declares with a proud shit-eating grin.

"Guess you got a lot of free time on your hands, don't ya?" snaps Larry, as he slaps the bill onto the counter and slams down the change.

"What's that you say?" asks Boss, feeling a bit miffed at what seems to be a hostile wisecrack.

"I said, you got a lot of time on your hands. Time you spend fucking around with matchbooks and packs of cigarettes, when you could have easily got off your skinny ass and walked out to the pumps to take my money."

Boss scrunches up his nose and narrows his eyes. He lets Larry dangle a bit after that last shitty remark because he doesn't give a rat's ass about this asshole. He's got a fully–loaded .45 pistol right under the counter, and if this wise-ass makes a move … well, it probably won't come to that, but he likes to be prepared, just in case. "You just never know who might walk into your store and want to steal your hard-earned money," he thinks.

"Looks to me as if you was gonna be walkin' over here anyways. You know, to get your pack of smokes."

Larry grabs the pack and tosses the book of matches back on the counter and grumbles, "Fuckin' smart-ass hillbilly."

Larry kicks open the clanging cow-bell door just as a delivery truck slows down as it nears David. It stops and David jumps up into the front seat.

"Son of a bitch!" Larry hustles over to his car, steps on the gas and quickly peels out of the station.

"Have a nice day, mister," waves the grinning gas jockey.

The air conditioner begins blowing cool air while Larry waits for the cigarette lighter to pop out of the dashboard. He turns on the radio and searches through a number of stations until landing on one playing a corny pop hit by Bobby Goldsboro, titled, "Honey."

A light mist begins to fall. Lost in thought, he stares at the windshield and is fascinated by the little droplets covering the glass. He thinks it's pretty neat the way they reflect the color of the trees, then laughs when he turns on the wipers and sends them sailing off onto the road. "Adios, water!" he laughs.

He lights the cigarette and for the next minute enjoys the song's sweet lyrics, which sadly lead up to the death of poor little Honey.

> ... I came home unexpectedly
> And caught her cryin' needlessly
> In the middle of the day.
> And it was in the early Spring
> When flowers bloom and robins sing
> She went a ...

The song's heartbreaking ending is cut short when static

drowns it out. For the next fifteen seconds it fades in and out before disappearing altogether.

Larry hits the steering wheel and yells, "God damn it to hell!" Fuming, he turns off the radio, his window and tosses the burning cigarette out of the car. "Shitty-ass state!"

Five miles down the road Larry spots the truck on the side of the road and stops a distance away. He watches David climb out of the truck and wave to the driver and watches it drive down the dirt road of a cattle ranch kicking a large cloud of dust.

Larry laughs to himself as David gawks at the rooster tail of rain and dust as it heads off in the distance and wonders why in the hell would that interest anybody?

He patiently waits for David to turn his attention back to the road and when he does, Larry puts his car in gear and eases onto the highway. He checks himself out in the rear view mirror from a couple of different angles and licks his fingers and presses his thinning hair down over his bald spot before slowing down and opening the window.

David sticks out his thumb and is delighted to be greeted by a beautiful 1965 Pontiac Grand Prix slowing to a stop. He walks the short distance to the car and offers the driver a wide friendly smile as he looks through the open window.

"Howdy partner," says a cheerful Larry. "Looks like we're goin' the same direction. Let's get you outta this drizzle before it gets worse—hop in!"

David opens the door and throws his backpack on the bench-style front seat and watches Larry use the power window control console to close the passenger side window. "Thanks, mister. The rain sure is a surprise."

"Rain or not, it's still hotter 'n Billy-H, " smiles Larry. "Where ya headed to?"

"Beeville," says David.

Larry takes a quick glance in the rear view and side mirrors before accelerating onto the road. Once up to speed he looks over to David with a big smile. "Well, I'll take you as far as I'm going."

"Like you said, at least we're going in the same direction," replies David. He takes a look out at the landscape for a few quiet moments and takes a sideways glance at Larry and wonders why this guy looks so familiar to him. "I've seen you somewhere before, haven't I?"

Larry turns to David with a wide grin. "You ever been out to George West … the Red Barn?"

"Sure."

Larry offers his hand and replies, "I manage it. My name's Larry, by the way."

"I'm David. That's a pretty rocking place. I like that it's far out of town. You probably don't get many complaints about loud music."

"It used to be strictly country, but with the Enlisted Men's club out at the base doin' rock shows, I said to myself if the kids want to hear that kind of stuff, that's what I'm gonna be playin'."

"Smart move. I really dig your dash," says David.

"It's a beauty, ain't it? Say, you've got a California accent!"

David laughs. "It sounds like you're the one with the accent."

Larry howls a smoker's wheezing laugh.

"You got that right! One hundred percent pure Dixie. Maybe you've seen me somewhere else, too."

David searches his memory. After a few moments of looking at Larry, he replies, "No, can't say as I do."

Larry reaches into his back pocket and pulls out a fat wallet. He opens it to an identification card in a plastic picture holder and drops it on the seat.

"You ever hear of Sheriff Lawrence Rainey, Neshoba County, Mississippi? It's okay, go on and take a good look."

David studies the identification card thoughtfully. Behind the yellowed plastic holder the photo shows a younger Larry with a bit more hair. And when he does remember where he's seen this guy before, his heart drops.

"Jesus," he exhales.

"Remember now?"

"You were on the cover of *Life* magazine a few years ago. You had your feet up on the courtroom railing at a trial."

Larry lets out a snigger. "Bingo! They was tryin' to hang me for killin' those Yankee college kids and their colored friend."

"The Freedom Riders—the civil rights workers."

"Yeah, those guys. Remember the caption?" asks Larry.

"Yeah, it was something about 'Red Man'?"

"That's it!" beams Larry.

"I never knew what that meant."

Larry guffaws and pulls a pack of chewing tobacco from the pocket in his sun visor and shows it to David. "Chewin' tobacco— Red Man, that's what I chew!"

"Didn't you go to jail?"

"Hell no! I got a jury of my peers. Ha! They was mostly my cousins, so who are they gonna believe, me or that spoiled Yankee rich kid Kennedy? I did get booted out of office for knockin' the shit out of that smart-ass, Stokley Carmichael."

David takes a deep breath to calm himself and thinks, "Just my luck to be riding with a racist killer. What are the odds?"

Larry reaches over and pushes in the cigarette lighter.

"That black bastard was standin' in the middle of the street yellin' some bullshit about black power and had traffic backed-up all over the place."

Larry stops his rant when the lighter pops out. He takes a couple of puffs and blows the smoke toward David.

David makes a mental note to prepare himself for some kind of trouble because this ride is about to turn sideways at any moment. He follows the smoke as it floats past his face and escapes out the open wind wing.

Larry resumes his rant, "Hell, all I did was to get out of my car and tell him to move his black ass. He starts in given' me a bunch of shit and I said the hell with that nonsense, and smacked him with my club. I lost my job and got six months probation! The South is turnin' to shit when decent folk get treated like I did!"

Larry sits back with a satisfied smile and enjoys his cigarette. His tirade over for the moment, he changes the subject and asks David if he's ever been to Mississippi and the Gulf.

"I hear it's nice," replies David. "I've been trying to make it out to Padre Island."

"Padre Island? Shit, Mississippi is like heaven compared to that dump. We got clear blue water and fishin' everywhere. Not like this brown muddy scum Texans call water."

Larry inhales deeply then blows another long stream of white smoke out. This time he aims for his wind wing. "Along with the dance hall, I also do work as a management representative."

"What's that?" asks David.

"Pretty simple work. I'm paid to run off troublemakers. Sometimes I gotta kick some ass, you know what I'm sayin'? Take these Mexicans we got in Texas for instance—half the little bastards don't even speak American. You know, if they don't like the way they're being treated up here, they can always pack up and go back to where they come from. What do ya think 'bout that?"

Juan Costino whispers in David's ear." Amigo, this conversation is truly going to shit. You are in grave danger at this moment and you need a plan. *"Ataca a este tonto ahora mismo o salta del auto."* (Attack this fool right now or jump out of the car.

"What do I think?" replies David. "That *Life* magazine article opened up a lot of eyes to segregation and racism. Maybe you don't know this, but most Americans regard those boys as heroes, killed in action for the Civil Rights Movement."

David lets his comment hang in the air, and except for the slapping of the windshield wipers, and the sound of the road under the wheels as they speed along the empty highway, the ride becomes eerily quiet.

Larry scowls, staring straight ahead for a minute, then says, "Well, most people don't know what the hell they're talkin' about."

Larry reaches past David and opens the glove compartment. He fishes out a folded piece of paper and lays it on the seat. David takes a cursory look—it's the boycott flyer he handed out at the dance at the Big Barn.

"This is you, right?" asks Larry.

David considers his options. If there was ever a time to "be courageous," this would certainly be it, as the man driving this car is a violent murdering racist.

David takes a deep breath and decides to take Juan Costina's advice—screw this pig. "Yeah, that's me. Why? Are you interested in contributing to our cause?" snaps David.

"Highly unlikely," sneers Larry.

"Is that why you picked me up?"

"You were the one hitchin'," replies Larry. "Look, we're just talkin', buddy. You seem to be good at that and you've made your point. And maybe the Mexicans do need more money, but you've pissed off a lot of powerful people, and they don't like outsiders waltzing into town and start messin' with them. I'm tellin' ya, you've already pushed them too far."

David tries one last chance at reason—maybe it'll get him out of this car alive.

"So if they won't change, which they've proven they won't, how do we transform their behavior unless someone forces them? All I've tried to do was to help a few workers get decent wages—the same pay the whites get for doing the same job. And it's not just the Tejanos who are supporting our efforts, we have a lot of whites backing us, too. So, I think those important friends of yours are in the minority on this."

Larry shakes his head in disgust.

"Boy, you sure are a tough one, ain't ya? Well, as much as I've enjoyed our little chat, this here is my offer, which I am going to say only once. How about I take you to the nearest bus station, and you get on back to where you come from. How's that sound?"

David shakes his head. "I haven't come this far to suddenly turn and run because Gene wants to scare me off. Those boys you and your friends killed in your so-called heavenly Mississippi? You guys accidentally created a wave of sympathy for Afro-Americans across the entire country. Most Americans weren't even aware of civil rights until those kids were murdered. Those days are going, mister, but I'd like to thank you for helping to bring Jim Crow and segregation to an end in a large part of this country."

Larry's face is flushed bright red. He wags a finger at David and says, "Now you listen to me, 'cause I know the way shit works down here. This ain't California, and you don't want to fuck with us. I'm trying to do you a favor here 'cause the people I'm working with ain't interested in settling this peacefully. Do you understand what I'm sayin'?"

"Yeah, I'm kinda getting that feeling," replies David. "But if you really want to do me a favor, pull over so I can get out. And you can tell Alamo that the right path is for him to work with us."

"Okay," shrugs Larry. He glances in the rear view mirror and checks for other cars. "Fine, if you're gonna get all huffy about it. But don't say I didn't try and warn ya."

The smooth rumble of tires pressing against asphalt turns to the crunching sounds of gravel as Larry slows the car and begins to pull to the side of the road. Relieved to be nearing the end of this tension-filled ride, David relaxes and looks out the window. He spots three young colts running about an open field chasing each other in play, bucking and kicking up their heels, before suddenly stopping in unison when something catches their attention. They crane their heads skyward and watch a low-flying fighter jet racing overhead, creating a deafening roar.

Juan Costino is nearly yelling at him.

"¡Deja de soñar despierto! Este hombre huele a muerte."

(Stop daydreaming! This man smells of death.)

A violent concussion follows the jet's passing and David wonders if it dropped a bomb that exploded in his head. Disoriented from the blind-sided punch he's just received, he wonders how he ended up in a bowling alley.

David blinks his eyes and shakes his head attempting to snap back to reality. It's not the first time he's been popped in the face. Growing up in East Los Angeles as a surfer, David had to fight his way through high school because *vatos* hated surfers. Instinct takes over and he puts his weight behind a right hook that connects solidly with Larry's face. Blood explodes from Larry's nose and splatters all over the front of his green shirt.

Larry screams in pain as a shooting, bright white lightning bolt blasts into his brain. Stunned by the blow, he stiffens in shock and accidentally presses on the gas pedal. The car races from one side of the road to the other while David pummels Larry with a barrage of hard blows.

In spite of David's attack, Larry recovers and slams on the brakes, forcing David to brace himself with both hands against the dashboard. It's enough of an opening for Larry to turn and slug David on the side of his head, and knocking him into the passenger-side window, shattering the glass, and knocking him out cold. David slumps over and falls onto his knapsack.

Larry sighs in relief as he gains control of both the car and David. He stares in disbelief at his blood-splattered green shirt and curses, "Fuckin' shit!" Pulling the car to the side of the road, he stops and spends a minute catching his breath. From habit, he pushes in the cigarette lighter, and taps the pack in his hands while he waits for the lighter to pop out. He looks in the rear view mirror and rubs his sore nose, rolls his aching jaw, and hopes that neither isn't broken because both sure as hell feel like it.

Larry looks over in reluctant admiration at the unconscious David. "Love and peace my ass, hippie! I give you credit, at least you went down like a man."

Larry tosses the backpack into the rear seat with a grunt, and hits David three times to the back of his head before shoving him to the floor. He huffs out a deep breath and stares down the road lost in thought, wondering why he's always the one stuck with doing the dirty work for pricks like Gene or those Brownsville ranchers. He asks himself, "Where's my payoff? Hell, I'm still making shit wages running a night club in the middle of nowhere."

Closing his eyes, Larry listens to the scraping of the wipers on the dry windshield and wonders how long it's been since the rain stopped falling.

"I was wondering if you had forgotten about me."

César Gaspard, the man in the tree, often looked to the heavens wondering why he had been left alone for so long. He, who had led such an exemplary life helping the poor and downtrodden: was it fair that he be left to rot on this branch? Over the past three months, he has learned that God prefers we pray for others instead of only for ourselves. So he prayed constantly that his daughter Ramona was safe and cared for.

But, today, the revenge he has sought is close at hand—his murderer, the tall man known as Pete, has returned.

He tells himself to quiet his thoughts and listen.

Pete leans against a pickup truck drinking a beer under the shade of a massive oak tree, complaining to Gene who is standing in front of him biting his nails. "Damn piddly-ass rain didn't do shit, Gene. Feels hotter now than ever."

Above them, a man is hanging from a branch with a wire noose wrapped around his neck. From the condition of the body, it appears he's been hanging there for some time—the man's checkered shirt and filthy jeans have turned to rags and hang loosely from his withered body.

Pete reaches into an ice cooler on the truck bed for another beer and pierces the beer can top with a church key opener. Foam bubbles spit out of the small opening which Pete quickly sucks up noisily.

"Damn, Pete, that is one disgusting sight. Aren't you worried someone might find this guy?" says Gene as he takes a nervous glance up in to the tree.

"Ain't likely, Gene. Harold's grandfather had a long history of punishing miscreants out here and nobody's been arrested yet. This character is just the latest in a long line of Mexican troublemakers. He was the braceros big-shot leader that me and the boys arrested down in Brownsville."

"I heard people talking about it," laughs Gene nervously. "You are one cruel bastard, Pete."

"Cruel is a bit harsh, Gene. I do what's right for this country, but more importantly what's good for Texas."

"Are you sure nobody knows about this guy?"

"It's not like we paraded it through town like they used to. We gotta be discrete, which is why we are out here on the most remote spot on the Rancho. Cattle don't even like it out here."

"Why's that?"

"'That scarecrow up there—spooks 'em."

"You're shitting me, right?" asks Gene, glancing up into the thick, gnarled branches and the hanging man.

Pete laughs after he takes a long swig of beer. "Sounds good though, don't it? Harold says it's the Navy jets. We're right under their landing path and the cattle don't like all the commotion. Just wait 'til one comes in for a landing."

"Does Harold know about this guy?"

"Nope. Talk about bullshit. Nothin' at all like his daddy."

"He's okay," says Gene. "He's just kind of opinionated is all, and he cusses too much. You know these past few months with this boycott and all, it's been one tough summer. But this thing you're about to do, I'm not sure I've got the stomach for it. Maybe I should talk to the workers again before this gets out of…"

Gene's words are drowned out by the scream of a low-flying fighter jet as it approaches the airfield for a landing. Pete rushes out from under the tree covering his ears to watch, while Gene reacts by ducking in fear. The ruckus lasts for only a few moments before the jet drops out of sight beyond the trees.

"Son of a bitch, Pete, you weren't shitting me!"

"What was that you were saying about throwin' in the towel?"

"Pete, I'm not getting any younger and I'd hate to see the factory shut down. Hell, I've got enough money to last me more than a dozen lifetimes. I think we should call this off."

"Are you seriously gonna let that communist agitator make a fool out of you? That doesn't sound like the Gene I used to know. Where in the hell are your balls?"

"Pete, I've never done anything like this. I mean, you're in law enforcement and you're used to stuff like this. You understand, right?"

Pete stares at Gene with a clenched jaw and tells himself he needs to straighten him out before they all get arrested. "There's nothing pleasant about killin' someone, Gene. Look, if you let the Mexicans pull you down, what do you think is gonna happen next? I'll tell ya what, those uppity bastards will start votin' and elect a Mexican mayor who'll call the FBI down here and throw us all in the shitter. I'm sorry you want to quit, but it's too damn late to stop it. This is what you wanted, remember?"

Gene fidgets with his mustache, knowing that Pete is going through with this murder, and he had better go along or Pete will end up killing him just to save his own ass.

Pete grabs Gene by the arm. "You need to remember what you asked us only a week ago."

Gene pulls away from Pete's grasp and says, "I didn't think we were talking about actually killing him. I guess I wasn't thinking clearly. You know, I've been pretty frustrated about all this."

Gene wishes he could escape from this nightmare. The entire

summer has him at his wits end, what with all the labor trouble and now being a part of a murder. But as folks say in a situation like this, the cow has left the barn.

"So, how much longer do we have to wait for Larry?"

"Be patient, Gene, I'd rather be doing something else too." Pete points to the ice cooler. "Why don't you have another beer and relax a spell until he gets here."

Halfway through the beer, Gene spots Larry's car racing toward them before sliding to a stop in the dirt and kicking up a cloud of a dust.

Larry rolls down the window and yells out, "Hey, you wanna help me with this?"

Pete and Gene dust themselves off as they rush to the car and stop in surprise when they see Larry's swollen lip, broken nose and his blood–soaked shirt.

"What in the hell happened to you?" asks Pete.

"What does it look like? That hippie peace creep turned out to be a hell of a lot more violent than we thought."

"Let's get him out of the car," orders Pete.

They drag David over to the base of the tree and dump him to the ground and spend a few moments studying his unresponsive body.

"That's the troublemaker all right," says Gene. "Jesus, Larry, did you already kill him?"

"I don't think so. He put up a hellava fight, so I might have overreacted a bit. The son-of-a-bitch was tryin' to beat me to death!"

"What do you want me to do, Pete?" asks Gene.

"Take Larry's car back to town and park it at Alamo. I only needed you here to meet the man you hired us to kill."

"I honestly didn't think that was the plan," whines Gene. "I thought you were just going to scare him off—run him out of town or something."

Larry scoffs, "You chicken-shit. You pretty much begged us to take this guy out. What did you think was happening when Pete picked you up and drove you out here, huh?"

Gene shrugs his shoulders. Maybe at one point he did think about killing the troublemaker, but that was just wishful thinking.

Pete grabs Gene by the shoulders and squeezes tight so he can't squirm away. "Gene, the Mexicans ain't gonna do anything, just like they didn't do nothin' for that guy up in the tree. We are sending a clear message that this is what happens when you step out of line, just like what happened to Pancho up there. And I want you to understand what we're about to do, just in case you feel bad later and start crying in your Martini at the club."

"I would never," says Gene.

"Good, that's what I want to hear. Remember, you're an accessory to a first–degree murder, and that is a hangin' offense. And don't lose any sleep over this, 'cause we're doing what's right."

Gene nods. "I get it. It's just been rough with all this trouble and such. I just want it to end."

Gene extends his hand to Larry. "Thanks Larry. I owe you."

"Thank Pete. This is his party."

"Not necessary, Gene," replies Pete. "Maybe a few golf tips. Now get back to town and try and settle down, okay?"

Gene ambles over to Larry's car talking to himself.

"God, this is not what I wanted. I didn't want anyone to die. I make soft drinks for Christ sakes, I don't kill people." When he opens the door he's stunned by the aftermath of the violence that took place in the car. He removes his sports coat and places it on the seat to avoid the large amount of dried blood on it and stares at the blood splattered all over the chrome dashboard and the white vinyl side panel. He can't take his eyes off the shattered passenger window. He curses to himself, deeply regretting his decision to ever let Pete get involved in his business.

"Are you okay, Gene?" calls out Larry.

Gene waves that he's good to go.

David's eyes begin blinking erratically, then stares glassy-eyed at the sky. Larry pokes him with his foot and yells over to Pete who is placing the ladder up against the branch. "He's wakin' up! Shit, I was afraid I did kill 'em."

Pete walks over and kneels down for a close inspection. He takes David's pulse, looks into his eyes and checks if he's reacting to light. "You almost did 'cause if there's anyone home they sure as hell ain't answering the door. Let's sit him up now that he's doin' so well."

"I'd just as soon shoot his ass for breaking my nose," says Larry.

"Then what? You wanna spend all day digging in this heat? We're not in the Mississippi mud Larry, this is Texas hard pan. And, in case anyone else needs to be taught a lesson, we'll have two guys hanging up there instead of one—let the Mexicans know there's always room for more."

"Somebody still might find them accidentally," says Larry.

"God damn it, Larry," growls Pete in frustration. "Nobody is going to find them but us. This guy's been up here for months, undisturbed except for the bugs. Look, Gene still has the Mexicans on his back, so the next guy we bring out here is gonna think twice when he sees just how serious we are."

Pete searches through David's pants pockets and pulls out a half dozen folded sheets of paper. "More boycott flyers. What a damn shit storm this guy started."

Pete wads up the papers and tosses them to the ground. He pulls out David's wallet and rummages through it, finding a folded paper with a San Francisco phone number and reads it out loud.

"Vivian. Humph, I can just imagine what kind of druggy sex freak she might be."

He wads it up and chucks it into the grass. Pete fishes through David's shirt pockets and pulls out a pack of rolling papers and a small amount of marijuana wrapped in aluminum foil.

"Check this out Larry ... reefer madness! I tell ya, we're doin' Texas a favor by gettin' rid of this guy—god damn drug dealer."

Larry takes the marijuana from Pete. "Pretty good loco weed by the smell of it. Mind if I take it for evidence?"

"Jesus, Larry, you're such a degenerate. Sure, roll up a big one and grow what's left of your hair."

Pete walks to the tree and begins climbing the ladder with a roll of wire and a rope looped around his arm and shoulder.

"At last! That bastard who killed me is coming. Come closer," whispers César Gaspard.

More than halfway up the ladder, Pete wraps the wire around the branch a dozen times and forms the rest of it into a partially completed noose. Satisfied, he tosses the rope around the branch and lets half of it drop to the ground.

A blinding light hits David like a flash of lightning and forces his eyes open. Juan is Cortina squatting before him shaking him by the shoulders.

> "Do you want to go to Mictian with its nine cold underworlds, where you'll disappear into nothingness? Quit horsing around and pay attention, *pendejo*. *¡Levántate, espantapájaros sin cerebro!* (Get up you brainless scarecrow!) They're trying to kill you! Wake up!"

David is confused when he clears his head and finds Larry,

the racist killer staring at him with a shit-eating grin and sporting a bloody, swollen lip and a crooked, blood-caked nose.

"What the hell is he saying?" asks Pete.

"Gibberish. This guy is a goner," replies Larry.

David notices the Texas Ranger standing high up on a ladder, and tells himself he might be dreaming because a man is hanging by his neck from a wire next to the Ranger, and the Ranger doesn't seem to care or notice.

For so long he has been clinging to that last infinitesimal bit of energy of what was left of his soul, waiting for this moment, and now, the time has come to exact retribution. César looks beyond the canopy of leaves to the blue sky and clouds, and says farewell to this life and to his daughter, who he loves more than anything on this earth.

"Ramona, my love. Please forgive me."

César lets go. His head separates from the wire noose and his body which throws the weight of his torso into Pete, who screams in horror and loses his balance, and flips backwards off the ladder. He hits the ground hard with a sickening *thump* and a *crack*.

César's body bounces off the dirt and flops over on top of the man who killed him, and ends up with his arms wrapped around the bastard in a death grip.

Howling like a frightened child, Pete frantically pushes the body off his chest and attempts to scramble away from the headless corpse but his broken leg gives way and he ends up on the ground grasping his leg and cursing loudly in pain,

"Shit! Dammit to hell!"

Larry races to Pete's side.

"Jesus, Pete, are you okay?"

"No, I'm not fucking okay, I think my leg's broken!"

Larry stands slack-jawed, unable to take his eyes off César's head lying just a few feet away.

"That damn thing attacked you! I swear it was like watching a horror movie!"

Juan Cortina is yelling at David to flee.

> "*Muévanse!* Race the wind, fly faster than *el águila mi amigo.* Mescalito has saved your life with the assistance of César Gaspard, the man trapped within that noose for many months. *¡Maldita sea, corra!* We are with you, but you must fly!

"Stop screwing around Larry, and get me my first aid kit out of the truck! Son-of-a-bitch, my leg is killing me!"

David ignores Juan Cortina's command to run. He knows something about being invisible, and slowly rises to his feet with a wobble before quietly walking away into the woods. Once he has distanced himself from the two guys trying to kill him, he takes off on a run.

Larry turns back to check on David and is surprised to find him gone. "Jesus Pete, the hippie has disappeared!"

Pete rolls over and curses, "Oh son of a bitch, god damn it! Well don't just stand there with your thumb up you ass. Go get him, Larry!"

The blur of branches and brush swat and punish David, every one reaching out to scratch and pull at him as he staggers aimlessly through the woods. In spite of his splitting headache and wobbly legs, he's outdistancing the man chasing him. He's not sure how long or how far he's run but his lungs are burning and he needs to rest somewhere safe. He squats behind a large tree and scans the ground for a weapon. Picking up a baseball-sized stone he holds it tight in his fist, ready to use it once his pursuer comes within sight.

David hears a voice far in the distance yelling to him.

"Next time I see you, hippie, I'm gonna shoot your ass! You hear me, you're dead in this town!"

Larry shuffles back to Pete with the first aid box wiping his forehead and neck with a handkerchief. He lays the kit on the ground then pulls a cigarette out of the pack and lights it.

"Smoking?" complains Pete. "Really Larry? You gotta suck on one of those things right in the middle of this shit? Put that damn thing out and hold the splint still while I wrap it up tight."

"Gimme a second, will ya? I gotta catch my breath."

Pete curses and bitches as he wraps gauze around the splint with Larry squatting in front of him holding his leg still. Larry looks over and studies the body of the man, then the head lying a few yards apart.

"What should we do with this?" he asks.

"Just leave it," says Pete. "Let the bugs and coyotes finish their work."

"I don't like leaving this mess. If anyone finds him, we're in for big trouble."

Pete lets out an exasperated breath. "Damn it, Larry. That thing has been out here for months and no one has found him yet. Jesus Christ, what a clusterfuck!"

David stumbles through the woods before entering a large green pasture filled with hundreds of cattle grazing on sweet grass. Based on the position of the sun, he has to cross the meadow and do so without disturbing the livestock. *Be invisible—move slowly.*

The cattle ignore David as he calmly strolls through the knee-high grass humming the tune, "What the World Needs Now." All is going smoothly until he stumbles over a gopher hole. He curses, "Shit!" and spooks a nearby steer who bellows out a loud complaint.

Two Brahma bulls grazing at the perimeter hear the threat to one of their charges and begin pushing their way through the herd. Bleating and carping erupt from the cattle, unhappy at their treatment as the bulls blindly focus on the unwelcome, two-legged visitor in the distance.

David turns around and is horrified to see the bulls coming for him and immediately takes off running. A few animals stubbornly impede his flight to safety, but he's fleeing for his life and now is not the time for good manners. He yells loudly and shoves a couple of them out of his way as he focuses on a large tree in the distance and hopes he can make it before the bulls catch up to him. His head is pounding and his legs are wobbly from Larry's blows, but one quick glance over his shoulder provides him with just enough adrenaline to make it to the tree before his pursuers stomp him to death. Using his last bit of strength, he jumps up and grabs onto a sturdy branch, pulls himself up and holds on tight.

The bulls arrive snorting and begin bashing the poor tree repeatedly trying to knock him off his perch. David can't help but laugh at the irony—the bulls attempting to do what Larry and the Texas Ranger had failed to do.

The grazing steers are blissfully indifferent to the commotion under the big tree. With the sun sitting low in the sky and their bellies full, they proceed to follow their nature and begin heading back to the safety of the rancho's protective corrals. With no one left to impress, the bulls give up too, and follow the herd.

From his perch David watches the meadow empty of cattle. When he's absolutely certain he's safe he slowly descends back to earth and makes his way across the pasture. Soon, a low fog begins to rise up, hugging the ground like a cool white blanket. He walks carefully through the waist-deep fog until it becomes so thick he can't see his feet, obstacles, or biting creatures. His jaw is still killing him from Larry's punch and the back of his skull is pounding for some odd reason. He guesses that Larry must have slugged him a few more times after he got knocked out.

A large dark shape racing through the woods freezes David in his tracks. While he wonders what else will try to kill him today, a massive black deer sporting an immense set of antlers charges out of the trees. It leaps fifteen feet through the air with each bound and effortlessly crosses the meadow before disappearing into the forest.

In the deer's wake the fog has parted, creating a wide path for David to follow. Stunned by the dazzling virtuosity of what nature has performed, seemingly for his benefit. He gives thanks to whoever is in charge of stuff like this—maybe his luck is beginning to change.

As the light dims' with the setting sun, David arrives at the end of the meadow before a thick stand of oaks and is forced to find a cattle or deer trail to lead him through the forest. Cold and exhausted, David hopes he's not hallucinating when he hears the sound of an accordion echoing through the woods and comes to an old wooden barn with light pouring out of an open door. He carefully climbs over a wooden split-rail fence and slowly walks to the barn.

"Hold it right there, asshole!"

Blinded by a bright light shining directly into his eyes, David holds up his hands.

"Okay, okay, I don't want any trouble."

"What the hell happened to you?" asks a man's voice.

"Some guys jumped me," replies David.

"No Shit."

The man's voice goes silent for a moment before exclaiming,

"Hey, wait a fucking minute, I know you! You're Luis' friend, the hippy union guy! *Hijo de puta* (Son of a bitch), it's me, Popeye! Remember?"

David falls to his knees and gasps, or maybe it's a cry, and quietly moans, "Shit, this is good news."

"Who in the hell did this to you? Was it that *pene pequeño (Little dick),* asshole, Benny?"

"No, it was our local Texas Ranger and his Mississippi buddy."

Popeye shakes his head and whistles. "Man, you're lucky to be alive. That Ranger is a murdering psycho. We should really get you to a hospital."

"Thanks, but can you give me a ride to Luis' house?"

"You bet. But seriously, you need a doctor, 'cause you look pretty fucked up."

"I can imagine, and I feel even worse. But I've got to get back to town without anyone finding me. I'm pretty sure they're still out looking for me."

"When Luis sees what they did to you, they better hope he doesn't find them first."

"I'll keep him cool, but if I can't, Carolina can handle him."

"Okay, it's your call. Let me get you a jacket."

"Thanks, man. I think it's the first time I've been cold since I got to Texas."

"Shit, you ain't cold, *ese*, you're going into shock."

The Foot Soldier

In spite of Carolina's insistence, David stubbornly declined any treatment and remained in his filthy, bloody clothing, thanks to Larry's nose erupting in a torrent of blood from David's blow. He was right about Carolina, who kept Luis from going crazy and jumping into his car with a baseball bat.

When he finally calmed down, Luis listened to David's talk about his plan to end the strike with Gene.

"Don't worry about my wounds. They'll give me the dramatic effect I'll need when I confront that asshole tomorrow."

While David slept that evening, Carolina placed a cool towel on his forehead. He was feverish and there was a little swelling from his beating. When she leaned in to kiss his warm lips she heard him talking in his sleep, speaking in Spanish with Juan, his guardian angel.

> "Amigo, I thought you were a goner. That was some punch you survived from that white bastard. But, with the assistance of César Gaspard and Mescalito, you conducted yourself like a true soldier, and for that you will win this battle. I am very proud of you.
>
> Tomorrow when you confront the man responsible for your abduction, trust me, he will fall to his knees when he faces the radiant glow of righteousness and verity surrounding your beaten figure."

A dust devil spinning madly about the empty Alamo-Cola parking lot tosses litter, dead weeds, and anything else in the way on its journey of destruction. The feisty little whirlwind smacks into Luis' car with force just as David exits and violently slams the door shut.

"It looks like Texas is still trying to kick your ass!" laughs Luis. "Are you sure you want to do this, 'cause I've never seen you this pissed off. You're not going to kill him, are you?"

"No, I'm cool. I've just been too nice to this guy."

"Gene might have a gun in his desk drawer and you know, the way you look, you're gonna scare the shit out him and he might shoot you out of fright."

David shakes his head. "I'm pretty sure his friends have told him their shitty plan backfired."

"I'll guard the entrance in case any of the *pendejo* cavalry shows up."

David kicks open the front door of Alamo-Cola and takes a quick look around the deserted office. He walks up the stairway to Gene's office thinking about his abduction and his near-lynching. The huge black deer and the fog in the meadow still seems like a dream to him, but it was a miraculous event, a heaven-sent gift in his mind. When he had made it safely to Luis and Carolina, he had decided that if God, in the image of a huge black buck, wanted him safe, then nothing would keep him from confronting Gene and demanding he accept the workers' demands.

David stands quietly in Gene's doorway, bruised and beaten, wearing a blood soaked shirt, and looking more like a ghost than a living person. Looking up from his Bible, Gene gasps at the sight and falls back into his chair.

"What are you ... how did you get in here?"

"I'm sure you already know that I escaped from those two

thugs you sent out to kill me."

Gene begins groveling and whining. "I ... I had nothing to do with what they did to you. You must believe me! I only wanted to scare you off, to get you to leave town! I am so sorry you were injured. I've been praying all day and night, begging for forgiveness. I was desperate, that's all it was. My business was failing and I blamed you. Please, let me pour you a drink. We can work this out."

David waves him off.

"This isn't going to be settled by a glass of your dumb-ass bourbon. Look at what you did to me. Your friends tried to kill me and they nearly succeeded. The only reason I'm here is to give you one last chance to make amends. Because if you don't, I'm on my way to the FBI in San Antonio."

Gene stands and goes to the bar to pour himself a drink. He spills a small amount of whiskey on the bar, stunned when he looks out the window to find his lot filling with cars, trucks, and dozens of workers. He turns to David with an embarrassed smile.

"Did you know about the man hanging on a limb out there? I'm sure the FBI would like to find out about that, and how you guys have been running things in this town."

Gene whines, "I knew nothing about that poor man, I swear! I had no idea just how murderous our Ranger had become!"

Gene continues to glance out the window, wondering if the men below are going to loot his business and burn him out like the Negroes did in Watts. "I'll do anything, just please don't go to the police. It will ruin me, and if I go down so does the plant. Your men will be left with no work. You don't want that, do you?"

David crosses his arms and glares. He wonders why Gene would let everything get so far out of control. Is he that greedy?

"You're right, we don't want the plant to close. But we will continue our boycott until you agree to our demands."

Gene grows quiet and stares into his drink.

David is in too much pain to put up with Gene's nonsense any longer and turns to leave. "Enjoy your prison sentence."

"No, wait! Wait a minute," pleads Gene. "Hold up, please. I promise I'll sign—the God's truth. I am so ashamed. And as a sign of good will, I will give the men even more than they asked for, I swear!"

"I will hold you to that promise." David holds out his hand and Gene takes it with a firm grasp. "No going back on your word or you will be seeing the inside of a cell."

As David leaves he turns back to issue a final warning, but Gene is already down on his knees next to his desk, praying with his head bowed.

Gene looks up, his hands in prayer. "Yes?"

"Where is Larry?"

"I fired him, he's gone. He told me he was leaving the state."

David leaves Alamo-Cola with a "thumb's up" to the anxious workers waiting for him, and his throbbing headache disappears when they form a supportive gauntlet for him to walk through. They joyfully slap him on the back and cheer him on as their struggle is nearing a successful end, It's not every day in this part of the world that brown skin wins.

Maybe it's the concussion, but this scene reminds him of the movie "On The Waterfront." In the film, Marlon Brando is severely beaten and nearly killed fighting gangsters who had taken over the dockworkers union. When David approaches Luis' car, he turns to the men, and like the union boss in the movie he cheers, "Let's get to work!"

The men chant, "LA UNION! LA UNION!"

The exuberant rally is brief as it is clear to the men that David is in need of medical attention. Ruben and another man help him to Luis' car, and once he's seated the workers return to their vehicles quietly repeating, "La Union, La Union."

Luis pulls out of the parking lot and steps on the gas in the direction of the Bee County Hospital. He looks over to David and sighs, "Son of a bitch, you got him to sign."

David leans back in the seat with his eyes closed breathing deeply and sighs, "Verity and virtue—that's what I've been told. Jesus, I hope this kind of work doesn't always end up with me nearly getting killed. I feel like shit."

"What about that Mississippi fucker, Larry? For sure he needs a beating," growls Luis.

"I thought Carolina got you over all that violence."

Luis laughs, "I don't think I'll ever be cured—tamed maybe."

David thinks about taking a vacation to Mexico, and recalls a surf trip to Matanchan Bay in Mexico, a year before the draft sent him into hiding. He dreams of dropping and climbing across the face of a sparkling green wave peeling down the mile-long point.

> Juan Cortina whispers to him, "My friend, the first step has been taken and the rest will follow. *Hasta que te vea de nuevo.*" (Until I see you again.)

David is jerked out of his daydream when Luis suddenly pulls off to the side of the road and slides to a stop. Luis jumps out of the car and cups his hand over his eyes and stares skyward, transfixed on some occurrence taking place behind them.

"What's up?" asks a puzzled David.

Luis points upwards. "Look!"

Ten Clicks South
of Beeville

Metal fragments are raining down from the sky and hit the ground with an explosive force all around the young pilot who is frantically clawing at his flight helmet as he stumbles through the woods. Finding safety behind a large tree, he bends over and takes in a deep breath and exhales slowly to calm himself, exercises he learned in flight school to avoid going into shock. He was taught that accidents are a process and remaining calm can save your life. First, go to plan A, and if that doesn't work, try plan B and so on. Still, he's struggling to keep from passing out.

But the hair on the back of his neck is tingling—something is watching him. He slowly lifts his eyes and gasps in horror as he is greeted by a human head lying on the ground less than ten feet away, its face crawling with insects. At that very moment a massive explosion erupts from the jet's burning fuel tank. The concussion knocks him to the ground and rolls him through the dirt until he stops when he runs into an object lying on the ground.

A log, he thinks, but it's much more alarming, it's a headless body. A scream is caught in his throat and all he can do is emit short hyperventilating gasps and scramble to his feet slapping at his arms and torso trying to wipe away death. No amount of training could prepare him for this scenario. The shock he tried so hard to avoid takes hold and all he can do now is run as far away as possible from this frightening nightmare.

Michael is feeling sorry for himself because he's worked all week and now he has to stand watch in the photo lab in case there's an emergency … on a Sunday. In the past year, there has never been an emergency on a Sunday. Most of the base is out enjoying the weekend with friends or family. With the photo lab available to him for the next twenty-four hours, it's a perfect time to smoke a joint and do a little experimenting in the darkroom while listening to music as loud as possible, free of his First-Class Petty Officer who always hassles him because he thinks Michael is a hippie.

Of course the Emergency Phone goes off in the middle of a unique weird texture he had just created by using Agfa developer on Kodak paper. He has no choice but to turn the lights on and ruin the print.

A young sailor standing wheel watch at the foot of the base runway stops the Navy pickup truck and excitedly tells Michael and the driver, "I fuckin' saw it! It fell like a rock!"

"Yeah, that's what happens when they run outta gas," snaps the driver. "Get the fuckin' gate open, we got work to do!"

Now free from the confines of the base, the driver steps on it and begins tearing through the brush toward a tall column of black smoke about two miles away, bouncing and lurching over the rough terrain. The driver is laughing like a maniac and hanging onto the steering wheel with a death grip. Branches smack the hood and windshield, and the muffler that got knocked loose a half-mile back bangs against the undercarriage with every lurch. Michael's window came unhinged shortly after they left the base and he's got his palm firmly pressed against it, fighting to keep dust out and hoping it doesn't fall into the door panel.

Michael yells at the driver, "The jet has already crashed! Slow down!"

The driver laughs back, "We're in the country now, buddy, this is the way you drive in the country!"

Their destination comes into view and they're awestruck as the towering flames rising high above the trees.

"Holy fucking shit!" exclaims the driver. "I swear to God, it's going to set the whole goddamn place on fire!"

Michael lurches back in his seat when a Navy pilot jumps out of the bushes screaming at the top of his lungs. He drops the window into the door panel and yells, "Stop the truck!"

"What?" asks the driver.

"Stop the fucking truck!"

The driver slams on the brakes and Michael jumps out and tries catching up to the pilot. "Hold up!" he calls out. "It's okay! Stop!"

The pilot has already put a great distance between them, and all Michael can do is stop and watch the poor guy race away and hope someone will wrestle him under control. Michael trots back to the truck shaking his head in disbelief and tries opening the door. It's jammed and now won't open, thanks to the driver, so he ends up climbing in through the open window.

"What in the hell was that?" asks a confused driver.

Michael laughs, "The pilot!"

The first on the spot is a Navy fire crew which proceeds to empty massive amounts of water from their pumper truck onto the burning trees and grass before two larger fire trucks arrive blasting their horns. Barely a minute passes before the crew covers the wreckage in fire retardant foam and smothers the blazing jet. In less than an hour, the area is secured and the crash investigation can begin.

Lt. John Rayburn is the officer in charge of the investigation. He and Michael met each other when he blew a tire on take off. Michael captured his plane stretching the arresting gear to the max, barely seconds before landing softly without any damage, and resulted in a spectacular photograph. The crystal clear shot showed every rivet on the fuselage as the plane floated just a few feet off the runway with a shredded left tire dangling from the landing gear. Michael was so proud of the photo, he gave Rayburn a large print and the two became friends. Rayburn gave him twenty-five dollars for the photo, too.

Rayburn darts about the smoldering wreckage searching for clues to help his investigation, pointing out areas to be photographed such as the burned out cockpit, the instrument panel, or anything else that might tell him why this plane fell from the sky. He stops abruptly and peeks into a fairly intact section of wing and shines his flashlight into a small structural compartment and spots a crescent wrench still attached to a large nut. Astonished, he steps back and complains, "What in the hell is that? Blackwell, look at this!"

Michael takes a cursory peek into the compartment and stares at the undamaged wrench. He knows this will not be good news to the jet mechanic who signed off on his work. It might have kept the aileron, used to control lateral balance, from working properly at a critical moment—such as when landing an aircraft.

"Is that a wrench?" asks Rayburn again. "Shit, it is a wrench, isn't it? Son of a bitch!"

Rayburn stares into the compartment in disbelief.

"I knew this was going to happen! This is the exact kind of bonehead shit the Captain was worried about—enlisted personnel making critical mistakes because they're fried on loco weed."

Rayburn turns to Michael and asks, "Am I right?"

Michael shrugs.

"Well I am right! God damn fucking base is falling apart! And right here is proof of it. Make sure you get a couple of good close-ups of this damn thing."

A stuttering, shocked gasp calls out in the distance. "Some… someone! Over here! Help!"

Michael and Lt. Rayburn turn in the direction of the voice as Michael's driver running out of the woods yelling, "Over here! Over here! Hurry!" He stops fifty feet away and anxiously motions for them to follow him, then takes off running with Rayburn following.

Michael gathers up his camera bag and walks down a narrow path through the woods that opens up to a pretty meadow and sees Rayburn frozen in place with a ghastly look on his face.

The driver points out an crumpled mass lying on the ground.

It's difficult to make out what he's pointing at—it looks like a bunch of old clothes, but upon closer inspection the mass turns out to be a headless body lying on the ground. Hundreds of insects crawl about the body, but the most sickening sight of all is when Michael expands his view and discovers the head a few feet away covered with yellow jackets. In the tree is a wire noose dangling from a large limb.

Rayburn finally turns away from the body, dry coughing and hyperventilating. He bends over to catch his breath and gasps out an order to the driver. "Get on the horn. Tell them we need Shore Patrol and Naval Intelligence out here. Tell them to notify the local authorities too!"

Then Rayburn begins dry heaving and finally vomits. "Take some shots. It might be a sailor," he gasps.

Michael has witnessed a few jet crashes, two resulting in the death of the pilot, but those were accidents; depressing as hell, but nothing like this—a new low in his life as a Navy photographer. This is a murder scene, and even worse, a lynching. The kind of creepy shit in history books about racism and the South, but not in his wildest dreams did he ever think he would be a witness to it.

To keep himself from vomiting like Rayburn, Michael takes off his shirt and wraps it around his mouth and nose. The medical officer will need detailed photos, so it's important for him to get in close, which would be impossible if he were ill.

A lot of guys envy him, saying he's got the best job on base as a photographer. Most of the time they're right, but today is not one of those times.

Michael doesn't know anything about forensics but wonders how long this guy had been hanging here—a month, six months, a year?

Lt. Rayburn mumbles, "The local authorities should be here shortly, let's get back to work."

Michael picks up his equipment and quietly follows Rayburn back to the smoldering wreckage, happy to leave the gruesome scene. The affects of the weed he smoked earlier wore off long ago, probably when that pilot came racing out of the bushes screaming.

A half-hour later, Michael and Rayburn return to the body, when Naval Intelligence and the local Sheriff show up.

Michael asks Lt. O'Neill, "Did anyone catch the pilot yet?"

"Did you see him?" laughs O'Neill.

"Yeah, we almost ran him over. How far did he get?"

O'Neill shakes his head. "He scared the shit out of the wheel watch when he jumped the fence. The Shore Patrol finally got him and took him to the clinic."

"He scared the shit out of me too," laughs Michael. "I tried to catch him, but he was hell-bent on getting the hell away from the crash, I guess."

O'Neill looks at the body, then to the wire noose. "Maybe it wasn't just the crash."

Sheriff Donny interrupts and asks, "Have you guys taken any pictures yet?"

Michael holds his camera up and nods.

All eyes turn to Ranger Pete when he shows up and climbs

out of his truck with his lower right leg in a brand new plaster cast. He slowly hobbles over to the men on crutches.

"What the hell happened to you?" asks Donny.

"I fell off a damn ladder if you must know," snaps Pete. "You got any ideas about this?"

"Just got here myself," replies Donny.

"Most likely not a local," says Pete confidently.

"Excuse me, Ranger, but there's no way of knowing until we get some prints," replies O'Neill. "If that's possible."

O'Neill turns to Michael and asks, "Print up a few extra and make sure you get them to these guys, will you?"

Rayburn tells O'Neill, "I'll get the fire crew over here to wrap him up."

Pete clicks his tongue and adds, "When you get that done, I'll take him 'cause this is off the base and outside the Beeville Sheriff's jurisdiction."

"Pete, it could be a sailor," says Donny.

Pete shoots Donny a sour look. "Donny, let me do my job."

O'Neill takes an instant dislike to this Ranger because this is Navy business, and no one is going to do anything without his permission.

"Any suspicious activity involving Naval personnel is Navy business, regardless of the location," says O'Neill matter-of-factly.

Pete glares at O'Neill in an attempt to intimidate him, and O'Neill fires back with one of his own tight-jawed stares.

Yesterday's shit storm which ended with him on crutches and a shooting pain in his leg, has all left Pete feeling pretty vulnerable. Uncharacteristically, he looks away and mumbles,"Understood."

O'Neill turns to Rayburn and asks, "Do you need the body or should we turn it over to the Ranger?"

"Fine with me if they want it. I've got a crash to investigate.

When the Captain reads my report, the shit is gonna hit the fan."

"You already on to something?" asks O'Neill.

Rayburn ignores O'Neill and turns away, then calls back to Michael, "When can I see the everything?"

"I'll have proof sheets ready in a few hours and the aerials tomorrow evening."

O'Neill watches with contempt as Rayburn struts back to the crash site, then he leans in and whispers to Michael, "I don't like that prick. A major ass-kisser if I've ever seen one. I'd watch my back with him."

"He's okay," replies Michael, "he's just Navy frat-boy uptight. Did you know he has a football injury, a bad knee? He asked me not to tell anyone, because they can take away his flight card."

O'Neill smiles and nods his head. "So now you can blackmail him, too, if we turn on you."

Michael nods and smiles. "Yep, I gotta protect myself from my masters. Feel free to blackmail him, though, if you want."

Donny can't take his eyes off the body. He studies the wire and the noose and wonders what this guy did to get lynched. Of course, everyone knows about the shit down in Brownsville, but if the Rangers took the law into their own hands, why would they bring him back to Beeville, fifty miles from the trouble? Donny is already piecing together a connection in his mind, and smack in the middle of it is Texas Ranger Pete. "That son-of-a-bitch knows something," he tells himself.

As Donny walks to his car, he thinks, "this is nineteen sixty-seven, this isn't done anymore in Texas." He takes a seat behind the wheel and stares past the woods to the meadow beyond, studying the crime scene—and it is a crime scene. This particular tree had a reputation in the old days for at least a dozen hangings. Harold's great-grandfather and his group of vigilantes used to lynch Mexicans out here, simply out of hatred for anyone who looked like the folks who killed their heroes at the Alamo Mission in San Antonio. That's the problem with some of the older Rangers and Pete is the worst of 'em. They still think they've got to defend Texas from all outsiders.

Pete calls out, "Hey, Donny! Snap out of it, kid. I'll let ya' know when I find out something!"

O'Neill calls to Michael as he leaves, "Get me a good shot of that noose, okay?"

Michael takes another photograph, a full frame composition showing the entire tree with the firemen placing the victim in a black plastic body bag. He watches them zip up the bag and carry the remains to the Ranger's pickup truck and gently lay him on the bed. Michael is impressed by the careful, almost respectful, way how they handle the body. It's a graceful dance, the complete opposite of the man's violent death.

Michael leans against the trunk in the shade of the giant oak and wishes he could be anywhere else but here. The world is in the midst of a cultural upheaval in music, politics, art, and even in his big love: surfing. Like everything else, it's changing and evolving, too. His friends have abandoned their long boards in favor of highly maneuverable short boards, some as small as six foot. Every picture he's seen about the Summer of Love shows hundreds of people of all ages and colors, happy and free, growing their hair long and shedding their clothes, and even making love out in the open, which is probably not true but it sure sounds like fun if it is. And where is he? Taking pictures of a lynching in Texas. Summer of Love my ass, this is a nightmare.

Pete lurches up next to Michael after thanking the Navy fire crew for their fine work. He stares up at the noose and wipes the sweat from his brow with a handkerchief.

"Yep, looks like a suicide," he says matter-of-factly,

The comment is so absurd that Michael can't help but laugh out loud. "What!? You gotta be shitting me! This guy wrapped the wire around his own neck? How did he even get up there? Where's the ladder?"

Pete steps in close and hisses, "Maybe you otta just take the fuckin' pictures and let me do the police work. Is that all right with you? God damned smart ass."

Michael is suddenly aware of the dangerous position he's just put himself in by criticizing a Texas Ranger.

"Sure, you're the expert," he replies flatly and begins packing up his equipment. He keeps his eye on the Ranger, hoping to avoid a kick in the ribs like what happened to Ruben. This guy has been acting odd all afternoon and as far as Michael is concerned, he probably knows who did this, or might even be the one who did it. He's heard plenty of stories about this guy. Rumors have it that he's killed sixteen people, one of them handcuffed to a post in a bar.

Michael looks around at the now deserted hanging site—just him and Texas Ranger Pete, and Pete is staring at him in a very hostile way. Michael notices the number of notches on the wooden handle of the Ranger's gun and guesses there's probably sixteen of them. He stands and gives the Ranger a half-assed salute, and says "I'll get some photos."

The Ranger snarls, "Your dumb-ass pictures ain't gonna tell me nothin' about this. Give 'em to the Sheriff for all I care."

Pete spits on the ground and mutters, "Fuckin' Navy."

Michael finds his driver staring off into space leaning against the truck smoking a cigarette. When he spots Michael, he tosses the cigarette to the ground and crushes it out.

"Pretty awesome, huh dude?" he yucks.

The jet crash that occurred today was serious business that cost the Navy a lot of money and nearly led to the death of the pilot. As much as Lt. Rayburn would like to blame this accident on the mechanic and marijuana use which he believes brought down a plane, the investigation will determine that on his approach, the inexperienced pilot failed to maintain proper air speed and was no longer able to keep his aircraft aloft. It was pilot error, not a crescent wrench left in the wing by a pot smoking mechanic who will be punished in some way and probably have his ranking lowered.

Once the aerial photo proofs are approved, Michael will add in text, arrows and dotted lines showing the spray pattern of parts that will determine the flight path of the jet on its approach before impact with the ground. The lines will also show that the pilot ejected from the cockpit at an altitude of one hundred and twenty-five feet and sailed through the air for another two hundred feet with a partially opened parachute. Where the dotted lines end on the photo is where the pilot slammed into the ground, directly in front of the exploding, disintegrating jet.

Michael can only imagine the pilot's view of hitting the ground still in his seat in front of the jet breaking apart on its path to consume him before he was able to flee to safety.

Nearing midnight, Michael pulls the last of the prints out of the drum dryer and shuts down the lab. He tries to sleep, but can't because the image of the murdered man is still haunting him. Twenty minutes later he's standing over the developer tray waiting for the image to appear. He watches it patiently until it's ready for the stop bath then the fixer. He prints up four photos. The first is of the hanging man's headless body lying in the dirt wearing the filthy, tattered remains of a plaid shirt and jeans. Then the man's head with thick, dirty hair, and an unrecognizable face destroyed by nature's cleanup crew of bugs. Next, he prints a close-up of the empty noose on the branch, and lastly, an overall shot of the crime scene with the tree, the noose, and the body lying on the ground.

After the final print is placed in the dryer, Michael cleans the lab once more and closes up shop. He crawls into the lower bunk in the lab's sleeping quarters and stares off into space reviewing the absolutely horrible day he's just experienced. He wonders who the poor man was and if any family or friends were looking for him. If so, had they given up on ever finding him? Certainly, now that his body has been discovered, his fingerprints or dental records, if he has any, will identify him to law enforcement.

Michael closes his eyes and remembers how the day began so harmlessly, smoking a little weed on what was supposed to be a quiet workday until the emergency phone began ringing. Even though he laughs thinking about his crazy driver and the screaming pilot running away from the crash, he can't erase the horrible sight of the murder scene. He wonders about the events leading up to the man's murder and the last moments of his life, which must have been terrifying.

Before he drifts off to sleep, Michael wonders what kind of person could do such a horrible thing to another human being?

Michael's First Murder

A noisy Navy helicopter is floating five hundred feet above yesterday's crash site with Michael hanging out over the edge of the gunner's door with a large format aerial camera between his legs. To keep from falling out he's held in by a canvas belt around his waist attached to four bolts on the bulkhead. The racket from the engine and rotating blades is so deafening that all on board wear flight helmets and communicate through the built-in microphone and headset.

After twenty minutes of taking every conceivable angle of the crash site, Michael tells the pilot, "I've got all I need!"

In the distance, Michael spots a pasture filled with hundreds of grazing cattle and calls out to the pilot, "Hey! Check it out!"

The pilot looks out his window and spots the herd about a mile away. "You wanna get a picture?"

"Yeah!" exclaims Michael. "Can you get in tight 'cause I don't have a telephoto."

"Roger that, buddy!" replies the pilot. "You want tight? Get your legs in, you don't want to lose 'em when I scrape those tree tops. YEE-HAW!"

The pilot immediately lowers the nose and races off toward the cattle. As they close in on the herd, the pilot sends the helicopter into a steep banking turn to set up an oblique angle shot Michael will need to capture the scene.

"Get closer!" yells Michael.

"You got it!" laughs the pilot and immediately whirlpools the helicopter and drops another fifty feet.

As he focuses on the animals, Michael becomes concerned when he observes some very surprised and terrified animals. Maybe he should have thought this out more carefully, because the cattle are not enjoying the photo shoot as much as he is. Even with the commotion coming from the helicopter, Michael can almost hear them complaining, and he can definitely see their tongues waggling about and their eyes opened wide in shock. He doesn't know anything about cows, but these guys do appear to be freaking out.

The pilot begins playing with a large bull that has decided to attack the shadow of the helicopter. "You better make sure you don't fall out, 'cause that crazy devil is lookin' to kill us!"

Five hundred head of cattle have their faces buried up to their eyeballs as they concentrate on their menu of lush, green grass and flowers, easily tuning out human activity less than a mile away.

An ever watchful Brahma bull spots a dark shadow racing across the meadow toward the herd and responds by lowering his head and charging his adversary. One thousand pounds of muscle races around the perimeter of the herd attempting to chase off the aggressive intruder.

The rest of the herd becomes agitated and start moving about erratically to escape the terrifying sounds overhead. A few of the younger steers think this is good fun and follow the bull in play, which only confuses the herd even more.

It takes only a moment before panic ensues. The herd forms into a single swirling entity with each individual steer hurtling itself into the center of the pack for protection. This action creates a circular race to avoid being left out on the perimeter and being an easy target for the screaming dark shadow.

The pilot's giddiness turns to horror when the sea of horns, heads and bodies—an ocean of hides, begins swirling en masse just under the aircraft like an enormous whirlpool.

"They're gonna stampede!" yells the pilot. "Whoa-ly shit, we're out of here!"

The shadow quickly retreats, but the bull continues his chase all the way across the meadow until it vanishes into the woods. Satisfied he's vanquished his enemy, he bellows out a victory cry, but it's only for a brief moment. When he swings around to confidently return to his charges, he's horrified to find himself about to be trampled by his own panicked herd barreling toward him. He immediately does an about-face and runs for his life into the safety of the woods. The herd does what instinct tells them to do: follow the bull.

Texas Ranger Pete finds himself limping around the hanging site muttering to himself. With every step a throbbing pain shoots from his toes to his kneecap. He's ditched the crutches for a single cane which has proven to be a good decision, making it a lot easier to push aside grass and brush while he searches for incriminating evidence he so casually tossed aside a couple of days ago that might tie him to a crime. With the Navy creeping all over the place lookin' for jet parts, he's way overexposed and blames them for sending up poorly trained boys in antiquated aircraft.

"Goddamn thing could've landed in the middle of town and killed somebody," he complains.

Pete reaches into a clump of weeds and picks up a crumpled boycott flyer. He takes a hurried glance at it before folding it up neatly and shoving it into his shirt pocket, then heading over to his pickup for a swig of water. It's been a long forty-eight hours and he's dog-tired. First, that hippie coming back to life and escaping, then dealing with all those Navy idiots snooping around, and then having to concoct some horseshit on the spot to convince them to give him the body. To make his mood worse, he's pretty certain Donny wasn't buying any of it.

After getting his leg taken care of, he stood by like a helpless invalid while Larry dug a grave in one of the most remote areas of Bee County that he's positive nobody will ever locate.

"I'm gettin' too old for this crap," he tells himself.

Pete glances at the wire noose still dangling from the branch then jerks spastically and drops his cane in surprise when a loud, low-flying Navy helicopter sails overhead and stops a few hundred yards away. It seems to hang over the crash site much longer than necessary just to take a few aerial pictures. He mumbles to himself, "God damn waste of taxpayer money."

Pete bends over and retrieves his cane with a grunt. He leans against the truck and watches the helicopter float in air with a sailor hanging out a big door with a camera between his legs. Probably that little shit photographer he wanted to shoot. Laughin' at me like he knows what the hell he's talkin' about.

Pete cups his hands over his mouth and yells, "Hey shit-for-brains, you better come not 'round me if you know what's good for you!"

The helicopter finally ends it's noisy task and sails off to parts unknown. All becomes quiet again, but the tranquility doesn't make

Pete any happier, especially when he parts the grass and retrieves a business card he tore in half. He picks it up and tries to decipher the name—another Mexican guy. Rosalio something or other.

Pete spends the next two or three minutes looking for the other half of the card when his solitude is overwhelmed once more by the deafening roar of the Navy helicopter as it passes overhead at a high rate of speed.

"Jesus Christ," he yells, "get a goddamn muffler!"

Another irritating sound, like the low pitch of a motor boat, is rattling around his head. Pete thinks it might be his ears doing something weird from the helicopter's loud engine. He sticks his finger in his ear and wiggles it around to clear it out. When that fails, he pinches his nose and tries to pop his ears, but the rumbling won't stop. Pete is truly concerned, especially when he finally realizes the noise is not in his head but is coming from the woods. He spots a large dust cloud rising above the trees and heading his way.

Instinctively, he makes a sudden jerky move toward the safety of the Hangin' Tree, only to be rewarded with a stabbing pain from his leg to his gut. He tosses his cane aside and hobbles over to the tree cursing, "Shit, shit, shit." He's got too much adrenaline racing through his body to be feeling anything except for saving his own life. Three feet from the trunk he leaps to safety, and just in time, as hundreds of stampeding cattle break free of the woods sounding much like a violent thunderstorm.

Pete holds on to the tree with all his strength and closes his eyes. "Shit, goddamn shit," he cries out as the stampede surges all around him.

Mixed in amongst the hooves and horns is a massive swarm of yellow jackets who were violently ripped from their underground nest by two-thousand hooves, and are now frantically sailing about in every direction to avoid being trampled.

Pete feels something, no, *some things* crawling on his face and arms, and is horrified when he opens his eyes and discovers hundreds of yellow jackets have sought refuge on the tree, which he is now a part of. They are everywhere—on his arms, crawling on his face and some are even trying to hide in his nostrils. He swats at them and is rewarded with dozens of painful bites.

Pheromones released from the yellow jackets communicate a dangerous presence to the other aggressive wasps, and they forget all about the rampaging steers who have already crushed or stomped to death hundreds of their fellow nest dwellers. When they begin attacking Pete, he swings wildly with one hand while desperately clinging to the tree with the other. But his struggle is futile, as each swat only enrages the yellow jackets who increase their attack with a vengeance.

Unable to withstand the yellow jackets' painful barrage any longer, Pete takes the one hand holding him to the trunk to cover his face and eyes and blindly steps a few inches from the trunk to turn his back on the assault. Unfortunately it is just far enough for the horn of a large steer to hit him in the ribs and spin him sideways.

Pete screams out in pain or shock, he'll never know which one it is, because immediately another set of horns plunges deep into his back and rips him off his feet. He becomes an unwilling passenger in the stampede, and with each collision, agonizing pain rips through Pete's entire body.

In the last seconds of his life, he emits the most pitiful howl from deep within. It is so unnaturally terrifying that the steer begins bucking and kicking to shake Pete off. With one final toss of its head, Pete is released from his host and sent cart-wheeling into a maelstrom of legs and hooves. The most feared law enforcement officer in South Texas, disappears into a cloud of dust, tossed about like a rag doll as a thousand hooves gouge and break him to pieces.

Finally, Texas Ranger Pete is unceremoniously kicked out of the stampede head first into a mesquite bush.

As the last steer lazily trots out of the woods, the frenzy of the past few minutes ends quietly and without fanfare. The dust kicked up by rampaging cattle dissipates into the air as a light wind takes it miles away, falling back to earth to fertilize another field or meadow. The herd unhurriedly makes its way home to a life of grazing and quiet rumination. The horrifying clamor of the dark shadow that attacked without warning also fades from their collective memories, because for the cattle, who live only for the moment, it's as if nothing happened of any importance whatsoever.

A peaceful stillness returns to the meadow. Wildflowers and grasses will quickly begin the process of renewal as they've done for a million years. It isn't long before the chatter of bees, flies, yellow jackets, and other creatures fill the air as is their nature.

Resurrection

With an pack on his face and his head cradled on Carolina's lap David is absorbed reporting to his friends about the events leading up to his abduction and his escape. Paul, Ramona, Luis, and Carolina listen attentively to every word until he tells them about the man hanging in the tree who assisted him with the aid of his spirit guide.

"Juan Cortina woke me, screaming that Mescalito and César Gaspard, the man hanging in the tree had come to my aid."

Ramona cries out, "Who did you say?"

"César Gaspard. How could I forget, him? He saved my life."

To hear her father's name is a kick in the stomach. She gasps, unable to catch a breath until the tears begin to flow, and there is no stopping them. Paul pulls Ramona to him and hugs her tightly. He too, is shocked hearing David say the name.

"David, that's Ramona's father's name. I told you about him, remember?"

"You just told me that he disappeared doing the same kind of union organizing," replies David, "but, I'm positive I didn't know his name. We were so happy to see each other again, I think you over looked telling me that."

"David, you were knocked unconscious. It could have been a hallucination," replies Paul.

"Maybe, but I know it wasn't. There *was* a man hanging in that tree, and that was his name."

Ramona wipes at her tears and asks, "David, what was he wearing?"

David closes his eyes and tries to visualize the scene out at the tree and the man's clothing.

"I was in a state of shock, and everything was happening so

fast; Juan was yelling at me to get up and run. But I know he had on jeans, and, his shirt—it was a blue and white checkered shirt."

Ramona pulls away from Paul and sits on the edge of the chair with her head in her hands. "The last time I saw him; that was what he was wearing."

David drifts in and out of sleep for the next hour while Paul and Ramona stare off into space in the quiet room. The deathly silence is interrupted only when she begins crying into Paul's chest.

Finally, Ramona stands and says, "I need some air."

"I'll go with you," says Paul.

"No, I need to be alone right now."

Ramona walks at a quick pace through the neighborhood with no goal in mind. The faster she walks, the more she is able to calm her mind. It's something she did a lot of in Nuevo Laredo after her father disappeared and El Papagayo only strengthened her resolve to remember who she truly is, to keep her dignity at all cost, regardless of the circumstance. That is what her father taught her.

It saddens her when she thinks of her Popi, alone and forgotten, dangling at the end of a wire. She knows it will take her many years, if ever, to overcome that image. But knowing he's been found gives her some comfort. Plus, he would be very happy to learn that in the midst of this tragedy she fell in love.

She remembers what he told her, and in fact can almost hear his voice when he said, "Think only good thoughts, my love, and promise me you will always be happy." She will forever return to her happiest memory of being with her Popi cheering, "Bravo, bravo!" as they watched the surfers riding the big waves in Mazatlan.

What is life but a collection memories? Ramona tells herself it's important at this moment to concentrate on the good ones to get through this difficult time. Maybe later on, when the dust settles, she could enroll in school and use her sadness and anger to counsel others going through similar circumstances.

In her heart, Ramona knows it is not in her character to break into a thousand pieces of self-pity. If that were ever going to happen, it would have been when she found herself being paid to have sex with a complete stranger. Now, having cried herself empty, she takes a deep breath and turns back to Luis' house. When she spots Paul sitting on the porch, her heart leaps with joy knowing that life will be getting better with each following day.

After Ramona left on her walk, Paul went to the front porch to plan his revenge. He's never revealed to Ramona about the man who looked like her father in his peyote vision, and would return to the underground for her to tell him that she is safe. But maybe he's not even there now that his body has been found. That would be fine, too, because as remarkable an experience as his vision was, it scared the shit out him. He wonders if a relationship can be healthy if some things are kept a secret. For the moment, he convinces himself that it is possible.

He looks up the street and watches Ramona as she returns from her walk. He can't take his eyes off her, even from a distance it's plain to see what a beautiful young woman she is. He laughs to himself thinking why such a remarkable person could fall for him.

Ramona sits on the steps next to Paul without a word, and wraps her arms around his shoulders and kisses him. Paul tastes the salt on her lips from her dried tears and makes a silent vow that he will spend the rest of his life searching for her father and his killers.

Ramona ends their kiss and takes his face in her hands.

"Everything that has happened to us in the past few months, including how we found each other is a wondrous tale. I do want to find out about my Popi, if David's tale is true or not. But for now, I want to do my best to keep a promise I made to him when we left Mazatlan. I cannot be sad any longer."

"Don't you want to find out for certain if that man was him or not?"

Ramona shakes her head. "I think it was and I will tell you why. A month ago I had the strangest dream, or maybe it wasn't a dream because I felt that I was awake. A glowing blue orb appeared over my bed, quivering rapidly as it floated in the air. I knew it was my father, but it scared me and I wanted him to go away—but I also didn't. All I could do was to say, 'I love you, Popi. But if you are dead, you have to go to where you belong. Then, right before he vanished he placed an icy cold kiss on my cheek."

Paul shakes his head. "I don't even know what to say. Is that what you believe?"

"Yes, I do. Someday we'll find out how he ended up being murdered in this town, I know that for certain. But you and I have our own story to live and I want it to begin as soon as possible."

Ramona buries her head in Paul's chest and hugs him.

"I have something to tell you, too," says Paul.

Michael finishes up the last of the prints for Lt. Rayburn and looks forward to taking the afternoon off. After so many hours in the darkroom cranking out prints and having to sleep on the photo lab's thin mattress on a lower bunk, it will be nice to see the sun again and his own comfortable bed in his own house.

As he's leaving the lab, Photographers Mate Bob Hagood, calls out, "Hey, Blackwell! I forgot to tell you, one of your hippie buddies called while you were off duty."

"When was that?"

"Uhh, Saturday. Sorry man, I've got his number for you if you need it."

Michael got Paul on the phone. "David got beat-up by some local cops," he said, "you should stop by on your way into town."

When Michael walks into the living room of Luis' house, he looks at David and exclaims in shock, "What the fuck happened?"

David is lying on the couch with a bruised and swollen face, being attended to by Carolina, with Paul and Ramona holding each other on the couch. He tells him of his nightmarish ordeal of almost getting lynched, while Michael sits mesmerized, almost holding his breath until David lays his head back down on the pillow.

"Oh man, I wish you listened to me about hitchhiking," says Michael.

David nods, yes. "I'm still not over the shock of nearly getting killed by those assholes."

"This is whole thing is really weird," says Michael, whistling out a breath, "A jet went down, and we discovered a scene just like what you described right next to the crash. That's what I've been working on."

David lifts his head and asks, "Is that where I was? Luis and I saw the smoke on the way to the hospital."

"I can't believe you were out there!" exclaims Michael. "And you're right about the Ranger falling off the ladder because he was wearing a cast and was on crutches. He even threatened me when I laughed at him when he said the hanging was a suicide. Any idiot could clearly see that it was a murder."

Hearing this, Ramona gasps.

Michael stutters out an apology. "Oh shit, I'm sorry."

"Don't be," says Paul. "We think you're probably right. The man could have been Ramona's father."

Ramona scoots up and sits on the edge of the couch. "Can you describe the man's clothing?" she asks.

"Well, it was pretty tattered, but he was wearing jeans and a blue and white checkered shirt."

Ramona shakes her head and quietly curses, "Shit."

"What happened to the body?" asks Paul.

"The navy let the Ranger take him," replies Michael.

"That's not good. We can't go to him, he already tried to kill David," says Paul.

"After laughing at him, I think he wants to kill me, too."

Michael takes a knee in front of Paul and Ramona. "I might be able to find out what's going on. I'm delivering photos to the Sheriff tomorrow and I don't think the Ranger and him like each other much. If he tries to give me the runaround, I can take the photos to my friend in Naval Intelligence. I know he'll do something."

Uncle Art was Sheriff when Donny was a kid. It's the reason he always wanted to go into law enforcement. He loved waving to his uncle when he'd catch him standing in front of his large office window staring off into space. He often wondered what Uncle Art was thinking about, because he'd have to whistle a couple of times to get his attention. He liked to think Uncle Art was in the midst of solving a crime, but when he would ask, Uncle Art would always whisper, "No can do. Loose lips, sink ships."

Today, Donny finds himself in front of the same big window overlooking the town square wondering if he might have made a mistake not following Janie to Austin when he still mattered to her. He could have enrolled in school and worked on a law degree or something along those lines. Like most teenage love affairs, their attraction was mostly physical. They were always breaking up after some petty argument, then forget about it a day later and return to their passionate love affair. The truth is, he was never interested in leaving Beeville. And it wasn't in Janie's nature to get involved in the sort of town activities expected of the wife of a community leader. It was as foreign to her as the man from Mars.

This momentary rewind into the past ends when a Navy jet rumbles overhead on its way to the base. It snaps Donny back to a nagging suspicion that's been bugging him for the past couple of days. He goes to his desk and dials the number on the black, rotary-style telephone.

"Texas Ranger Services, Southern Division," answers Alice with a bubbly voice.

"Hi Alice, is Pete around?"

"Hey, Donny! No, I haven't talked to him in a couple of days. He might be takin' time off. You know, with his leg and all."

"That doesn't sound like Pete."

"No it doesn't, 'cause he likes to stay in touch. That man is always on the lookout for desperados," chuckles Alice.

"It must get frustrating for him. I mean, things aren't as wild as they were in the old days."

"That's true in some ways, but I don't know, Donny. Did you hear about all those Negroes rioting up in Detroit?"

"I did. All this civil rights stuff is makin' everyone a little crazy. Could you have Pete call me when he returns?"

"You bet, Donny."

"Say Alice, has Pete given you any info about that hangin' out at Harold's ranch a couple of days ago?"

"A hanging, really? No, he hasn't said a thing to me about that. Two days ago? Who was it?"

"No idea, Alice. Just let him know I called, okay?"

"Will do, Donny."

Donny leans back on his swivel chair, puts his boots up on the desk, and mulls over the strange scene out at the Rancho. More than anything, he's thinking about Pete's behavior, which is downright suspicious. He hasn't thought about the labor riots down in Brownsville in months, but he remembers Pete and his Ranger buddies bragging how they beat the crap out of the braceros and sent them high-tailing it back to Mexico.

Donny picks up the phone and makes another call.

"Bee County Morgue, Chip speaking."

"Hey, Chip, it's Donny."

"Hey partner, I haven't heard from you in awhile. What's up, buddy?"

"I'm interested in a body Pete brought in a couple of days ago. You have time to get any prints?"

"I'd like to help you out, but if Pete brought something in, it would be his case. You'll have to get permission from him. Anyway, he didn't bring nothing in, the fridge is empty."

"That right? Okay, thanks Chip."

After hanging up the phone, Donny spends a few moments putting two and two together before kicking his chair away from his desk and cursing, "Son of a bitch!"

He crosses the office, yanks his cowboy hat off the coat rack, and grabs his gun and holster. "Be back soon," he grumbles to the secretary as he cinches down his hat and storms out of the building.

A mile onto Rancho el Abejorro, Donny stops the car a short distance from the hanging site and carefully studies the scene. *Something is not right,* which an experienced lawman can perceive it without even realizing why or how he knows. A good cop just feels it. Off to his left is Pete's truck, covered in dust and looking as though it's been through a hell of a beating with dents and scratches covering almost every square inch of the side.

Donny unlocks the safety of his gun and cautiously walks to the truck. He's concerned that Pete, with his back to the wall might be lurking nearby waiting to ambush him. He notices bits hair or cattle hide stuck in a portion of the rear bumper and the tail lights are smashed. He looks into the cab—the keys are in the ignition. Finally, Donny calls out, "Hey Pete, where the hell are ya?"

He receives no response except for the chirping of birds and the buzzing of insects. He follows a wide swath of flattened bushes, the ground chewed up and scraped clean of grass, like after a cattle drive. He follows the trail for a hundred yards until he surprises a number of crows who spring out of the brush with loud complaining. Flies and yellow jackets race about in a frenzy near a mesquite bush and it doesn't take him long to find the source of their interest.

Donny pulls aside a branch for a look and is nearly blinded by the bright reflection of a Texas Ranger badge on a torn, bloody, Ranger shirt.

He stumbles back in shock and stares open-mouthed at the mangled corpse of what used to be Pete, twisted and tangled deep within the branches. It looks like nearly every bone in Pete's body is broken. His left arm is wrapped behind his back and his blue eyes are now buried under a crushed brow. But the most horrifying sight is Pete's face, which has turned black from hundreds of yellow jacket bites.

Donny notices a small piece of paper sticking out of Pete's shirt pocket. It amazes him what survives and what doesn't in a disaster. Once, he found an unscathed greeting card still taped to a refrigerator in the remains of a burnt out house. He carefully pulls the paper out, unfolds it, and sees that it reads, BOYCOTT ALAMO-COLA. As he stares at the flyer he begins making a case in his head. Was Pete actually investigating the hanging, or did he want to run the investigation to cover his tracks because he played a role in killing the guy?

What he does know is that Pete got surprised by a stampede and ended up getting trampled. To Donny it looks like a series of events that began with a man being lynched and culminating with his killer returning to the scene of the crime and getting trampled to death. The missing body could only mean that Pete wanted this to end without anyone discovering the man's identity.

Donny can't help but laugh to himself. Dumb-ass steers killed the most dangerous and hated crime fighter in Texas. Who would have thought? It might be funny as hell if it wasn't so pointlessly tragic. But, that's the mystery of funny shit—it pops into your head when you least expect it.

Donny takes a last look at the massive oak tree with the wire noose still in place. Then he turns around and walks back to his car, and out of frustration, yells out to nobody in particular, "Every little fuckin' change is a god damn battle to the death!"

He reaches in through the open window of his patrol car and brings the handset to his mouth to call Alice at the Texas Rangers office, Southern Division—this is their jurisdiction after all."

What The Hell is an Icon?

Michael patiently taps on the counter to the tune of, "My Best Friend," by the Jefferson Airplane rolling around in his head. He's watching Sheriff Donny through the glass door who is on the phone with his feet up his the desk.

After a moment, Donny swings around in his chair and waves him into his office. Michael enters quickly and remains quiet while enjoying the tree top view from the large window while listening to the Sheriff's conversation.

"I agree, Alice, he was a man's man. They don't make 'em like Pete anymore. There's a lot of folks around here who are gonna miss him. So, I hate to bring up business at a time like this, but could you please have headquarters give me a call? I'll be here all day. Bless your heart, Alice, I am sorry for your loss."

Donny ends the call and turns to Michael.

"I've got your photos," says Michael stiffly.

"Thanks for bringin' them in so quickly. Do you mind shuttin' the door? Donny points to a metal chair against the wall. "Pull up a chair, please."

Michael grabs the chair and makes a racket as he drags the chair across the linoleum floor to the front of Donny's desk. He lays the packet down and watches Donny eagerly begin flipping through the photos before stopping and staring at one in particular, and wonders what Donny is thinking. Like, what goes through a cops's mind with murders and other horrific bad behavior? Because once he's out of the Navy, he never wants to do this kind of work again.

"Did you print them up?" asks Donny.

Michael nods.

"Pretty good. Beats the hell out of what we usually get from our local newspaper photographer."

"Thanks."

Donny holds the photo of the oak tree with the wire noose, and studies the image in earnest.

While Donny has his eyes glued to the photo, Michael checks out his office, walls filled with a gallery of past Sheriffs casting stiff, stern poses. One might assume that was just the way people acted back then—strong men of few words. But Michael knows it was also the film they used in the old cameras that required the subject to be absolutely still for at least five or ten seconds. He also wonders if any of them took the law into their own hands—lynching horse thieves or other desperados. Kind of like what he just witnessed out at the crash site. How many were Ku Klux Klan? He guesses that at least a good number of them were.

"This is a very strange photo," says Donny. "Almost like, uh, like uh..."

"An icon?" says Michael.

Donny lays the photo down. "What the hell is an icon?"

"It's something you pray to, like a religious symbol."

"Who'd wanna pray to this?"

"I don't know, how about a guy nailed to a cross?"

Donny laughs, "You got me there buddy. Yeah, that is pretty weird when you think about it." He grows quiet for a moment then asks, "How's Nancy?"

Michael appreciates the attempt at familiarity, but that was a quick jump in the conversation, so he returns the favor.

"You dated her sister, Janie, right?"

"Yeah, I sure did. All through high school. At one time we thought we might even get married."

"Really? If you don't mind me asking, what happened?"

Donny fumbles with the photos before answering.

"I don't know, maybe she's got a bit more wanderlust than me. Not everyone is cut out for small town living. You know how those Jensen girls are, right?" Donny stares at him a few seconds too long and it creeps him out.

"I should go to O'Neill in Naval Intelligence," thinks Michael. Instead he asks, "Anything else?"

Donny apologizes, "Sorry, I didn't mean to be starin' off into space like that. It's a bad habit, but you got me thinking about Janie. So listen, I have some questions about what we discovered out there at the crash. You know that fellow who was livin' here a while back in your house and is now stayin' in Mexican Town?"

"You call it Mexican Town?" asks Michael cynically.

Donny nods. "That's what it's always been called, long before I was born."

"Naval personnel aren't supposed to be messing around in local issues, and I don't have that much time left in the Navy to be doing anything that keeps me in any longer than I'm obligated."

Donny chuckles.

"Look, you're not gonna get into any trouble telling me a few things that might help me find out why I found an Alamo-Cola boycott flyer out at the hangin' scene. This isn't about your friend, I promise. Do you know his name?"

"David Macias."

Donny scribbles the name down quickly.

"Ma … ci .. as. You know where he's from?"

"Uh, not really. I know he was born in L.A."

"Anything else? What about his friend?"

Michael shrugs. "Paul? He left town after you ran him out."

Donny lays down his pen and pad, then cocks his head and gives Michael a stern look. "You know, I did those guys a big favor. I found out that some of our boys were gettin' uptight about hippies livin' in our town and were plannin' to bust their asses whether they found anything wrong or not."

"Busting them for what? Because they had long hair?"

"Sometimes that's all it takes. But they were most likely doin' drugs, too, just like your old roommate, JC. Hell, for all I know, you might be a pothead, too."

"Okay," thinks Michael, "the real Donny has finally shown up. Just another redneck cop, not the friendly good old boy who dated Janie. Now I know why she left your ass."

Michael abruptly pushes away from the desk.

"I think I've done my job and delivered the photos. I've got to get back to the base."

"Don't get all uptight now. I called off the raid on your house. Nancy told you I warned her, right?"

"Yeah, I guess I should thank you, but I didn't have anything in the house, and neither did the other guys."

He was telling the truth too. After watching his friend head off to Naval prison because he got sloppy with his weed, Michael became fastidious about pot in the house. It was pretty much the only thing he embraced of Navy life—being *squared away*. As for those kilos he brought back? As a photographer, Michael roamed all over the base and spent a fair amount of time photographing the wheel watch, the loneliest, most isolated spot on the base. A sailor's only function was to stand out at the end of the runway and watch jets land to see if their wheels were down. If they weren't, the watch fired off a flare gun that warned the pilot to figure out another way to land. Michael's weekly visits to his stash stored in a metal footlocker in the woods were always appreciated by the lonely, and very bored sailor on watch.

"Sorry I spoiled your party, then," replies Donny. "Did your friend ever have a run-in with our Texas Ranger?" .

"He never complained to me about it if he did. Speaking of Texas Rangers, have you talked to him about the lynched man?"

Donny flinches. "No, I haven't, and we don't know if it was a lynching or not. No one has any idea what the hell we were looking at, so don't be callin' it a murder."

"Well, it wasn't a suicide either," replies Michael. "You saw that Ranger out at the crash site. He was pissed off that the body was even discovered. Naval Intelligence told me the guy had been hanging up there for at least a few months, and it looked like a murder to them."

"The Navy seems pretty sure of themselves."

Michael shrugs. "Have you even talked to the Ranger?"

"Listen, you need to stop before you get yourself into some serious deep shit. That Ranger has some very powerful friends and you don't want to be pissin' on them."

Michael has had enough tip-toeing around with this guy, so he blurts out, "Okay then, look up César Gaspard, a labor lawyer from Mexico. He was working on the big farms in the Rio Grande Valley and disappeared three months ago. That's the name of the headless guy we found out at the crash site."

"How do you know this? Does the Navy already know?"

"I know because that Texas Ranger and his friend Larry tried to kill David the other day. They beat him up and took him out there to lynch him next to César, the man who had been hanging in that tree before rotting and falling to the ground. Did you know that Larry, known by most as Lawrence Rainey, is the same guy who helped kill four Freedom Riders in Mississippi? They were college kids helping register voters. It was on the cover of *Life* magazine."

"Larry? The shithead who works for Gene?"

"Yeah, he's a real piece of work. He nearly killed David, who barely escaped with his life. David also told me about the Ranger falling off the ladder and breaking his leg, and the name of the lynching victim. How would he know that unless he was there?"

"That's mighty interesting. Your friend could help me tie up a lot of loose ends. Do you have his phone number?"

"Now that the boycott is over, it might be safe for him to come out of hiding. He still thinks the Ranger and Larry are looking for him."

"It's over, really? Son of a bitch, I didn't think that old bastard Gene would ever give in."

"He did when David gave him one last chance to cooperate. Apparently, Gene was involved somehow, then saw the light after the whole thing headed south."

Donny's face reddens. "Son of a bitch! I'm supposed to know this shit first, not some Navy photographer. God damn Gene didn't say shit to me about this."

The two grow quiet for a few moments until Donny huffs, "Oh, hell." He lowers his voice and says, "What I'm about to say stays in this room. Do you understand?"

"I'm not sure I should agree to something without knowing what it is."

"Just promise me you'll give it some thought. Recently, with all this hippie shit everywhere, *Newsweek* magazine had an article on Karma. I had never heard of Karma before, but this morning I believe I might have witnessed it in all its glory. I've just returned from the hangin' site where I discovered the mangled body of that same Texas Ranger you'd like me to question. Karma? I don't know about that, but down here we like to say, you reap what you sow."

"The Ranger is dead?" asks a stunned Michael. "The same guy who tried to kill David?

"Yep. It appears he got trampled by a herd of the Rancho's cattle in what appears to have been a stampede. God only knows what spooked 'em. And by the looks of him, he also received multiple bites from a couple hundred yellow jackets, too."

"When did this happen?"

"I'm pretty sure it was the day after the plane crash."

Michael suddenly feels light-headed. He takes a deep breath to calm himself and rubs his hands together because they're feeling clammy. He stares at the floor and thinks, "Shit, I only saw one stampede that day and I started it. Hell, talk about Karma."

Donny pushes away from the desk and walks to the window. He leans against the sill and looks down to the square below to clear his mind.

While Donny occupies himself, Michael thinks about what a first-class, murdering prick that Ranger was, who would have killed David if things hadn't turned out differently. "Screw him," he thinks. Michael laughs to himself thinking how funny it is that David's beating led to his role in the asshole Ranger getting his ass kicked by a bunch of cows that he spooked. Whether it's Karma, or reaping what you sow, life truly does work in mysterious ways.

"Ha!" Michael laughs, when he realizes there really was a reason for him to end up in the Navy as a photographer—someone has to document this crazy shit.

Donny turns around in surprise.

"Sorry," offers Michael.

Donny shrugs.

"This has got me a bit puzzled. I'm pretty certain it's all tied–in with the boycott and what happened to your friend. If the story of how he was able to escape Pete and Larry is true, I would truly be interested in hearing it."

Donny doesn't have to worry about him telling anyone in the Navy about this—no one would believe that he was responsible for the death of a vicious Texas Ranger. Although he would love to tell Donny that it was the ghost of César Gaspard who knocked Pete off the ladder and saved David from being lynched. And that Paul's girlfriend is Ramona Gaspard, the daughter of the murdered man in the tree. But then again, that would really be too far out for a Texas cop to believe. Hell, it's almost too far out for him to believe. But then again, this is the Summer of Love, and these *are* magical times.

"As far as the man's identity," says a dejected Donny, "that's a problem because the body has gone missing. It's not in the morgue where it should be, but my gut tells me that once he took the body, Pete, and probably Larry, buried him at some isolated spot far out in the country."

"You're kidding me? How about arresting Lawrence Rainey, then? He probably dug the grave 'cause the Ranger couldn't have with a broken leg!"

Donny nods his head and clicks his teeth.

"My thinking exactly, but he left town in a big hurry. When I told Gene about Pete, he told me he fired Larry, and I'm beginning to think it was because of his part in your friend gettin' snatched."

Michael slumps in his chair feeling especially impotent now that he'll be returning to Ramona and Paul without any information on her father. He glares at Donny and wonders if he's getting jerked around or not.

Donny notices Michael's demeanor, but all he can offer is a shrug of his shoulders. "That plane crash got me thinkin' in a way I'm not used to, like how so many things in life are connected. How an inexperienced pilot or engine failure, set in motion a series of events that lead to the discovery of a murder victim, and the death of the man who might have killed him. If only the dead could talk. But, as of this moment, I don't believe we'll ever find out the true identity of that poor man, or what really went on out there. "

"Fucking Texas," grumbles Michael.

"Yeah, sometimes it is," agrees Donny.

★

Two weeks later finds Sheriff Donny standing at his favorite perch, watching the sunset. He spots an Alamo-Cola truck below rumbling past with Luis, one of the leaders of that troublesome strike behind the wheel. He's still curious why Gene turned over half of his company to the workers. He also wishes he knew more about the lynched man's murder. Unfortunately, the hippie who started all the trouble at Alamo told him one of the most far out tall tales he'd ever heard, even by Texas standards. Even if half of it was true, he still doesn't have any witnesses, hard evidence, or even a body.

While Donny meditates, he hopes that life will return to the way it used to be, before drugs and hippies, the Vietnam War and the Navy, and the end of labor struggles like those of Brownsville and Alamo-Cola. Thank god, no one ever found out about Pete's criminal activities. All he needed was the FBI to show up and start making a federal case out it.

He continues watching the Alamo-Cola truck as it leaves the business district and enter the surrounding neighborhood of single-story, ranch-style homes before disappearing under the thick foliage of the large oak and linden trees that shade and conceal the small ranching community of Beeville, Texas from the world beyond.

Good Ol' Blackie

itting atop Junior, his champion Morgan horse, Harold is exploring the latest addition to Rancho el Abejorro. After years of coveting an adjacent tract of exceptional quality, two days ago he took ownership of this prime real estate that features lush meadows, an ancient oak forest, plenty of water, and most importantly the tallest hill in the county that offers exceptional views of his vast holdings.

For over one-hundred-and-fifty years, the previous owners had refused to develop this property, being devout followers of the author Henry David Thoreau, an early American conservationist, thereby leaving this one of the last unspoiled plots of land in all of Texas.

The most recent family caretaker was a man named Richard Fox, who lived with his small family in a brightly painted bus parked in a meadow. They were gentle souls and good neighbors who raised chickens and sold eggs, and preached the Gospel to anyone who cared to listen. When Mr. Fox was offered his own church in San Antonio, he and his wife Shirley, and their two children, Angel and Faith, were more than happy to accept Harold's generous offer to purchase their extremely valuable inheritance.

Harold promised in writing that the land would remain free of any development with the one exception that he be allowed to build a modern, arts and crafts style, wood and glass house on the very top of the hill.

Today, he is engaged in one of his favorite pastimes, watching the world's smartest hunting dog go through his paces. Blackie has got his nose to the ground taking in information far beyond human perception. One square foot of dirt might contain a long history of critters, varmints and birds that once came this way and stopped to peck at a worm, or gnaw on a lizard. Harold knows that his dog is capable of discovering odors so infinitesimal and ancient, that in many ways he's like a walking encyclopedia. He has said on many occasions that if he could be granted just one wish, it would be to sit down with Blackie and have a long, serious conversation with his favorite companion.

Harold is delighted to be back to a routine they had been sharing for almost five years until a Navy Jet crashed on his property a couple of months ago and uncovered a possible murder. Then, that damn ol' Texas Ranger Pete got trampled to death in the middle of his investigation when the Rancho's stock went on a stampede for some unknown reason. With those dumb beasts it might have been almost anything that set 'em off. Sheriff Donny paid him a visit a couple of times to ask a few questions about the murder victim, but all his Tejano workers were accounted for, so that was that.

Blackie races back and fort, darting into the bushes to shoo a bird or two out of hiding, then, without warning, he takes off racing out to a rocky butte known more for bobcats than birds.

Harold calls out, "Hold up there Blackie!"

Blackie ignores Harold because he's on to something good.

"Hold up you damn dog! Stop!" Harold's order has no effect on Blackie, which Harold finds very unusual. That dog will stop on a dime whenever he's commanded to do so.

"What the hell?" he asks himself.

Blackie's behavior is just puzzling enough for Harold to give Junior a nudge and trot over to where his dog is kicking up a cloud of dust as he enthusiastically digs deep into the dirt. Harold laughs out loud watching Blackie race in circles trying to get a better angle on the object of his desire.

"What ya got there 'ol boy?"

Harold expertly dismounts before Junior comes to a complete halt and runs over to where his obsessed dog tosses up a dirt clod that hits him in the face.

"God damn it!" he cusses, wiping the dirt from his eyes. "Get out of the fuckin' way so I can see what ya got there."

Harold squats down with a grunt and holds his crazed dog by the collar to keep him still as he clears away the diggings with his free hand.

"Let's see what's got you all excited. You find some buried Spanish treasure, huh boy?"

After a bit of digging, he exposes a portion of a thick black vinyl sheet. Harold brushes away the dirt carefully then grabs onto an odd shape rising out the earth. It takes him only a second to realize he's grasped the remains of a human foot. The horror jolts him and he ends up stumbling back and landing on his butt.

"Holy fucking SHIT!" he yells out loud.

Extremely proud of his work, Blackie jumps on top of Harold and excitedly licks his face. Harold laughs while trying to push him away. "Come on now, get off me ya crazy dog!"

Blackie immediately obeys the command. He leaps over Harold and sits down on his haunches with a proud smile on his very expressive face. In appreciation, Harold sits up and rewards him with an enthusiastic head scratching followed by a bear hug. Blackie returns the attention by nuzzling his nose deep into Harold's armpit.

Harold stares at the foot for a moment before rising to his feet and dusting himself off. He shakes his head in wonder, huffs out a deep breath and looks at Junior and Blackie: "Whadaya say boys, think we should give Sheriff Donny a call?"

EPILOGUE

2016 SAN ANTONIO, TEXAS

A large exultant crowd has assembled in the city's Military Plaza to celebrate the election of Texas' newest congressman. The plaza has been the scene of everyday business and social events of San Antonio for over two-hundred years, as well as many skirmishes between Texas and Mexico. But today's gathering is to hear Paul "César" Macias deliver his hard-fought victory speech. Under banners and flags, the fifty-year-old Tejano steps up to the podium facing the thunderous cheering crowd and waves a "V" victory sign with both hands held high.

Paul César waits a moment for the applause to quiet before speaking.

"All my life, I have been driven by one goal, one vision: to overthrow a system that treats some of its citizens as if they are not important. That dream grew from the emotions I felt watching my parents as they traveled the state organizing labor unions. They were jailed, sometimes physically assaulted. Even as a young boy, I could not understand how some could abuse and exploit my people.

During this struggle, many have suffered from the forces of hatred, racism and ignorance. Some gave up their lives, so that one day we Latinos might enjoy a better life. It is those people, foot soldiers, who gave selflessly, and today, we honor and remember, and give our everlasting love and appreciation to them."

Inspiration for The Foot Soldier began when I was stationed as a photographer at Chase Field Naval Airbase in Texas. A couple of months after photographing a lynching as described in this story, I got picked up by ex-Sheriff Lawrence Rainey while hitch-hiking outside of Nuevo Laredo, Mexico. During our two hour ride, he talked about his involvement in the murder of three young civil rights workers, and the famous trial feature in *Life* Magazine.

When I asked him what he was doing in Texas, he showed me his business card and said he was a Management Representative.

"What's a Management Representative?" I asked.

Mr. Rainey replied, "Mostly kicking ass on troublesome farm workers."

Above right: Lawrence Rainey enjoying his favorite chewing tobacco "Red Man" alongside Cecil Ray Price. This photo ran on the cover of Life Magazine when both men were on trial for their part in murdering three civil rights workers in Neshoba County Mississippi, in June 21, 1964.

Lawrence Rainey died from throat and tongue cancer in 2002 at the age of 79.

TOM TRUJILLO
U.S. Naval Photographer 1967–1968

ABOUT THE AUTHOR

Tom Trujillo lives near the beach in Central California with his wife of many years, and is the father of two adult children and two grandchildren.

As a designer, Tom spent his professional career as an art director and illustrator, producing book covers, posters, architectural graphics and more for over thirty years. As an artist, he has many of his paintings in private collections, exhibited in art galleries throughout California, and was featured in a one-man exhibit at the Museum of Art & History, in Santa Cruz, California.

OTHER WRITTEN WORKS

HERESEY: JESUS, THE TEENAGE YEARS

In three intersecting stories about discovering love in difficult times, an artist who creates a controversial painting titled "Jesus, The Teenage Years." A group of radical evangelicals set out to destroy the art but fail. The attack, instead, results in more publicity and fame for the artist. After the unsuccessful attempt an assassination of the artist is planned, but a life changing miracle ends the assassin's quest and her relationship with her radical pastor.

A nineteen year-old Jesus finds himself working as a building contractor and fighting the Roman occupation. He meets and falls in love with a young woman named Mary, and they end up traveling to Bethlehem to escape Roman soldiers after a riot. In Bethlehem, Jesus learns the truth behind his family's flight to Egypt and leaving the innocent children to be massacred by Herod's troops.

In 2009, a young Marine is fighting his own battles in Iraq, disillusioned with the pointless invasion and its tragic consequences. Finally, he lays down his weapon after a horrific event involving the death of innocent civilians, and wonders what Jesus would have done had his family been killed by invaders

MIRACLES AND MURDER: AND OTHER TRUE STORIES

A fully illustrated collection of Tom's true life short stories accompanied by dozens of colorful illustrations. Tom weaves his way through tales of wrangling back rent out of a murdering motorcycle gang, escaping an attack from a vicious dog thanks to the miraculous appearance of a metal pole in the middle of a stream, his "First Murder," plus many other inspiring and humorous tales told in the tradition of American Folklore and Tall Tales.

> *Whoa Weeee, what a ride! Thank you Tom. Your book was a joy to read and your artwork is fantastic! It was a sad day when I finished reading the last of your stories. Kind of like saying goodbye to a fun evening of feasting with friends. I look forward to more books...love your sensitivity and your consistent voice. So many fun adventures and I can only imagine you have a ton more up your sleeve.*

> *With Much Appreciation, Emily Bording*

(FILM SCREENPLAY) THE BROTHERHOOD OF DOLPHINS

Sylvia Cruz, a heroic Latina firefighter battles Bill Johnson, a psychotic arsonist and killer who believes he has been ordained by ancient Chumash mystics to destroy the culture of the European invaders. His task is too deliver "The Word," that when heard will remove the malignant flint holding Latinos captive to the white invader. The Dolphin Brotherhood also assigns Bill the task of finding *La Reina*, a queen who will produce a new race of *Californios* to usher in a new society based on respect for nature and the environment.

Made in the USA
Middletown, DE
03 December 2020